ADVANCED PRAISE FOR
OVERKILL

Author Andre Charles has crafted an engaging experience filled with intriguing clues and clever plot hooks that kept me hooked from start to finish. The well-crafted plot, intriguing characters, and clever puzzles made for a captivating mystery that unfolded with suspense and unexpected twists, but I'd especially like to highlight the atmosphere and detail of setting at Cactus Heights, which was a delight and immersed me from the get-go. With this unique backdrop to the investigation in place, Charles utilizes some really stellar dialogue to express the dynamics between Mike and Molly, furthering their relationship, delivering clever banter, and giving us naturally occurring plot clues and surprises at the same time. Overall, *Overkill* is a delightful mystery that keeps you guessing until the very end, and I would highly recommend it for your next cozy read.

K.C Finn, Readers' Favorite 5-star review

Overkill by Andre Charles is a thoroughly enjoyable, excellent contribution in the world of senior sleuth mystery novels. The two amateur detectives, complemented by a cast of interesting characters, solve a compelling mystery that keeps the reader guessing until the end.

Mike Befeler, author of Last Gasp Motel, Old Detectives Home, The Front Wing, The Back Wing, Death of a Scam Artist, The Tesla Legacy, and the Paul Jacobson Geezer-lit Mystery Series.www.mikebefeler.com

In *Overkill,* Andre Charles gives us an engaging tale that evolves from clue to clue faster than the police can keep up with it. It's a good thing that Molly and Mike are on the right side of the law. The narrative is descriptive and the plot moves at a comfortable pace, uncovering one surprise after another as the circle of suspicion widens and hitherto long-hidden secrets are revealed. I enjoyed the tenacity of Molly and Mike to go where the detectives had no interest. Molly and Mike's romantic relationship is woven into the storyline. Both have issues to resolve before they can move forward. A highly satisfying story, and I look forward to more Molly and Mike sleuthing adventures in the future.

Kimberly J. Bent, Readers' Favorite 5-star review

This is a captivating read that pulls you in and doesn't let go. Clues are sprinkled throughout the story and each one adds more depth and more questions. As soon as you think you have it figured out, a new clue will have you questioning your own sleuthing skills.

The story is full of relatable characters, but the

lead duo is a powerhouse couple. Mike and Molly face real life issues, bicker back and forth, and use witty banter which keeps the reader entertained. Molly is a strong female lead who knows what she wants and doesn't take no for an answer.

If you enjoy mysteries, desert settings, or entertaining characters, I highly recommend this book. Overkill is a fantastic addition to the cozy mystery/amateur sleuth (sub)genres.

Trish Arrowsmith, author of Ink or Swim: A Dakota Maddison Tattoo Shop Mystery

OVERKILL

OVERKILL

A MOLLY AND MIKE MYSTERY

ANDRE CHARLES

aka
Dorothy Leonard
+
Walt Pav, ...

KONSTELLATION
PRESS

Published by Konstellation Press, San Diego

www.konstellationpress.com

ISBN: 979-8-9868432-3-0

Cover design: Teresa Espaniola

To our children, grandchildren and (gasp!) great-granddaughter

PROLOGUE

DECEMBER 5. A STATE PARK IN SOUTHERN ARIZONA

As Mike Landry later recalled to the police, the hike started normally. There were the usual minor dramas, but nothing to suggest what was to occur later.

Three members of the hiking club were late to the gathering spot behind the library in the Sunrise Acres active adult community. Barry Sturges had forgotten to bring a hat. Mike, drilled by years of university teaching into obsession about punctuality, grumpily explored the trunk of his Lexus for an extra one. The Detroit Tigers baseball cap he extracted and handed to Barry was crushed and spattered with the remains of old painting projects, giving the originally white cap an unsettling resemblance to roadkill. After a few seconds inspection, presumably to confirm it was a hat, Barry shrugged and stuck it on his head. In southern Arizona, where skin cancer threatened bald domes and prominent noses, everyone—especially seniors—prized sun protection over style.

Peter Jackson was leader for the day. "Trailhead is a couple miles past the Safeway on Boulder Drive," he reminded the group. After a few minutes of chaotic milling, the hikers sorted themselves into shared cars.

Mike groaned inwardly as retired judge Tom O'Day squeezed into the back seat beside the other two occupants.

"Know where you're going?" Tom demanded as if he were in an Uber. Mike did not respond. He glanced in the rear-view mirror as he backed out. Barry was squashed into a corner by Tom, who was fishing awkwardly around the backpack on his lap for the seatbelt.

"Hey Judge," Barry said, "watch the hands!" The two other passengers grinned. Tom O'Day was not universally loved.

In the trailhead parking lot, the hikers pulled on their equipment. Mornings in early December were typically cool, even cold, but today was predicted to be unusually warm. As temperatures rose, the group would shed layers of clothing. Of course, everyone carried plenty to drink.

The narrow trail forced the hikers into single file. Opportunities to socialize were limited to those with the person in front or behind. Delayed by the need to check his car for any orphaned equipment left by absent-minded passengers, Mike brought up the rear. His view featured Tom O'Day's backside.

The ascent was gradual at first. The spiky agaves and prickly pear cacti were succeeded by scrub juniper and mesquite, their gnarled branches over-hanging the path. As the trail became steeper and rockier, Peter shouted back frequent reminders to hydrate. Mike's daypack held a reservoir of water that allowed him to sip from a tube without stopping, but Tom's bottle contained what looked like a red sports drink in the side pocket of his pack. He had to stop mid-trail to laboriously reach back and fish it out. Mike fidgeted, wishing he could sidle around Tom on the narrow path, but it would seem pushy, so he reminded himself to enjoy the views during the enforced stops. Tom seemed disinclined to chat.

Except, increasingly, to himself. About a half hour into the hike, he started mumbling. Mike couldn't make out any words, but Tom's tone was angry. *Who the heck is he arguing with? He couldn't be on his phone. I don't see any ear buds and there's no cellular reception until we get up to the ridge.*

Mike and Tom were the last to arrive at the first rest stop, a widening of the trail at the top. Boulders afforded a welcome spot to sit and have a quick snack. Some large creosote bushes provided modest shade and respite from the surprisingly warm morning. The other hikers had already taken their break and had packed up to continue along the ridge. Far below, the wash, which flowed freely during the summer monsoon rains, was now totally dry. The view was spectacular. The morning air was so clear that even the University of Arizona's famed observatory on distant Kitt Peak was visible. But Mike was focused on Tom O'Day, who was now sitting on one of the boulders. His face was extremely red. Yet he was not sweating.

"Tom, you okay?" *Maybe he's about to have a stroke.*

That final mile was rough. Tom didn't appear to hear him. "Tom?" Mike said a bit louder. *I don't think he's hard of hearing.* "Hey, Tom? Judge?" Still no response. Tom was staring at the horizon talking excitedly to some nonexistent person. Mike was thoroughly alarmed now. He looked for Peter, the only doctor on the hike, but the group had continued on. None were still in view except Barry Sturges, who was adjusting his pack about fifty yards up the trail.

"Tom! Tom! Talk to me, Tom. You're acting kind of crazy." Mike could see there was something seriously wrong with Tom, whose face had turned deeper scarlet. *He must be feverish. Why isn't he sweating? Should I run ahead and get Peter?* Tom suddenly jumped up, pushed past Mike, and walked rapidly towards the edge of the ridge where it dropped precipitously to the dry creek bed.

Then, to Mike's astonishment, Tom unhooked his backpack, hurled it over the side, and began tearing at his shirt, popping the buttons. He was still talking nonstop. "There it is!" he said excitedly, looking towards the horizon. He started laughing, his voice rising. "Yes! Yes! I'm telling you. There it is!" He lurched closer to the edge.

"Tom!" Mike yelled and grabbed Tom's arm, pulling him backwards. Tom finally seemed to hear him and stared, wild-eyed, at Mike.

"Leggo!" Tom yelled as he staggered towards the cliff edge again, dragging Mike behind him.

The next few seconds were a confused struggle as Tom stretched out his hand and shook the taller man off his other arm with surprising strength. Mike reached again, only catching the remnants of Tom's shirt. "Leggo! There!" Tom roared, his eyes fixed on the object he was reaching for—and stepped off into space.

PART I

1

MID-OCTOBER

Two months before the fateful hike, Mike Landry and Molly Levin were preparing to host a dinner party as members of the Prepare and Share Club. It was one of over a hundred clubs in their retirement community, Sunrise Acres, in the town of Cactus Heights, outside of Tucson, Arizona. Each month, three or four couples gathered at the home of an assigned host. The objective was primarily social; people who had not previously dined together could become acquainted through planning and contributing dishes to the meal. Each dinner was designed around a theme that had been selected by vote of the entire membership. Themes could focus on ethnic cuisine such as German or Ethiopian, but typically a few were chosen to spur the dinner groups to more creativity: "food from movies" or "colors." Recipes from the 1950s featuring canned mushroom soup were not encouraged.

Usually, such dinners were friendly get-togethers full of comradery. Usually.

This month's theme was French Bistro. As host, Mike had decided on *boeuf bourguignon* as a main course. He reviewed the rest of the menu with Molly, stooping slightly as he habitually did when talking with someone shorter than his six feet. "Tom O'Day signed up for appetizers; he's bringing *gougères*. Conrad and Christine Konsinski are responsible for salad—something with baby arugula—and Ellen and Ed Featherstone are making *crème brûlée*. They should all be here in an hour or so. Can you set the table? I'm gonna check on the beef."

"Wow, fancy!" Molly commented as she placed silver and china on Mike's dining room table.

Through the door linking kitchen to dining room, Mike watched her slim form as she moved gracefully around the table. Her black slacks were topped by a red V-necked blouse with long sleeves that spread wide at the wrists and fluttered as she moved.

"You're a scarlet tanager," Mike observed admiringly. "Beautiful birds!"

"Then what are you?" Molly asked.

He glanced down at his brown slacks and beige golf shirt with narrow brown stripes.

"Common English sparrow, I'm afraid. No, wait— a lark, I think." Mike's gaze rose towards the ceiling as he retrieved a quotation from memory:

Haply I think on thee, and then my state,
Like to the lark at break of day arising
From sullen earth, sings hymns at heaven's gate...

"Whoa, impressive!"

Mike bowed to her, doffing an imaginary hat. "Taught my Shakespeare course at least a dozen times to undergrads—and one of my graduate students wrote her thesis on Shakespeare's sonnets," he said with a grin. "I've read Sonnet 29 ad nauseum."

Then he reverted to the topic of table settings. "You're right about the fancy place settings. Haven't used the china or the silver since we left Michigan. I don't know what to do with it all. I've offered to send at least the silverware to my boys, but Andy and Brent were fervently altruistic, each insisting I should give it all to his brother. Back when we got this stuff as wedding presents, a single spoon cost ten bucks."

Molly smiled. "I know. I've tried to give Megan my crystal, but she insists her family would just break them. Guess she thought her kids would take up goblet juggling."

"Anything that can't go into the dishwasher is an abomination to the younger generation."

"Maybe they've got the right idea," Molly said as she eyed the number of items on the table that would need to be hand washed, and mentally inventoried the dirty pots in the kitchen. "But at least we don't have *all* the KP duty. The best part of these club dinners is that some of the dirty pans are left in other peoples' kitchens.

"So, we have seven all told," she said, setting out water and wine glasses. "Do you know Conrad and Christine?"

"I know Conrad from Monday night poker, but I've never met Christine. I did all the planning by email. Hold on a sec." He pulled out his phone. "Huh. A text from Tom. In our last email exchange, he said Audrey would not be coming. But now he's adding someone named Shelley Goossens. So, it's eight after all."

"Oh boy!" Molly exclaimed, shaking her head. She tucked a lock of salt-and-pepper hair behind her ear. Mike cocked an eyebrow at her and waited.

"Shelley is the young woman Tom's been, uh...seeing for a couple months. Tom introduced us a week or so ago when I asked around for recommendations for web designers—you know, for the library's site. I'm hoping she'll agree to help me. Anyway, I'm not surprised Audrey isn't coming. She and Tom are probably headed for divorce if the Sunrise grapevine is up to date."

"Aki?" Mike smiled.

"Yep. She's not the only source of gossip. But she kind of specializes in romance rumors."

"Please tell me we aren't included in regular updates on her personal true romance channel."

"Why not?" Molly chuckled at Mike's horrified expression. "No worries. She's a good friend, but I would never confide in her. Might as well go on Oprah." Thinking of the big-eyed innocence that served Aki so well in unearthing scandal, Molly added, "Good thing she's not coming tonight. But I believe Ellen is a close friend of Audrey's, so..."

"Sounds as if we are in for a very, um, interesting evening."

Mike inspected the half bath off the family room. Seat down? Check. Guest towels out? Check. Plenty of TP? Check. They would serve appetizers and drinks in the seating area off the kitchen, where a brown leather couch and five chairs rimmed an oriental rug in shades of light rust and beige. Then dinner in the rarely used formal dining area. The walnut table created by Amish craftsmen seated eight easily. Again, it sat on an oriental rug, this one in shades of sea green, mauve, and beige with touches of light turquoise. Mike's late wife Andrea had loved oriental rugs, even though they were certainly not Southwest décor. "These rugs can withstand spills and wear," she had observed.

The walls of both rooms were still covered with Andrea's artwork. Her oils featured stylized landscapes of clouds so solid they looked organic, and cacti abstracted into design elements. *This house still reflects Andrea everywhere. But I don't think Molly minds. Maybe if we decided to live together, it would be an issue.* Mike knew that unlike china and silver, these paintings would be happily inherited by Andy and Brent. *I should send some of them to the boys. But not all of them.*

True to Sunrise Acres norms, everyone was a few minutes early. The first to arrive were Christine and Conrad. Christine was a trim, petite woman with short curly white hair. Conrad was so tall that he ducked his head going through their six foot ten-inch doorway. After she greeted Christine, Molly tilted her head up to Conrad's face.

"Six-eight," he said as he enveloped her hand in a human baseball glove. At Molly's puzzled look, Conrad explained with a grin. "Sorry, so many people spend time visibly trying to estimate how tall I am— before finally asking me, that I've found it saves time just to satisfy their curiosity right away. But maybe you weren't even wondering."

Molly flushed. She had been. "Guilty," she said with a smile hoping he couldn't read her other, rather more inappropriate, thought that he'd have to bend in two to kiss his wife. She turned to the other guests as they arrived.

Mike's prediction of an interesting evening, given Tom O'Day's last minute decision to include Shelley, turned out to be an understatement. The drama started as soon as introductions were over. Shelley was not only at least twenty-five years younger than everyone else but overdressed in a tight black dress that clung to her curves like melted wax. *Hope that dress has a strong zipper,* Molly couldn't resist thinking. Shelley's low neckline displayed a youthful décolletage. Her above-the-knee hemline was shorter than any of the other women would have considered, and her four-inch heels lofted her a couple inches above Tom. He was dressed much more conservatively, but still a bit formally for Sunrise, in tan chinos and a long-sleeved dress shirt patterned with small warm brown loops.

After an embarrassingly open visual assessment of Shelley, Ellen Featherstone was blunt. "Wow, I haven't worn heels like that in twenty years."

Molly held her breath. She thought swiftly of a couple snarky responses Shelley could justifiably make. "I can see why." Or, "Well, I probably won't wear them when I reach your age." But although Shelley's mouth tightened for a few seconds, she then smiled.

"That's smart," she said. "These darn things are so uncomfortable. I'm already sorry I wore them." Everyone visibly relaxed.

"Well, they look fabulous," Molly said. "Now, what drinks may I get for everyone? We have white and red wine open, and margaritas with Mike's homemade prickly pear syrup. Or beer. Ladies?"

After shaking hands with the other men, Tom stood staring at Conrad, brows wrinkled, head tilted as if puzzled. Molly had to repeat his name to get his drink order. The two men differed a lot physically. Tom was rather short, wiry, and compact. His gray beard was neatly trimmed, and his black-rimmed glasses set off deep-set almost black eyes. Conrad towered over him. In the past, Molly thought, Conrad must have been muscular and physically imposing. But now he was a model for the "before the exercise program," with multiple chins and a bowling ball stomach. His open-collar blue golf shirt draped unattractively over the bulge. His white hair was so close cropped around the sides that it bristled like a cholla cactus, but across his otherwise bare dome, a few wisps of longer hair sprouted like sparse weeds on barren soil. *At least no comb-over.*

Ellen's husband Ed had an obvious toupee, coal black, perched on his head like a nesting raven. Tall and rangy, he dwarfed his wife--at least in size, if not in presence. Ellen was as loquacious as he was taciturn. The years had blurred her features, but she still had the air of a pretty woman expecting admiration. She posed a bit languidly in one corner of the sofa, her dark blue pants suit set off with an ivory silk blouse and large silver bangles that jangled on her wrists with every gesture. And gestures accompanied every utterance.

"So, Mike, you're here year-round? And, uh, Molly?" Ellen added awkwardly, unsure of the depth of the relationship. Without waiting for confirmation, she continued. "We're here just for six months. Not sure whether we're sunbirds or snowbirds." She smiled as if the comment were witty and patted the cushion beside her for Ed. "But honestly, I don't know how you stand living here in June. Everyone says it's dry heat, but so's my oven and I wouldn't live in it!" Ed said nothing but watched her with a small indulgent smile as if she were a precocious child or talented pet.

Everyone else settled down on the matching leather armchairs spread around the family room. Mike and Molly served drinks and Tom passed the *gougères*. Christine, legs sheathed in black jeans, appeared to be at least ten years younger than her husband. She perched on an ottoman beside Conrad, who fit comfortably in a large recliner. She made an effort at light conversation telling stories on herself about checking out books at the local library only to realize twenty pages in that she'd already read them —even recently.

"I've found a way to avoid that," Mike said. "I keep a spreadsheet of books as I read them, with a few words of description. I rate them one to five in case a friend asks for my recommendations."

"But," Ellen said ignoring Mike's last comment, "I suppose you are too young to have memory problems, Shelley."

Molly glanced desperately at Mike. The inquisition had begun. Shelley deftly sidestepped the question. "A personal bibliography. Mike, that's brilliant. I wish I had started that years ago. I envy Christine and her twenty pages. I was on page a hundred and something not long ago when I realized I'd read it a year earlier."

Ellen was lining up for another shot, but Molly was relieved when Tom took on the role of goalie. "So, Conrad, where are you from?"

"Minnesota," he said. "We used to be migrating birds as well." He acknowledged Ellen's prior remark about snow or sun birds with a nod in her direction. "We just sold a house on Lake of the Isles in Minneapolis that we'd go back to during the summer. But now we're here permanently."

"I'm originally from St. Paul," Christine chimed in.

"Is that where you two met?" Molly asked, continuing to shepherd the conversation away from Ellen's focus on Shelley's youth.

"Yeah," Christine said. "I used to work for Conrad. He retired a couple years ago when he sold KCS.

"KCS?"

"Sorry. Konsinski Cyber Security," Christine clarified. "Well, it was originally Konsinski Computer Systems. But Conrad changed the name when he shifted the focus to protecting companies from ransomware and worms and stuff like that. Anyway, Conrad is a software guru."

Conrad looked uncomfortable at the characterization. "Hardly a guru," he said. "I *hired* software experts. I'm sure some of them would like to be thought of as gurus."

"Do you deal with cryptocurrency?" Mike asked. "I'm waiting for someone to give me a clear explanation."

"Not directly. KCS is a small company, and it's not really in our business model. But you probably know that digital currencies involve blockchains." At the baffled looks around him, he continued, "You might think of blockchains as sort of a Google spreadsheet, not on a single server but distributed among a network of computers all around the globe. Blockchains are more secure than usual record-keeping systems because no single person or organization can alter the contents. There's a complex algorithm that creates consensus about what's in the database." He flushed as he glanced around and realized from the blank faces that he had completely lost his audience. "Sorry about the tech-talk. Uh, Mike, I could send you links to a couple good articles. They'd do a better job of explaining than I can."

"Or you could talk to Jamie," Christine interjected. "Our seventeen-year-old is into anything having to do with computers—and he'll be home for school break in a couple months."

Conrad shot her an annoyed look. "Uh, maybe better if you talk to me." Seeming uncomfortable that they had become the center of attention, he looked hopefully at Molly. She took the hint and deflected attention back to Shelley. "Shelley is also computer-savvy. She designs websites."

Everyone looked expectantly at Shelley, but she seemed even more uncomfortable than Conrad at being in the spotlight again. She glanced around nervously and sent what appeared to be a silent plea for rescue to Tom. He picked up the nearly empty plate of *gougères*. "Um, can I persuade anyone to take this lonely last *gougère*?" Tom looked pointedly from the dish to Molly. Mike was watching the conversational ping-pong with a bit of amusement, but he left the direction of the game to Molly.

Quickly she announced, "Shall we move on to the

next course? I believe Christine has already put out salads for us." She led the way into the dining area.

As they sat down to dinner, Tom returned to the topic of peoples' origins. "I'm rather surprised you don't have any Minnesota accent," Tom said to Conrad. "You sound more like someone from Illinois, maybe, or—Kansas." He stared steadily at Conrad as if waiting for some reaction.

"Oh, no," Christine said. "What gave you that idea?" She glanced around the table. "Not all Minnesotans have that 'yah sure, you betcha' Norwegian thingy. Anyway, I hope I'm not offending anyone," she said shaking her head with a small smile, "but Kansas seems so..." She paused, searching for an inoffensive descriptor. "Um, flat. I'd never agree to live there."

In contrast to his wife's relaxed response to Tom's statement, Conrad had stiffened. His eyes widened. He looked hard at Tom. Then he grabbed his water glass and took a large swallow. Sitting next to him, Molly was struck again by how huge the hand gripping the glass was—twice the size of her own. His fingers seemed abnormally long, although she had earlier noticed that the ring finger on his left hand was truncated. An accident perhaps? As if he sensed scrutiny, he set the glass down hurriedly before looking across the table again. "I guess everyone from the Midwest sounds about the same, Tom," he said. Molly thought the casual tone was deliberate but strained.

Oblivious to her husband's discomfort, Christine babbled on. "I once saw a US map of 'standard English,'" she said adding air quotes. "You know, without any distinct regional accent like Southern or Bostonian. What used to be considered the only way to talk on radio and TV. Anyway, the map included most of the Midwest. Probably includes Illinois and Kansas. I don't remember."

"How about you, Tom? Where are you from?" Conrad asked. It sounded like a challenge.

Tom leaned back in his chair—a pose that seemed artificially nonchalant. "Oh, quite a few places. I was in the military for twenty years, and we moved around a lot. California, Florida, even Alaska. Oh, and Kansas. Spent some time at Leavenworth. The Army base part, not the prison," he added with a smile. It sounded like a well-used joke.

At Tom's mention of Leavenworth, Conrad paused cutting up the meat on his plate and looked up sharply. He seemed relieved when Ellen—Ahab with harpoon at the ready—homed in again on the errant husband and Audrey's apparent successor. "Where did you two meet...Shelley is it?" she asked. Molly thought the feigned lapse in memory seemed intended to emphasize Shelley's outsider status.

"Turns out we're both alums of the U of A," Tom said, parrying the slight. "It was reunion week at the end of August, and I was on a panel about the legal difficulties some universities have complying with Title IX, you know, equal representation for girls on athletic..."

"I'm sure you mean 'women' Your Honor," Ellen interrupted. "But please, do continue."

"Women, of course." Tom looked a little put out but went on. "Anyway, this lovely young *woman*," glancing at Ellen, "came up to me afterwards to ask about—I forget what—we talked a bit, one thing led to another, and I asked for her phone number."

"Really! Reunion week. Was Shelley celebrating, what, her tenth reun..."

Smiling pleasantly, Shelley spoke over Ellen. "Where did you and Ed meet?"

Ellen frowned at the interruption but proceeded to describe, in some detail, Ed's immediate passionate attraction to her in a college history class, his avid pursuit of her, and her eventual acquiescence, culminating in a big wedding in her church. "Fifty years in June!" She concluded triumphantly. Ed listened stoically to the well-practiced history without dissent or comment.

Wonder what his version would sound like, Molly thought idly. *Still, fifty years....*

But before Molly could comment on the longevity of their relationship, Ellen switched gears abruptly, turning once again to Shelley. "So, your big reunion was a couple months ago. Why did you come back?"

Like Ellen's other contributions to the discourse, the question bordered on rudeness. But Shelley continued to appear unruffled. "A combination of things. I've been scouting out retirement communities for my aunt, and there are a lot of them around Tucson. I went to school here, as Tom said, so I know the area well. I love the climate—well most of the time. Now I'm thinking of moving here. As Molly said, my job is designing websites, personalized websites. And I don't need to meet clients face-to-face. I mean, I *like* to meet directly, but I do almost all the work virtually, so I can live anywhere. If I have to choose between shoveling out my car from a Chicago blizzard or wearing sunscreen and a hat—well, it's not a hard choice."

I have to hand it to Shelley, Molly thought. *She's showing a lot of restraint in responding so calmly to Ellen.*

"So, you didn't know anyone out here before moving?" Ellen asked pointedly.

"Oh, I haven't moved—yet. I'm just renting. No, I was just lucky to meet Tom and thankful that he was willing to introduce me to his friends."

Ellen made a little noise that turned into a small cough, leading Molly to wonder if Ed had kicked her under the table. Before Ellen could speak again, Molly hastily addressed Shelley. "Well, I think your being, um, around here will be opportune for me. I'm supposed to help our library with their website. I missed the meeting where I was 'volunteered.' But honestly, I know about as much about web design as I do about, well, nuclear physics. Would you be willing to give me a bit of guidance? I'll introduce you to some other residents here. I'm sure they'd be happy to help you get local clientele if you wish."

After Shelley said "Sure—yes to both," Molly steered the discussion to more general topics.

Everyone avoided national politics. But the turf wars between tennis and pickleball could arouse similar passion, if based less on ideology. A current hot issue was the relative space devoted to a dwindling population of tennis players and overcrowding at the increasingly popular pickleball courts. Mike was an enthusiastic convert to the newer sport. "We've simply got to have more pickleball courts," he said. "The tennis courts are practically deserted a lot of the time, and ours are almost always filled except in the middle of the day in summer. We could create three or four pickleball courts out of one of theirs."

With no tennis players present, the pickleballers at the table were free to vent about their common rival. Shelley looked on with a bemused expression at their near religious fervor.

As soon as Molly and Mike started clearing the entrée from the table, Conrad looked at his watch. "Time to go. Early tee time tomorrow." He stood. Christine looked startled, and opened her mouth as if to protest, but after glancing at her husband's face, she obediently pushed her chair back.

"But you haven't had my dessert yet," Ellen exclaimed. "It's *crème brûlée*."

"Ellen's perfected it," Ed added loyally. Everyone looked as surprised as if a table leg had spoken. "She even interviewed a couple of chefs about their techniques. Turns out what's crucial is the cream to egg ratio, and Ellen..."

"I'm sure it's delicious," Conrad interrupted, "but I'm trying to watch the waistline." He patted the ample protuberance that made it doubtful his waistline was ever in view.

Christine looked embarrassed. "I'm so sorry, Molly, Mike. I..." She frowned at Conrad, but he had already pulled Christine's cardigan off the back of her chair. "It's been a, a lovely evening," she said hurriedly, as Conrad unceremoniously handed the sweater to her, took her elbow, and steered her towards the door. "Thank you so much," she called back over her shoulder as they left.

When the door closed, the rest of the party sat avoiding each other's eyes. Finally, Mike broke the silence. "I think he's going to catch hell," he said with a smile. Nervous titters rounded the room. Tom O'Day did not join in.

"Maybe the beef disagreed with him," Molly said. "Now, who would like decaf coffee or tea with their *crème brûlée*?"

MIKE WASHED the silverware and Molly dried it, laying each piece carefully on a couple of dish towels to finish drying before storage. After setting down the last spoon, she wrapped her arms around Mike, who was now elbows deep in soapy water scrubbing the large pot he'd cooked the beef in. She gave his back a deliberately loud kiss.

"Great bourguignon," she said. Molly felt what she always termed a "happy bubble." *It is wonderful to have a partner again. I am so lucky!* She surveyed the remains in the serving dish. "There's a ton left. How many nights can we eat it? Or should we freeze some? You must have thought you were cooking for your boys."

"Yeah, I should have remembered that it takes three Sunrisers to match one Andy." He handed her the large pot to dry. "Although I would have expected a guy Conrad's size to eat a double Andy portion. I'll package up some leftovers for Irwin. He can always use a good meal." Mike's bridge partner, Irwin Robeson, had become a good friend despite the age difference. "I know he doesn't cook, and I don't think his lady friend, uh..." He rummaged through the jumble of female names in his head and finally emerged victorious. "Maeve—I don't think she cooks either." He retrieved the large Tupperware container he had put the leftover beef in, spooned some out into a smaller container and set it aside.

Molly continued her review of the evening. "Aside from the food, not the best one of these dinners I've been to. The conversation ricocheted between boring and hostile. If we hadn't been hosts, I'd have been tempted to bail. But I don't think Ellen got all the lowdown she was hoping for on Shelley. Where does that expression, lowdown, come from, anyway?" Molly was often distracted by curiosity about the origins of some peculiar expression.

"Means information or true..." Mike started to respond.

"I know what it means," she said a bit impatiently. "But where..."

This time he interrupted her. "Did you notice what was going on between Tom and Conrad?"

"Yeah." Molly paused in wiping down the front of the stove, where deposits around the controls bore testimony to serious, if messy, cooking. "Tom seemed to be kind of baiting him. That odd question about whether Conrad was from Kansas."

"What did Conrad say? I was just going to the kitchen for more wine."

"He didn't directly respond at all. Just said something about having no accent in his speech. Didn't seem relevant." She hesitated. "You're going to think I'm nuts, but..."

"Never!" he smiled.

"Well, I could see both of them clearly from where I sat. And when Tom asked him about Kansas,

Conrad was cutting up his meat." Molly mimed securing meat with a fork in her left hand and sawing with her right. "He stopped, put the fork and knife down and then he put his left hand down on his lap. The rest of the meal, I never saw him use his knife again. Cut his meat with his fork using just his right hand. I remember thinking it was a good thing the meat was so tender."

"Okay, so what if he didn't use his knife? Does Emily Post disapprove?"

"You're missing the point. I think Tom was looking at Conrad's left hand and so Conrad hid it. Did you notice? His left-hand ring finger is a lot shorter than the rest. Looks as if it was cut off at the knuckle."

"I didn't notice. But you think he's embarrassed about it?"

"He wasn't embarrassed until he saw Tom looking at it. Then he looked, I don't know, either angry or scared. And he sure bolted out the door. And look, they left in such a hurry they forgot their big salad bowl."

"CONNIE, WHAT THE HELL?" Christine said as she pulled the car door shut. Conrad was already behind the wheel, ready to pull out onto the street. When he said nothing, she sat a moment in confusion and then tried for a lighter tone. "Why are we scampering off as if we stole the silver?" She sat a few more minutes in silence as he drove towards home. She eyed the speedometer uneasily but said nothing. Finally, as he turned on to their street, she said, "I know Tom O'Day upset you with that reference to Leavenworth. But rushing off like that is only going to make everyone notice. I think you overreacted."

"Overreacted! Geezus, Christine. He recognized me. I know he did."

"Did you recognize him?"

"No, dammit. I don't think I've ever seen the man before in my life. But it was so long ago. People change. Unfortunately, people remember a guy my size," he said. "And I think he noticed this too," he added, holding up his left hand. "I've been racking my brains. Who could he be? How does he know me?"

"If you don't know him, maybe he just thinks he knows you. Or maybe he knows you from before it happened. I don't think we can assume..."

"Don't be naïve. He was threatening me, Christine!" Conrad pounded his fist on the steering wheel. "The bastard could ruin our lives!"

Conrad repeatedly pressed the garage door opener while they were still too far away for the signal to work. When the door finally rose, he drove quickly into the garage. They had suspended a tennis ball from the ceiling to mark the furthest they could park to avoid hitting the cabinets built into the back wall. Christine automatically stomped her foot down on her side of the car as Conrad seemed about to ignore the ball. But he brought the car to an abrupt halt. The tennis ball banged and rebounded against the windshield as he leaped from the car and dashed into the house. With uncharacteristic rudeness, he let the house door swing back into Christine's face as she hurried after him.

"Connie, what are you doing?"

He was in his office, leafing through the Sunrise directory. "O'Day, O'Day—I want to see where he's from and what he did for a living." The directory listed hometowns and careers before retirement. "He's from Michigan, not Kansas. And he was a..." Conrad stood frozen, the small paperback directory hanging limply at his side, his thumb holding it open at the O's.

Christine waited for a few seconds before taking the directory from her husband and looking at the entry for Tom O'Day. "Okay, a judge. He used to be a judge. I don't get it. So, what if he was a judge, Connie?"

Conrad still stood immobile. Only his huge hands moved, nervously massaging the abbreviated finger. "Somehow, he knows," he said, ignoring her question. "I don't know how, but he knows. And the SOB was putting me on notice."

"What are you going to do about it?" Christine asked quietly.

"The more important question is: What is *he* going to do?"

2

MID-OCTOBER

"Whew! I've been cleaning the house all afternoon. I'm ready for a drink," Molly said as she plopped down in a seat across the table from Shelley at The Hole-in-One. As the name suggested, Sunrise Acre's only restaurant also served as a golf course diner. A couple days after the Prepare and Share dinner, Molly invited several friends to meet Shelley at Happy Hour and suggested that Shelley arrive a few minutes early so they could chat before the others arrived. They each ordered a glass of wine.

After going over some of the possibilities for the library website design, they turned to more personal matters. "Love to have the grandkids visit," Molly explained, "but I swear they shed toy parts like dandruff. I keep finding mysterious little objects under cushions and in corners. Maybe they're critical to some now non-functioning vehicle. Who knows? Bottle tops, little green smears that had better not be what they look like, pens without tops and tops without pens. And rocks. Lots of rocks that they picked up on our desert walks that their parents refused to haul home."

"My little brother Brian used to collect bones," Shelley said with a small smile. "He'd find them on the street or in the woods—even in the trash. They were all fascinating to him. Bird bones, squirrel bones —who knew what critters they came from? I'd discover them in his pockets when I did the laundry."

"I hope he grew up to be an anthropologist or maybe an orthopedic surgeon!"

Shelley's smile vanished and she slowly lowered her Chardonnay. She stared across the restaurant where a white-haired woman and her bald companion sat eating mounded taco salads in silence. But clearly Shelley was not seeing them. She appeared to have gone somewhere inside herself. Molly was startled at the discomfort her innocent comment had caused.

Shelley seemed to be considering whether to respond, and after a few awkward moments, she said, "No. Either of those could have been wonderful careers."

Molly wondered what she meant. But Shelley's closed expression suggested that she would not welcome questions.

To their mutual relief, Molly waved at several women just entering. "Here come the gals I wanted you to meet." Charged with finding a designer for the library website, Molly had followed an unofficial, but proven vendor identification process: the Sunrise "Yelp" network. Whenever a group of Sunrisers were waiting for a class, a sport, or a meeting to begin, often someone would ask for a recommendation: Good hip replacement surgeon? Dog psychologist? Nail salon?

A few weeks ago, a sizable audience, including Molly and Mike, had sat in rows of folding chairs awaiting the well-known author J.A. Jance to arrive. Molly passed her inquiry for a web designer down their row. Sitting behind her, Tom O'Day had leaned forward, tapped Molly's shoulder and suggested Shelley as "a talented professional."

"Ladies," Molly said to the group after everyone was seated, "This is Shelley Goossens. As I mentioned in my email, she's a web designer helping me with the Sunrise library website. And she makes it sound so easy, I'm going to have her help me set one up for my real estate business." Given that Molly had heard about Tom's romantic involvement with Shelley, his referral was not unbiased, but Molly had taken the precaution of speaking with clients and references. Shelley's qualifications checked out.

"Shelley doesn't live in Sunrise, but she comes highly recommended by a close friend of hers who does," Molly said.

Aki as usual was the first to sniff out romance. She peered nearsightedly at Shelley through large round glasses. "A very close *male* friend?"

Shelley shifted in her seat and frowned at Molly. "Um, sort of," she said.

"Sort of male?" Aki teased, "Or sort of close?"

Molly intervened, shaking her head at Aki. "The main reason I suggested that Shelley meet you all is that I thought maybe some of you might know other organizations or clubs here in Sunrise or maybe local businesses in Cactus Heights who need websites. She can create one from scratch and honestly, she charges so much less than others I've contacted."

The women were quick to follow Molly's lead and move to slightly less intrusive personal questions than Aki's. Sunrise residents had a canine compulsion to sniff out a newcomer's background—origin and political leanings in particular. Any hint of liberal or conservative? Midwest outgoing or New England reserved?

After Shelley obliged by acknowledging her Illinois roots, the conversation moved on to her profession. Shelley explained what a web designer does and some of the pitfalls. She spoke as if she were accustomed to an audience—her voice more authoritative than conversational. She used clear short sentences as if delivering a lecture.

She's good in front of a group, not just when it's the two of us, Molly thought with some relief, as Shelley would have to present her design to the Library Committee. She studied the young woman. *What has so attracted Tom that justifies destroying what's left of his marriage? The attraction can't be purely physical.* Shelley was tall and sturdily, if curvaceously built. Her strong features were even, maybe a tiny bit masculine— Glenn Close handsome, especially when she smiled broadly, as she was doing now. *But it's hard to see her as a seductress. Maybe the pull is her energy, the way she strides into a room. She's coiled for action. Or maybe it's simply her relative youth. Given how long the O'Days have been together, Audrey O'Day must be considerably older than Shelley.*

The women were posing questions to Shelley—

some of them only remotely relevant to designing websites. "How do you get rid of trolls?" one woman asked.

Shelley responded politely. "One strategy is humor. Humor is kryptonite for trolls. I remember one of my clients getting a nasty comment on her website telling her to 'go bugger yourself,' along with some even more colorful, er, suggestions. She responded with, 'What you suggest is anatomically impossible.'" The women smiled, some of them a bit uneasily. Younger generation humor.

Discussing trolls released a flood of personal stories about the hazards of social media. Shelley gamely passed out business cards as the conversation veered like a flight of starlings on to another subject that was absorbing many Sunrise residents: the huge renovation project underway at one of the main buildings. There had been considerable controversy over space allocations: the ballroom and stage for dances, musical performances and lectures, or the numerous smaller rooms for club meetings.

"The Cactus Swingers have the largest club here," Aki said. "But the new auditorium will be barely bigger than the old one. We'll still have to limit membership, or we'll be kicking each other black and blue every dance."

"But that's just one club," another woman protested. "We need more rooms for the other clubs: mahjong, bridge, euchre..."

"Stained glass studio," Christine Konsinski added. "And all the regional clubs like the New England Club...."

"Molly," Lauren Fleek interrupted. "What was all

that brouhaha last week between Mike and Tom O'Day about the renovation?"

Molly was careful not to look at Shelley but could sense her stiffening. "I don't know that I'd call it a brouhaha," Molly said cautiously, picking her way through the mine field. *How did Lauren get here? I didn't invite her.* Then Molly recalled that she had told her friends, "And bring anyone you think might be interested." She didn't feel comfortable with Lauren, who was quick to attribute malicious intent to innocent interactions. If she was cut off in traffic, it was not because she was in the driver's blind spot but because the driver was malevolent or, at best, an idiot. Both verbal and sign language escalated from there. Lauren's beautifully manicured middle finger had seen some exercise.

"Well, I heard Tom and Mike really got into it at the committee meeting—loud and furious. Didn't he accuse Tom of fraud or something?" The women at the table eagerly homed in on Molly. The breakfast was getting decidedly uncomfortable.

"Not fraud or anything illegal," Molly said. "It's just that the committee decided on a single source bid on the renovation. And Tom really pushed hard for Audrey's nephew's company to get the work. Mike thinks that was, uh...."

"Nepotism!" Another woman chimed in.

"...unwise," Molly finished. "Especially since some of the provisions in the contract seemed to favor the vendor over community interests."

"I always said that Tom is a jerk," Lauren nodded. "I know he's a judge and all that, but you know his wife moved out on him. She must have had a good reason!"

Shelley stirred uneasily. Careful not to look at her, Molly grabbed for a thread to take back the lead. "I can't wait to have the renovation finished. When I take prospective Sunrise residents around on orientation tours, one of the big draws is all our clubs. But a lot of them are not even meeting right now because of the construction." The discussion continued, with various estimates about how far behind was the renovation schedule.

But Aki, Molly could see, had not abandoned her quest to identify Shelley's "close friend." Her delicately pointed nose fairly quivered as she waited for a break in the flow. With her almost unlined face and oversized glasses, Aki always looked more like a schoolgirl than a sixty-year-old woman. People tended to underestimate her ability to extract secrets. "So, Shelley," she said innocently, sitting upright like a meerkat, "where are you staying now?"

Shelley smiled as she veered around the obvious trap. "The Radcliffe Apartments on First Avenue. But," she said with a glance at her watch, "I'm afraid I have to go. Another jolly virtual planning meeting with a client."

After she left, the women turned their attention to Christine, the most recent recruit to Molly's large circle of friends. *She looks so young,* Molly thought. *Not as young as Shelley, but maybe I just think all the new women I meet here look young.* She gave an audible sigh.

The topic was a bit out of Aki's usual focus, but she bent to the task of solving the mysteries on everyone's mind. Using the code words for establishing someone's age, Aki asked, "Are you and your husband still working?"

Molly noticed Christine's lips twitching a bit. *She knows what they're curious about and she's finding it amusing.*

"No, once Conrad sold his company, I retired along with him."

Well played, Christine, Molly thought. *They still don't know how old you are.*

Aki resorted to the customary "So, how did you wind up in Sunrise Acres?"

"Our son Jamie is in a small private college in Denver. Bromley. We wanted to be close enough for quick visits, but we're not helicopter parents, so we don't see him all that often."

Glances of astonishment bounced around the table, and there was a pause in conversation while everyone seemed to do a bit of mental arithmetic. A kid in college? Could the son be adopted? How much older was Conrad than Christine?

"Besides, we're certainly not concerned about him shirking his studies. But Jamie is...he is most comfortable with the other Bromley geeks." She smiled to show the term was affectionate.

"I think Bromley's where my college roommate's daughter went. Isn't that the school that *claims* every student is a genius?" Lauren asked.

Christine looked embarrassed. "Well, I really don't think they'd use that term. But they do tend to enroll students who show a special aptitude for some subject like music or math or physics. Or art," she added.

"What is Jamie's, um, specialty?" Molly asked. *Not exactly the right word, but how do you ask about what a kid is a genius in?*

"Anything to do with computers," Christine said. "You know, at his age it's fun to write programs and hack into something forbidden like, oh, I don't know, the nuclear codes."

"He could do that?" Aki gasped.

"No, of course not," Christine said with an easy laugh. "That was just the most outrageous possibility that I could think of. I'm sure the college keeps an eye on how all the students—especially the computer geeks—use their talents. Wouldn't want them getting into the school's computers and changing grades."

"Sunrise must be a kind of odd place for a kid that age to call home," Lauren observed, frowning. "Having to mingle with a bunch of us geezers."

Does she ever say anything positive? Does she enjoy carrying that big storm cloud around with her? Molly thought.

Christine's smile faded. "Jamie's not actually here that much," she replied. "He'll be home for Christmas and then we're off to Stockholm for a month's skiing and to see my parents."

She had clearly had enough of the interrogation. "If you or Shelley needs help on the website," she said to Molly, "I'm sure he would be willing to be conscripted." With that, she shoved her chair back from the table and nodded pleasantly around the table. "Nice to meet you all," she said, picking up her purse and heading for the door. All eyes followed her exit.

"Good grief," Lauren said once the door closed

behind her. "She's so young. Between her, the teenager son, and Shelley, the average age in Sunrise has gone down a decade!"

"Shelley doesn't live here," Molly reminded them.

"Yet," said Aki.

3

MID-OCTOBER

A couple days after introducing Shelley to friends, Molly drove her ancient golf cart over to Mike's, with her dog Jessie riding shotgun. Jessie always sat up tall in the seat as if she was watchdog for traffic hazards. Molly leapt out of the cart almost as fast as Jessie and was barely through Mike's door before she started talking. "You won't believe what I found out on the web."

"I believe, I believe." Mike raised his hands and waved them in a fair imitation of a revivalist preacher. "Hey, hold that thought. It's a nice morning. Let's take Jessie for a walk through the neighborhood and you can tell me all about it."

Molly hesitated, obviously eager to share her news, but she gave in. "Good idea. Let me grab my water bottle and a doggy poop bag from the golf cart."

It was prime weather for being outside, cool but sunny. Mike and Molly were exchanging "good mornings" with fellow dog walkers every few minutes. Most walkers used the street, giving them more room to socialize with friends and neighbors and to avoid the trios of mailboxes mounted on the sidewalks every fifty yards or so. Walkers with dogs moved slowly with erratic stops as their furry charges halted every few feet, sniffing bushes, rocks, and gravel to suss out which canine acquaintances had passed by and to find suitable spots to leave their own calling cards. Traffic was light and speeding was almost unheard of. Drivers going even thirty in the twenty-five-mph zone were likely to be scolded. -

After a peloton of ten or fifteen Lycra-clad bikers swept by, Molly launched into her news. "I was curious about Konsinski Cyber Security. You know, Conrad's old company." Jessie tugged at the leash and squatted. Molly obediently stopped as she explained to Mike. "I googled it. I thought I should know something about cybersecurity to sound halfway intelligent when I discussed the library website with Shelley. KCS has a minimal online presence, including its website. Doesn't even give details about what it does —just sort of general statements like 'teaches employees how to combat phishing.' And it has some kind of proprietary security-checking software that they maintain has never been hacked."

Molly pulled a plastic bag out of her pocket, covered her hand with it and retrieved Jessie's contribution to the landscape. "But here's what's interesting," she said, absently handing the plastic bag to Mike. "The About Us history section of the site credits Conrad as founder and former CEO, but there's no bio or photo for him at all! Just says he was 'an award-winning cybersecurity expert' but no details on the awards. No mention of education. Basically nothing. But the site lists four senior employees, all with bios and photos." She looked eagerly at Mike. "Well?"

"You must be Greek," Mike said, holding up by thumb and forefinger the little parcel she'd handed him and eyeing it dubiously.

"Huh?" Molly said. "What..."

"From the Aeneid. 'Beware of Greeks bearing gifts,'" Mike quoted with the bag now at arm's length.

"Are you even listening to me?" Molly was not interested in irrelevant literary allusions. "Mike!"

"Sorry." Mike pulled himself back to the thread of her narrative about the KCS website. "I'm not sure I follow. Maybe a company like that, dealing with secrets, doesn't provide a lot of information on past employees."

"Yeah, okay, maybe the company's secretive. But here's the thing. I googled Conrad Konsinski and other than the one reference on the KCS website, I couldn't find him anywhere. The website had a list of specialties, so it can't be a real tiny company. Seems really weird that the founder and former CEO isn't somewhere on the web. I found the current CEO, Janice someone or other, who has given lots of speeches about cyber security, but nothing about Conrad ever having given a speech."

"Maybe she's a better speaker. His explanation of cyber currencies at our dinner was about as lively as a brochure on mattress specifications. And once we sat down at the table, he hardly spoke at all."

"Okay, okay, but I thought it was odd that I couldn't find him in a dozen searches. I tried Bing and DuckDuckGo also. Nothing. Got all kinds of hits on

Konsinski and of course countless Conrads, but no Conrad Konsinski. You don't find that strange?"

"Not particularly. But why are you spending all this time DuckDucking or whatever on Conrad?"

"It's just weird, that's all. Like we had dinner with a ghost. Aren't you at all curious about why he doesn't seem to exist anywhere except here?"

"Why should I be? Probably a lot of cybersecurity experts fly under the radar."

"I don't follow that logic," Molly persisted. "Just because he deals with security doesn't mean he's had to hide from public view. Not if he wanted new clients."

By now, the dog walkers were out in force. Mike and Molly's walk was frequently interrupted by human and canine greetings alike. Mike was always entertained by observing who pulled whom. The younger dogs tugged enthusiastically at their leashes, dragging their owners. When the agility gap between pet and owner was too large, owners resorted to driving their golf carts while their leashed dogs trotted alongside. But there were also dogs with grizzled muzzles and the halting gait of an elderly body that required gentle tugging. And a few owners wheeled disabled dogs through the neighborhood in baby strollers.

Mike stopped to pet a large Labrador with huge brown eyes begging for attention. Jessie greeted her enthusiastically and the two dogs circled each other, checking out each other's butt. "She loves to meet everyone," the Lab's owner said, but pulled her dog away from the mutual sniffing.

"It's fine, just the doggy equivalent of checking out

someone's profile on the Internet," Mike commented about the rear end explorations. "I've read they can learn how old the other dog is, what he eats, where he's been."

"Still disgusting," the Lab's owner said, as she resumed her walk.

"Seems so to humans," Mike agreed. *But humans have equivalent customs—just not that one, thank goodness.* As he and Molly walked on, he returned to the discussion. "KCS is a private company, Molly. As the former owner, Conrad could have done whatever he wanted." Mike smiled at her. "I think you're getting bored. You're seeing a mystery where there's likely a perfectly rational reason for him to protect his privacy."

"So, don't worry my pretty little head about it?" Molly said sarcastically.

Too much talk about butt sniffing; too little listening to her, Mike realized. "Ouch. I guess I did sound a bit patronizing. Hey, I can always ask him about it when I see him at poker. He'll probably have a good explanation."

4

LATE OCTOBER

A couple weeks after they had hosted the tense Prepare and Share dinner, Molly and Mike had just finished a much more peaceful meal of chicken tikka masala that he had prepared. As Molly cleaned up, Mike sat on the couch, lounging against some of Molly's brilliantly colored throw pillows while he looked through Sunrise Notes, the community monthly magazine. "Tonight is try-out night for the Cactus Swingers," he said suddenly.

"You have to try out to join a club?" Molly asked incredulously.

"No. Sorry, I don't mean you have to audition or anything. It's just a night for people to come without joining the club, just to, you know, try out the dancing. Let's go. Andrea and I joined it when we first moved here. It's a lot of fun."

"I don't know," Molly said. "I'm not much of a dancer."

"Neither am I, but swing dance is easy. Ever

done it?"

"Not since college." Her tone was decidedly unen-thusiastic.

"Hey, it starts in fifteen minutes. Come on, let's try it out."

Molly just shook her head.

"Jeans are fine," he said assuming dress was an obstacle. "If you don't enjoy it, we can leave."

"Oh, alright," she said with a resigned sigh. She looked down at her pickleball "Carpe Dinkem" T-shirt. "But I've got to change my top." Mike sighed inwardly but said nothing. In a couple minutes, Molly emerged from the bedroom, holding up two hangers with shirts on them. "Which one?"

Mike hesitated. *Why do women do this? They know most men are either color-blind or style-blind or both. And if she's like Andrea, whichever one I choose, she'll wear the other!* He cocked his head and tried to look thoughtful and judicious. "Um, the pink" *or is it red?* "That one." He pointed at the nearest shirt.

Molly smiled. *She's on to me,* he thought. But when she came out wearing the blouse he'd chosen, he was unreasonably pleased.

MOLLY COULD SEE that Mike was enjoying himself. The music was not to her taste and was far too loud, but they immediately saw friends. Aki and Frank were members of many clubs, so Molly was not surprised to see them. Peter was there with an attractive woman whose blonde hair and English rose complexion contrasted dramatically with Peter's dark hair and skin. Her clothes yelled Western—shirt with silver buttons, large silver belt buckle, cowboy boots.

After introductions, Mike said, "Surprised to see you here, Peter."

"What, you think Black guys only do hip-hop?" Peter said with a smile.

Mike colored at the friendly taunt but rallied to tease in return. "No, I thought radiologists were too sophisticated for this country and western stuff."

"Oh, we are. But Lynn here," nodding to his companion, "dragged me."

Lynn grinned and affected a Texas accent. "Gotta knock some of that stuffin' outta his shirt."

"She'll regret it," Peter said over his shoulder as the two of them made their way to the dance floor.

For Molly and Mike, the first dance went fine. But disaster struck on the second number. Mike made one of his old swing moves: twirling his partner under his arm. As Molly started to pass underneath, Mike's arm struck her full on the forehead and launched her like a missile into the line of folding chairs set up along the wall.

"Oh my god," he yelled, extracting her from a tangle of partially collapsed chairs. "Molly, I'm so terribly sorry. Are you okay? I didn't...I haven't danced since...you are about four inches taller than Andre...than I'm used to," he concluded lamely. "Shall I get some ice?"

"I'm fine," Molly said firmly to the concerned group of dancers gathered around. She turned to Mike. "But that's it. We are leaving." She marched for the door with a very red-faced Mike trailing.

All the way back to her house, Molly huddled

behind a wall of silence. She tried to analyze her feelings before she allowed herself to speak. *Am I being unfair? It's not as if he knocked me over deliberately.* Hunched over the steering wheel, he glanced at her every few seconds, obviously uneasy but hesitating to speak. To her own discomfort, she recognized that one of the emotions she was feeling was self-righteousness. *It's his fault. I didn't want to go, darn it. Let him stew a bit.* But Molly prided herself on being fair. *I did agree to go.*

Mike parked and walked Molly to her door. She stopped abruptly and turned on him, despite her resolve to think a bit more before letting her feelings out. "Mike, I hated that. The music was too loud. Old people trying to be twenty again, flailing around, knocking into each other. I don't need this. I'm not an introvert, for heaven's sake. But...."

Mike tried to apologize but as he started to follow her inside, she put a restraining hand on his chest. "I'm fine," she said again. "Don't worry. But I've had enough drama for the evening. Let's talk tomorrow." She slipped inside and closed the door behind her. She glanced out the window as Mike walked back to the car, his shoulders slumped.

At the kitchen counter, Molly turned the kettle on. *It's too late for tea; it will keep me up—or at least get me up in the middle of the night.* But she wanted the comfort. As she poured boiling water into the waiting cup, an uncomfortable thought came unbidden. *Did I hate that dance so much because I know Andrea loved it?*

She set the kettle back on its base with a thump. *No, darn it. I'm not going to scrutinize every reaction I have to what Mike wants to do. If I don't want to do it, I'm not going to!* She thought of Princess Diana's famous complaint about then Prince Charles's love for Camilla Parker Bowles: "There were three of us in this marriage, so it was a bit crowded." *Change the word "marriage" to "relationship" and that's the way I feel sometimes.*

She pulled the tea bag out of her mug and dumped it in the trash can under the sink. It dripped a bit on the floor because she'd not pulled the trash can out far enough. She barely noticed. She took the mug into the living room and sat in her favorite brown leather chair. Jessie followed and settled her head on Molly's lap. Normally, the dog would have insisted Molly pet her or scratch behind her ears. But Jessie seemed to sense that this time it was her job to provide comfort. She didn't push Molly's hand but just left her head there and looked up with anxious eyes at Molly's face. She occasionally thumped her tail as her mistress continued to ruminate.

Mike says he'd never treat me the way Max did, and I know he'd never carry on an actual affair. But is he unfaithful to me in his mind? Is Andrea the "other woman"? How much am I willing to risk to keep this relationship going?

As Mike drove home after the dance disaster, he shook his head, berating himself for being so clumsy. And "let's talk" always set up a nervous thrumming in his chest. He stood miserably a long time in the shower before he realized how much water he was wasting— anathema to desert dwellers. He tried reading his usual twenty minutes in bed before turning off the light, but after an hour of staring alternatively at the ceiling and then at the taunting red figures on the clock face, he turned the clock to the wall to avoid counting the hours of lost sleep. At last, a welcome oblivion enveloped him, but he awakened several times with a tightness in his chest signaling that something bad had happened. It was only too reminiscent of the months before and after Andrea's death. Each time it took a few seconds to remember the source of anxiety and a lot longer to get back to sleep.

At about four thirty, he made coffee and debated with himself about how early he could call Molly. By five thirty, Jessie needed an early morning walk and exploration of scents left by doggy friends or the occasional coyote. On balmy summer mornings, Mike knew Molly rather enjoyed the dawn choruses while she walked Jessie. However, abandoning a warm bed for a dark and cool autumn morning was another matter. When Mike stayed over at her house, he habitually took Jessie out to allow Molly another half hour in bed. By the time she got up, her tea water would be boiling and, if it was chilly, the gas fireplace would be turned on. Mike could picture Jessie, leash in mouth, forlornly sitting alongside "his" side of the bed, wondering where he was. Giving up on him, she would then round to Molly's side and rest her head on the edge of the bed, breathing a bit loudly into Molly's face. *Nothing like doggy breath to get one up in the morning*, he thought, with a bit of an evil smile. *She shouldn't have kicked me out last night!* He was immediately ashamed of the thought, but a bit of moral indignation crept back in. *It's not like I hit her on purpose.* He went through his usual coffee-making ritual on auto pilot, grinding his coffee beans and checking the temperature of the water.

I should go over, let myself in as if nothing happened and walk Jessie before she can wake Molly. Kind of an apology for the dance accident.

When he reached Molly's house, he was surprised to see the kitchen lights on. He let himself in, expecting a frantic scramble of claws on the tile and Jessie bounding to greet him. The kitchen was silent. "Jessie," he called softly, thinking maybe Molly had left the kitchen light on last night and was still asleep. No response. Then he thought to check the electric tea kettle. It was hot, and there was a wet tea bag in a mug on the counter. *So, Molly is out walking Jessie and she took her insulated tea mug with her.*

Mike made himself another cup of coffee with the supplies he kept at her house and sat down at the kitchen table.

He heard Molly open the door and then came the familiar sounds of a happy dog rocketing in his direction.

"Good morning," he said cheerfully and scratched behind Jessie's ears as Molly entered.

She did not look particularly happy to see him. "Good morning," she responded evenly. She turned the tea kettle on again, stood at the sink, and did not meet his eyes.

"Let me see where I hit you," he said as he walked over to her. He cupped her face in his hands and examined her forehead. "No bruise," he said in relief.

"The bruises are on my hip, where I hit the chairs."

"I'm so sorry," he said again. "I wasn't aiming for you, honest," he joked, looking at her hopefully. "Forgive me?"

"You're apologizing for hitting me?"

"Yes, of course. I was clumsy. Out of practice."

She looked at him steadily, unsmiling. Then she shook her head a little and turned away. "I accept your apology for hitting me."

He looked at her in bewilderment. *That sure didn't sound as if she's forgiven me. What more does she want*? "Molly, you've always been frank with me. Well mostly," he amended, thinking of how long it had taken before she had told him about her disastrous marriage and her consequent difficulty in trusting men. "If you've forgiven me for my awful dancing, what is it that you have not forgiven? You're obviously still mad at me."

"It took me all night to figure it out myself." She fished a fresh Earl Grey tea bag out of the cupboard, took down the heavy aqua pottery mug she used every morning, and inserted the tea bag.

"And?"

Molly braced both arms outstretched on the countertop and stared down at the bright Mexican tiles for a long moment. Finally, she turned and faced him. "I don't know how to put this any other way. It feels to me as if you are trying to make me into Andrea." He started to protest, and she held up a hand. "Wait. Let me explain. You and Andrea loved Western dancing. Well, I don't. And the other night, you said that 'the natural next step for us' was for me to move in with you. Into the house you and Andrea completely re-built and decorated."

"I guess that was badly expressed."

"Oh man, you still don't get it. 'Badly expressed.' Like it's a matter of choosing the right words." She picked up the tea kettle but instead of pouring the boiling water into her mug, she set it back down heavily and turned away again. "I need some time to think, Mike. Let's give it a rest for a little while."

"It?"

"It. Us. Let's take a break from each other for a few..." She hesitated and Mike tensed, afraid to hear the time frame she'd decided on.

"A few...?"

She looked around at his desolate face and relented. "Days. Maybe a week or so."

5

LATE OCTOBER

When Christine Konsinski pulled into the driveway and son Jamie climbed out of the car, Conrad was kneeling by the large rose bush in front of their house. The fall bloom was starting, and Conrad was removing a few spent blossoms and doing some minor pruning. Jamie towered over his mother, but he hadn't yet acquired his father's bulk. *Small wonder his nickname at school is Bean,* Conrad thought. He stood up, brushed off his kneepads, and gave his son a hug, despite Jamie stiffening at the embrace. *Eventually he'll get used to it,* Conrad thought. *I hope.*

"Is that the burning bush of biblical fame, Dad?" Jamie asked with unaccustomed humor. "Or were you on your knees praying for rain?"

Conrad smiled, pleased at the teasing. "These roses have two flowering seasons. This is not as spectacular as the one in April, but still some nice color. I *am* praying, though—for a competent landscaper. This darned irrigation system sprouts a leak at least once a week and I'm getting tired of watering things by hand. I'd hate to have my roses die of thirst." He gestured at the shallow ditch he had dug. "There are three irrigation lines here—and one of them is definitely bleeding water somewhere. I just have to figure out which one and plug it. Wanna help?"

"Great way to start my long weekend, Dad. You do know that we live in a desert here, right? You should get rid of the roses and xeriscape the whole garden. I'm taking that course in desert ecosystems I told you about. You could spend an afternoon out in the desert and bring back all kinds of flowers and cacti. Free, too."

"Actually," Christine said, "Except for maybe collecting some seeds, it's illegal in Arizona to take plants out of public lands. But," she added thoughtfully, "the Tucson Cactus and Succulent Society rescues native plants from building sites—we could buy some from them."

"Better than wasting all that water on *roses*," Jamie said scornfully and headed for the house. "Gimme a few minutes to change. I'll come back out."

"Ah, the righteousness of youth," Conrad said with a grin after Jamie had left.

"Well, in this case, he's right," Christine said. "But Connie, can't you get George to come back and fix the leak? Jamie just got home."

"By the time George could schedule us in, we'd have a lake in the backyard. And it's something Jamie and I can do together, besides programming or video games. I thought you'd be pleased."

When Jamie eventually emerged from the house, Conrad had identified the leak. He cut a section out of the pipe and was attempting to fit a plastic connector to splice the two ends together. "Shit!" he exclaimed loudly, sitting back on his heels in frustration. He glanced guiltily at the house next door, hoping Mrs. Albertson hadn't heard him. *Probably never swore in her life.* He pictured her with both hands over her ears. "I cut too long a piece out," he told Jamie. "Now I'll have to find a longer connector."

"Like this one?" Jamie held out a connector he had plucked out of the clutter in the box of pipes and connectors Conrad had set on the ground.

"Thanks!" Conrad said, taking it from Jamie and forcing the cut ends into the connector. "That should do it—for now. I'm afraid I don't have a mechanical gene in my whole body."

"Um, me neither. And Dad, speaking of genes...I wanted to talk to you about that."

Conrad was shoveling gravel into the hole with gloved hands. "About what?" he asked distractedly.

"About your family." Conrad stopped moving the gravel back in place and looked up at Jamie.

"Your parents. I know you don't have any pictures of them because of the house fire. But what were they like?"

Conrad stood up and looked at him warily. "Where's this coming from, Jamie? I told you my dad was a firefighter, and my mom was a housewife. You've seen that one photo I have of them."

"Uh-huh. Dad, the thing is...their name wasn't Konsinski. And they didn't live in Alton, Illinois."

Conrad stared at his son. He started to speak, glanced again at the neighboring house, shook his head. "Maybe we'd better talk inside." He picked up the box and strode quickly into the garage, lowering the door almost before Jamie was inside. He washed his hands in the laundry room sink and dried them slowly and deliberately before turning to Jamie.

"I want to know," Jamie said, anger in his voice now, "why you've been feeding me a bunch of bullshit all my life. I'll bet your house didn't burn down with everything in it. Maybe my grandparents didn't even die while you were in college. It's all a big lie, isn't it? I've known for a long time that something was screwy, the way you avoid answering questions. But I figured there must be a good reason, and I really didn't care that much then, so I let it slide. Until...."

Christine appeared in the laundry doorway, drawn by Jamie's angry voice. "Jamie?"

He turned on her. "Has he lied to you too, Mom? Or maybe you know all about his family?"

Christine exchanged a glance with Conrad. "This is between you and Dad," she said. "Your father is a fine man. Remember that." She turned away and went into the kitchen.

"So, what evidence do you have that I've lied to you?" Conrad asked heavily.

"Okay, first, I've looked, Dad. And I'm exceedingly good at finding stuff online. Frankly, I could tell you when the FBI director's beagle had her last rabies shot if I wanted to. But I couldn't find Conrad Konsinski until about page 20 in the Google search. Then in the Albany Illinois newspaper I got a hit. It's that kind of small local paper that reports Thanksgiving visitors from out of town and high school teams' scores. Finally, I found a Conrad Konsinski."

"Okay," Conrad said guardedly.

"Same birthdate as you. At least, the birthday we celebrate."

"Uh-huh." Conrad looked at his son. *I know where this is going,* he thought unhappily. *We should have had an artist for a son instead of a computer whiz.*

"Yeah, except," Jamie announced triumphantly, "it was an obituary. He died of the flu at age three! And no more about Conrad Konsinski until just about when you started the company. And no Paul and Lorraine Konsinski either—at least not the right ages. So, there are two logical explanations: one, I'm inept at elementary web searches; two, for reasons unknown, you chose to change your identity decades ago or someone else changed your identity for you. Well, I think we can discard possibility number one. You didn't send me to college to watch me flunk out of Web Search 101. So, it's number two."

Conrad looked at him steadily but did not respond.

"I figured that much out over a year ago, but I let it pass. I guess I thought you'd let me know when the time came, but I got tired of waiting. There's really only one logical explanation. You have to be in federal witness protection. I haven't been able to get into WITSEC databases yet to confirm. I want to know what you did to get yourself into WITSEC. You had to have been in a position to put some bad guy or guys in prison. What if they've figured out where you are? Where *we* are? Dammit, Dad, I have a right to know. And I can't let it slide any longer."

Conrad's face registered relief. *Let him think that for now.*

"What makes all this so urgent now, Jamie?"

Jamie glanced at his mother who was now standing in the doorway, observing. "I'm going to apply for an internship for next fall. It's supposed to be for college seniors, but Professor Novacek says he can get me in."

"Your computer science prof?" Jamie nodded. "Well, where is the internship?"

"The NSA." Jamie ignored Christine's audible gasp.

"Professor Novacek used to work there; he was the one who started the internships for students, and he's good friends with the woman directing the program. I'm a shoo-in, he says. But of course, they'll do a background check. An extensive one."

Conrad looked at his son's flushed, excited face and then at his wife. She had her hand over her mouth in a cliché pose of horror. As she lowered her hand, she breathed softly, "The National Security Agency. Oh my god."

"What will they find?" Jamie demanded. "Come on, Dad, you gotta give me something. Who the hell are you?"

Conrad shook his head. *That kind of background check could ruin everything—the business, my reputation, even our family.*

"You're barking up the wrong tree," he said. "And it's the wrong time. I'm sorry, Jamie, but I can't...you can't apply for that internship. I'll explain why some time, but right now I can't. Honest, Son, I just can't."

Jamie's face darkened. "Wrong answer," he said, mimicking his father's tone. "I can find out, Dad. You know I can."

6

EARLY NOVEMBER

"You look like a man who needs a beer," Irwin said to Mike. "It's nice out in the sun on the back patio. If it gets too cold, I'll turn on my portable heater out there. Have a seat and I'll get us each one."

The view from Irwin's patio was one of the best in Sunrise Acres. It looked across the eleventh hole of the golf course to the Catalina Mountains to the east and the distant Tucson Mountains to the southwest. *This is a really prime spot. Molly would love to have this listing if Irwin, uh, ever decides to sell.*

Mike noticed that as Irwin walked towards the kitchen, he determinedly straightened his back and took a bit longer stride than his usual shuffle.

When Mike had once asked his age (a question permitted in the peculiar Sunrise culture, at least among the men), Irwin had responded, "Can't remember." Most people his generation were quick to inform others, even if the question had not been posed. It was regarded as a personal achievement to have survived that long. Not Irwin. But given Irwin's service in the Korean War, Mike knew that north of ninety had to be an accurate estimate.

Irwin was a small man, curved and wrinkled as a dried peach. His bushy white eyebrows stuck out straight from his brow like insect antennae. But the lively blue eyes beneath were sharp with intelligence. He returned with two beers and plunked them down on the glass-topped table. His Grateful Dead T-shirt with a faded photo of Jerry Garcia matched almost threadbare jeans. He sat down beside Mike and stretched out his feet. Noting Mike's glance at his outfit, Irwin observed: 'I'm wearing these jeans until they rip enough to be fashionable. Couple more years, I figure."

Mike and Irwin sat in silence for a few minutes. A hummingbird dived towards the bright red logo on Mike's T-shirt and veered off in disappointment.

Mike wasn't quite ready to broach the topic that had brought him. "What kind of leather is that?" he asked, pointing to Irwin's boots.

"Crocodile. Not Alligator," he added, as if Mike had confused the two.

"Huh. I thought you were an animal lover."

"Mammals. And birds. Reptiles, not so much."

"Somehow I never pictured you wearing animal skins."

"Why? You do. Don't you have leather shoes in your closet?"

"Well, yeah. But crocodiles?"

Irwin shrugged. "His choice," he said, waving a casual hand at the boots. "Nasty guy went after us when I was canoeing with a friend in Australia a few decades ago. Bad decision. My friend was nastier. Shot him, wrestled the carcass to shore and had him made into boots. Two pair. Ever eat croc meat? Some folks say it tastes like chicken. But I can say as a fact that this guy did not. At all."

Mike smiled, shook his head, but made no comment. After watching him for a few minutes, Irwin broke the silence. "Got one for your collection," he said, taking a sip of his beer and putting the bottle on the patio table. He knew Mike collected malapropisms as ardently as philatelists did stamps. "Heard it on the radio. NPR of all places. The guy being interviewed was talking about Arizona politics and he said the recent lawsuits 'would exasperate the situation!'"

Mike dutifully took out his phone and recorded Irwin's contribution, but with less than his usual enthusiasm. He put the phone away and sat, downcast, apparently absorbed in the progress of a large black beetle laboring across the pavers in the patio.

Irwin waited patiently.

"Irwin," Mike said at last, "It's good to have a guy to unload on. I usually bug my sister Frannie, but right now she's on one of those Viking river cruises somewhere in Europe, and besides..."

"So, I'm pinch-hitting for your sister?"

"No, no. Well, not exactly. I mean, Frannie's great, but sometimes I need a guy's advice. A guy with some experience with women. You've been married, what—twice? Three times?"

"Yep, thrice: died, divorced, died. Plus, of course, there's Maeve. So, Mike, I take it you're having woman trouble. Molly? How serious?"

Mike nodded glumly. "I don't really know." He recounted the scene with Molly. "And I'm afraid to find out if we're finished. But don't you think she's overreacting? I just don't get why she's so mad at me. Okay, she hates dancing. It's not as if I intentionally hit her."

"That can't be the only reason she's angry. You told me before that your enthusiasm on the dance floor makes up for your two left feet. But I seem to recall you also suggested that one of those feet sometimes finds its way into your mouth off the dance floor. Ring any bells?"

"Well," Mike said slowly. "I did suggest she move in with me."

"Huh. Not you move in with her?"

"Irwin, that wouldn't make sense!" Mike began ticking off his house's advantages on his fingers. "Her house is a lot smaller than mine. And it has no landscaping at all. I have all those flowerbeds, a couple citrus trees, and the fountain out back. Really nice for entertaining. And the orange tree is finally bearing fruit. Last winter, I had fresh orange juice every morning."

"And exactly how did you make this suggestion?"

"What do you mean?" he said defensively. "I just said I thought it would make financial sense."

"How romantic," Irwin murmured.

"But Irwin, my place has this great open floor plan and a terrific master suite. And a jacuzzi." Mike was running out of fingers.

"Which, no doubt, Andrea loved," Irwin added.

"Which Andrea...loved," Mike repeated in agreement, his voice trailing off uncertainly as he heard himself.

"Well, I had a cat once," Irwin said. "Name of Binky."

"Irwin, what the...?

"Bear with me a little. Any sudden noise and Binky'd get into a defensive crouch, ready to bolt."

"Okay," Mike said slowly, still unsure where Irwin was headed.

"We always figured he'd had some bad experiences before we got him from the rescue center."

"I'm not sure I like comparing Molly to a neurotic cat...."

"Binky wasn't neurotic!" Irwin said a bit indignantly. "He'd just had a tough life and he couldn't tell us about it. Mike! Just listen!"

"Okay, okay. So, how does this..." Irwin stared at him. "Sorry, continue."

"So, from what you've told me, Molly's had some rough times. Having her husband mowed down by some idiot driver while he was out jogging was bad enough. Then she found out only after he died about his longtime affair. And then that guy—what's his name—the best friend who knew about the affair and didn't tell her?"

"Kirk—that's his name. And maybe I didn't tell you the rest. After her husband, Max, was killed, Kirk and Molly dated, and he eventually proposed to her. And she might have accepted if she hadn't found out that he had betrayed her by not telling her about Max's affair."

"Okay, so maybe she has a right to be a bit guy-shy.

How did she take your suggestion that she move in with you?"

"Not well. Irwin, if I lose Molly...." The thought opened an abyss that he was afraid to look into. He remembered the time he realized for certain that he was going to lose Andrea. She had insisted that she be told the truth, and Mike could still hear Dr. Eubanks's words. The oncologist had delivered them as gently as he could, but they still pierced Mike's heart with their finality: *"Andrea, I'm so very sorry. How long? Two months, maybe three."*

"I've been incredibly lucky, to have two great loves in my life," Mike told Irwin.

"Uh huh. Me too."

"But you've been married *three* times! Plus Maeve."

"Yep. As I said. Me too."

Mike caught on belatedly. "Oh, got it." They sat for a bit, listening to Irwin's fountain. Another errant hummingbird whizzed by like a huge bumblebee and headed for the feeder on the corner eaves of the house.

"How's your love life?' Irwin abruptly cut into the calm.

Mike sat up startled. "What? Irwin," he began accusingly...

"Now SC! You probably think I'm too old to even think about such things, but Maeve and I find time for some intimacy. You don't have to have the 'little death' to have fun!"

I have no intention of discussing Irwin's relationship with his current girlfriend. Certainly not that aspect of it! "Not all problems can be solved in bed," Mike said, wincing as he heard the pompous note in his voice.

Irwin chuckled.

"And what the hell does SC mean anyway? You've been talking too much to your grandkids."

Irwin grinned at him. "*Great* grandkids! It means Stay Cool! They're teaching me text-speak."

"But text is just that—written, not spoken."

"How about LOL? Huh? Bet you've heard people say that, right? And TMI? Learning a new language is good for me. Helps keep my brain from going AWOL —that's 'absent without—"

"Leave," Mike finished. "Yes, Irwin, I know what AWOL means."

"My mind's going AWOL a lot these days. But when I forget six things, I figure that gives me room for at least three new notions. And it amuses the hell out of the kids to teach me."

"Irwin, you never cease to impress me. But I've gotta go." He put his bottle down on the glass table and started to get up, but Irwin waved him back down.

"Wait, now you came to the oracle for an answer."

"More cat parables?"

"Nope. Just a question: Would you rather wake up to freshly squeezed orange juice—or Molly?"

THE MORNING after his talk with Irwin, Mike sat in his family room admiring one of Andrea's paintings, *Datura*. Sunlight highlighted a saguaro in the fore-ground, a small mourning dove perched on a lower arm of the cactus. Another dove was partially hidden under a nearby shrub. The birds drew the eye of the observer down to the spectacular cluster of white trumpet-shaped jimsonweed (locally known as datura) blossoms set off against dark green leaves. Of Andrea's series of Southwest flora this was Mike's favorite and held pride of place above the fireplace. He liked the realism, although it was atypical of his late wife's more abstract style. The large flowers reminded him of Georgia O'Keeffe's marvelous works, although Andrea's point of view in the painting was much farther away.

*Andrea. That unbearable pain has been slowly receding. But this painting brings back so much. Her delight at having the time to paint, to redecorate this house, to....*Mike's thoughts returned again to Dr. Eubanks's shattering prognosis. In the drive back from the hospital, Andrea had broken their stunned silence. *"Mike, I know you don't want to hear this, I know you'll deny it, but please listen. You are still young. I don't want you to be alone. Find joy again."*

She would have liked Molly.

Okay, time for breakfast. Hot cereal and dried fruit, he decided. From the cherry cupboards in the spacious kitchen, he pulled out packages of cranberries and golden raisins, a bag of brown sugar, and ten-grain cereal. Several large store-bought oranges sat in a bowl on the counter.

Mike inhaled the citrus aroma as he squeezed the oranges. *Can't wait until my own crop is ripe!* He took a small sip and set the glass aside thinking about Irwin's stark question. *Right about now, she's taking Jessie out for the first walk of the day. And here I am with—fresh squeezed orange juice! No debate there. I'd opt for waking up next to Molly! If she'd have me.*

He was tempted to drive over to her house and grovel. But he couldn't let go of what seemed perfectly obvious. *What was so wrong with asking her to move in with me? This is a terrific house.* He looked around the kitchen at the carefully chosen Brazilian granite, the cherry cabinets, the sleek modern appliances, the large soft yellow ceramic floor tiles that complemented the countertops. *We made some really good selections.*

And then it hit. *"We." Andrea and me.* For the first time, he tried to see the house as Molly might. His late wife's large oil paintings on every wall. The muted earth tones that predominated in furniture, walls, tile and rugs. Very different from the bright colors Molly favored. She had never mentioned how she felt about a house she'd had no hand in planning and decorating. He thought about the story his older (and wiser) sister had once told him about weaver birds. The males made nests as part of the courting ritual, but the females would select mates depending on whether they liked the nests or not. A door opened in Mike's mind. *Birdbrain!* he chided himself as he suddenly "got it."

And I know what I need to do about it.

7

EARLY NOVEMBER

Jamie didn't call home often. In fact, usually his parents had to plead for him to take a break from whatever programming task he was deep into or from Dungeons and Dragons with friends to respond to a call.

So, Conrad was surprised to see Jamie's number appear on his mobile one morning in early November. He and Christine had just returned from a three-mile hike in the nearby Catalina State Park. It was perfect weather for hiking, and they usually liked to go further, up to where water tumbled into the Romero pools. But Conrad was glad they'd had to come home a bit early for Christine to attend her stained-glass art class. He would have hated to miss the call.

"Hi Bean!" Conrad said enthusiastically. "To what D & D conquest do we owe the honor of a call?"

Jamie did not respond to the teasing. "I called to warn you," he said grimly.

Conrad went on high alert. "Warn me about what?"

"I told you I'd find out. I know all about what happened at Leavenworth, you going AWOL, and why you changed your name."

Conrad's mind immediately flew to the one person he knew could reveal his own past. "Did Tom O'Day contact you?" he asked angrily. "That SOB. He had no right..."

"Dad, Dad!" Jamie almost shouted. "I don't know any Tom O'Day. Nobody told me anything. I found it all out myself. Not as hard as you probably have been thinking it would be after all these years. Have to give it to you. You covered your tracks fairly well, but once I compared your fingerprints..."

"My fingerprints! How the hell did you get my fingerprints?"

"Dad," Jamie said as if to a child, "Your fingerprints are all over the house, the car, the furniture. Not exactly difficult to pick them up on a piece of tape when I was home for my long weekend."

"But..."

"The genius part, if I do say so myself, was hacking into the military databases. And then searching for a comparison."

Conrad was almost speechless. "The military..." he repeated in disbelief.

"And once I had your real name, *Joseph Osterhous*," Jamie emphasized sarcastically, "I could track you back as far as I wanted. Back to grade school, high school—nice stats in basketball, by the way—enlisting in the Army. And then there were press clippings about your, um, misadventure as an MP at Fort

Leavenworth. I can see why you didn't want me to intern at the NSA. Even a half-assed background check would find it all. Guess I can kiss the internship goodbye for sure."

"Jamie, I promise I'll find you a super project at KCS this summer."

"Oh, great. Working for my dad. That'll look real impressive on my resume."

"Jamie, come on, you know I don't work for KCS anymore, so you won't be working for me. But the CEO and I are old friends, and I know she would be thrilled to have you. The shortage of programmers hit just after she bought me out and she can't fill the open positions. And you'd be working for a KCS client organization anyway. It'll be just as top secret as anything at the NSA—but without the background check."

Jamie didn't say anything.

"Okay?" Conrad asked anxiously. He took the grunt from the other end of the phone call as assent.

"I still want the whole story. And I want to know if I have living grandparents on your side."

"Jamie, give me a chance to explain what happened, please. And no, my parents have been dead for years. Can you wait until you get home? You'll be here for a few days in just a couple weeks. I want to tell you everything. But not over the phone. It wasn't as simple and straightforward as the newspapers made it out to be."

"And that's why you went AWOL? Because it was 'complicated'"?

"Son, give me a break. I promise I'll give you all the details. The truth—all of it. I have a couple things

I need to work out. After that you can decide what you want to do with it."

He disconnected the call and went into his office to wait until Christine returned from her class. He fired up his computer and brought up their brokerage account, intending to do work on their portfolio, but he couldn't concentrate. He had no sense of what Jamie would do with the facts he had now promised his son. *How could a seventeen-year-old possibly understand the circumstances that led to my going AWOL?*

He heard the garage door open and Christine calling his name.

"In here," he said loudly.

"You should see what..." Christine stopped in the doorway when she saw his face. "What happened?"

"Jamie called. He lifted my fingerprints while he was home and went through some databases to find a match."

Christine stood stunned and open-mouthed. Without even questioning how their much-too-smart son managed that feat, she finally asked weakly, "And did he?"

"He called me *Joseph Osterhous*," Conrad said.

Christine sagged into the leather chair Conrad had positioned opposite his desk. "How much does he know?" she asked.

"About my going AWOL, about the fire, about my parents. He wants the whole story."

"I suppose," Christine said quietly, "we always knew we'd have to tell him."

"But the worst of it is," Conrad said, "I screwed up. I asked him if Tom O'Day had contacted him."

"You told him about O'Day?" Christine asked incredulously.

"No. No! But I jumped to the conclusion that Jamie had to have gotten my name and the AWOL story from Tom...and so I asked...and now Jamie knows O'Day's name. He said he'd never heard of Tom, but what if he remembers the name? God only knows what he'll do with *that* information."

8

MID-NOVEMBER

As Mike backed the golf cart out of the garage, he admired the future bounty on his orange tree laden with ripening fruit the size of tennis balls. *They'll be ready in a month or two and last me into spring.* He mentally slapped himself. *Orange juice or Molly? Orange juice or Molly?* as he headed for her house.

When they had settled at her kitchen table, coffee for him, tea for her, he took a deep breath. "Molly, I think I've figured out why you're angry with me."

"Not really angry, Mike. More...disappointed."

"Okay. But I'm just trying to say I think I got it. You can tell me if I'm wrong."

"Sorry. Go ahead."

"I've been asking you to do things you don't want to—the dancing, moving in with me, in my house. The house Andrea and I renovated. I've been, um..."

"An ass?" she asked helpfully.

He smiled. "I was going to say 'insensitive,' but it's

the same thing. So, I propose a solution! Let's find a house here in Sunrise—there are always a few on the market and we can wait for one we both like a lot—and we buy it together and renovate it together."

A spasm of what he interpreted as dismay crossed Molly's face. "Or if you don't want to own it together," he revised hurriedly, "I'll buy it and you help me renovate the way you want."

"Mike, you are a dear." She reached across the table and placed a hand on his. "You've *sort of* got it. You understand that I was feeling pressured to be like...no, to *be* Andrea. And the fact that your house shouts her name from every corner does...intimidate me."

"Only sort of?"

"I know how you love that house and your garden. So, it really touches me that you'd give it up for a new place. But the fact is..." She hesitated a long moment and Mike willed himself not to interrupt.

But when she just sat there, head down staring at her lap, he couldn't help himself. "The fact is...?"

"The fact is," she said heavily, "that I don't want to live with anyone."

"Yet? Or not ever?"

"I don't know," she admitted. "I've been clear with you that I'm...sort of damaged emotionally. I still can't commit to...to the future. I still dream about Max. And every time I do, it's...I'm miserable. In the dream he's not dead, he's divorcing me. And sometimes Kirk is there too. And he's telling me I should have known Max was cheating."

"I had hoped we were past all that by now," Mike said quietly.

"I'm getting there, I think. But every time I feel you thinking about Andrea, it reminds me what it's like to be betrayed."

"Wait a minute. How can you *feel* what I'm thinking? That's not fair, Molly. You don't know what's in my head. And the very day we were told she was...she was dying (*that word still sticks in my throat*), she told me to find someone to love. To find joy."

"And you're just following her dictates? Nice to know." She got up from the table, walked to the sink and dumped her tea.

Mike felt a swell of anger. *What the hell is going on? I can't say anything without getting slapped down.* Out of nowhere came a vision of a cat crouching and ready to flee. Binky! He almost smiled at the memory of Irwin's cat parable. He got up from the table and put his arms around Molly as she stood at the sink. He kissed the back of her head and turned her around to face him.

"No, love," he said. "I am not betraying you in my head, in my heart. Ever."

He felt her relax against him. *Finally, just maybe I've said the right thing.* And then he ruined it with one of his ill-timed jokes.

"But you won't mind going this weekend to the karaoke bar Andrea and I loved?" She pulled back her head and looked at him in alarm.

"Kidding!" he said, bending down to deliver an emphatic kiss.

"Not funny, idiot." Her exclamation was a bit muffled.

Mike savored the feel of her familiar body against him. He gave her a little squeeze and stepped back, looking at her face to be sure he was interpreting her returning hug correctly. *Thank god she's going to forgive me* was his first thought. The second was a somewhat rueful realization: *She's "getting there." What does that mean?*

9

MID-NOVEMBER

About a month after Molly introduced Shelley to her friends at the Hole-in-One, the younger woman called, suggesting that they have coffee together. They decided on a coffeeshop at a nearby mall.

Molly was just climbing out of her car when Shelley pulled up. They met at the front door, then stood in line behind a young woman in heels, a white blouse, and a navy suit who rattled off four complicated orders.

"Must be a law firm nearby," Molly whispered to Shelley.

"Yes," Shelley whispered back, "I'll bet she's the paralegal sent out for coffee. Impressive memory—she probably does this every morning."

The barista was a thin Black youth with his hair pulled back in a "man bun," piled high on his head, the style reminiscent of a Sumo wrestler. After he had taken their orders (skinny soy latte for Shelley and chai latte no water for Molly) and had written their names on the paper cups, Shelley pulled out a credit card and insisted on paying. "My treat," she said. "I just got a nice gig through Lauren Fleek. So, a tiny thanks for introducing me to your friends."

"Lauren? I thought..."

"Yeah, I know. I was a bit surprised as well. She wasn't exactly Ms. Congeniality at the Hole-in-One happy hour. But she gave my card to her landscaper, and he gave me a call."

"Good for Lauren," Molly said, feeling a bit guilty but unwilling to confess that she hadn't even invited Lauren to that meeting. "And good for you, of course."

"Did Aki ever find out that my 'friend' was Tom O'Day? Man, she is persistent, isn't she?"

"A bit of a terrier," Molly agreed. Retrieving their respective orders, they sat down at a small window table at the back of the shop next to the narrow corridor leading to restrooms. "When Aki scents a mystery—especially one involving romance—she'll go down any number of holes to pounce on her prey. But no, Aki didn't give you away then. By now, though, probably everyone in Sunrise Acres has figured out your relationship with Tom. How's that going, by the way?"

There was a long pause as Shelley removed the top on her latte and took a sip. "Fine," she said cautiously. "He's awfully generous. Embarrassingly so. We eat out at least twice a week, and it's always some fancy restaurant I'd never think of going to myself. And he gave me a diamond and sapphire bracelet yesterday. I'm still trying to figure out how to return it graciously."

"Wow! Sounds beautiful."

"Yeah, it's gorgeous. But honestly, I don't know where I would ever wear it. Very few people around here wear that kind of jewelry." Molly thought back to the dinner the night she had met Shelley. *Tom should have warned her not to overdress the way she did. And she's right about jewelry—at least in Sunrise.*

"But that's typical Tom. Guess he's awfully well off. Usually pays in cash for everything. He must have a money tree out back that grows hundred-dollar bills."

"If I had one," Molly mused, "it would grow quarters!"

Shelley smiled. "Know what you mean. Mine might even be nickels. But it seems as if that's the only denomination he's been carrying the last couple months." Shelley turned her cup in her hands, staring into it as if there were tea leaves instead of coffee. "I guess he's trying to impress me. And it's working— but more intimidating than impressive. I don't like the fact that he carries so much cash around. Makes me uneasy. Tom's awfully casual about safety. He keeps a key to the house in the backyard."

Shelley rotated the cup again and put the top back on it. "My brother Brian and I didn't grow up with money. Far from it."

Molly wondered if she was going to say more. *Is she deciding whether she can trust me?*

Shelley sat for a few moments longer. Then she surprised Molly by asking, "Molly, were you close to your parents? I mean, did they really love you?"

"Still do," Molly said, almost apologetically, sensing that Shelley's relationship was very different.

Shelley blew a small snort. "We didn't even have parents caring for us. My father left when Brian was a baby. A newborn, in fact. For a while my mom held it together, but she began to leave Brian with me more and more. I basically raised him." She set the cup down and shook her head. "At least I tried to. I can empathize with teenage girls who have babies in high school because that was essentially my situation. I wanted to play basketball, but anything after school was out of the question. Plus, we had no money. Dad sent some now and then, at least at first, but we couldn't count on it. By the time Brian was in middle school, Dad didn't even call, much less send money. We got by on Mom's salary as a receptionist and what I earned in odd jobs." She looked a bit abashed. "Sorry. TMI?"

"No, Shelley, not at all. I'm glad you confided in me."

"I just wanted you to understand that being with someone as wealthy as Tom is...awkward." She smiled. "Guess his wife didn't have that problem."

"Have you met Audrey?"

"No, thank goodness." Shelley seemed relieved to be talking about something else—even if it was Tom's wife. "I hear she's a terror and she can't be very happy that Tom's making such a big play for me. I know they're...separated." She looked at Molly as if pleading for understanding. "Otherwise, I wouldn't...you know...go out with him." She wiped a drop of coffee off the table with her paper napkin. "A few days ago when he called to say goodnight, Tom said Audrey had been at the house looking for something while we were out hiking. But she didn't stay overnight. Not that he wanted her to," she added quickly.

"My guess? She probably wanted to see if you had

left anything there—nightgown, toothbrush—anything that suggested you'd moved in with Tom."

"Oh lord. I'll bet you're right."

"Would she have found anything?

"No! Absolutely not!"

"So, your relationship..."

"I told him we're going to take it slow and that's what we're doing. That's why I've got to give this bracelet back. It's too much, too personal, and too soon."

Molly laughed. "Yes, I can see that a diamond bracelet might suggest a bigger *quid* than the *quo* you're willing to provide."

"I know that he doesn't have the greatest reputation around here, but I do like him. You'll think I'm terrifically shallow, but...well, I've never been treated this way before, like... like someone special. Face it, I'm not really pretty, but he treats me as if I'm beautiful. He thinks I'm not willing to get more...involved because of the age difference. But that's not really it. Sure, I wish he was younger. But I don't really care. He's still an attractive, vital guy. A lot more fun than most of the men my age. And he works at staying healthy. He's in the hiking club and he's mentioned kind of proudly that he goes on their more strenuous hikes." She drained the last of her coffee before continuing. "It's more what other people think. I do worry that I'll look like a gold digger or something."

"I don't think," Molly said, "that anyone would assume that. Tom has..." She started over. "Um, people who know Tom...." She broke off awkwardly again. *Oh boy, how do I get out of this one?* "Everyone knows that Tom enjoys younger companionship," she said at last. *Just like Max,* she thought about her faith-less husband. *The age difference between Max and his lover wasn't as much as between Tom and Shelley, but that woman was a lot younger than me.* Molly felt a flash of anger at the thought. For a moment she looked at Shelley as the "other woman," and considered how wounded Audrey might be by Tom's infidelity. *But I can't help seeing Shelley's side of this also. Audrey moved away from Tom before Shelley came on the scene. And now Shelley's gotten pulled into a problematic relationship a long way from home, where she doesn't seem to have any friends.* Shelley's next words echoed Molly's thoughts.

"Tom's friends make it clear that I'm an outsider in Sunrise. You saw that at our Prepare and Share dinner in October. At the time, Tom and I were still getting to know each other, and I had no idea what he was taking me to. I'm sure that everyone at that dinner expected him to bring Audrey. It was embarrassing. I didn't fit in at all. That was my first introduction to how small this community is, and how...um...." She broke off in embarrassment and grabbed her coffee again although the cup was empty.

"Old everyone is?" Molly finished the sentence with a chuckle. "You're right. And that it's small, but it's basically a friendly place—especially so in Prepare and Share. The whole point of that club is to meet new people socially."

"Yeah," Shelley said slowly. "But I got the feeling Tom didn't like the Konsinskis. Or at least not Conrad."

"Kind of odd, wasn't it? I had the same feeling--like they were wary of each other. Two dogs deciding whether to wag tails or growl."

"I asked Tom about it later. All he would say is, 'Conrad and I have had a little talk.' Oh my gosh," she exclaimed suddenly as she glanced at her phone. "It's almost ten. I've got to go. Hey, do you think we're ready to present the library website to the committee? Can I try out my presentation on you tomorrow?"

"Sure," Molly said. "My house? How about nine again?"

As she climbed back in her car to leave, Molly reflected, *I wonder what kind of 'little talk' Tom had with Conrad.*

10

MID-NOVEMBER

The short flight from Denver arrived on schedule. Conrad met his son at the foot of the escalator down to the baggage level. Jamie had only his backpack as luggage, so they were able to leave immediately for the forty-minute drive north to Sunrise Acres. After exchanging brief greetings, both were silent as they made the short walk to the parking lot. "Hey Dad," Jamie said as he stowed his backpack in the back seat, "I'm not coming home for Thanksgiving after all. Is Mom going to be mad?"

"No, not mad. Disappointed probably. Why aren't you coming?"

"I don't have final exams this term except for one course. For the others, I just need to turn in software programs and papers. So, I can finish up early. And Justin asked if I could come home with him to Boulder. We're gonna build a D&D table in his basement. He's got the wood for the top, legs, a TV screen—everything. Just have to put it together. It'll be really cool."

"Why do you need a special table to play Dungeons and Dragons?"

"We don't exactly *need* one to play. But four out of five of our group live in Boulder, so we can, you know, have a place to play in person and just, kind of...spend a whole day or more together. Justin is the DM right now, but I'm taking over," he added as if that explained the whole plan.

"DM"?

"Dungeon Master," Jamie said, with exaggerated patience, as if his dad were a bit slow.

Gads. Is that the way I sound when I'm trying to explain something to him? "Sorry, Bean, but I don't quite get it yet. What's the advantage of this table?"

"It's hard to explain if you've never played. You know we have battles and have to figure out how to get in and out of places, like special rooms and stuff, right?"

"Uh, yeah." *Not really.*

"So, if we have, like, a physical table we can all sit around, we can download different detailed back-ground screens, like maybe a fort that players have to capture, or at least get into. The TV will be mounted under the table with the screen side up. Then we can put our characters—little plastic figures—right on top of the screen. And we can move them around and see how close the players are to each other. Like, are they close enough to fight."

"Sort of like chess pieces on a board?" Conrad asked, trying to visualize the game.

"Uh, maybe," Jamie said doubtfully. "When we get it built, I can send you photos."

"Well, let's see what your mom thinks about your

going home with Justin," Conrad said as he backed cautiously out of the parking space.

Once he was strapped in, Jamie said, "Okay, Dad, how about we have that explanation you promised me."

Conrad's first impulse was to stall until they got home before launching into what he knew would be a difficult conversation. *But there's no better place to trap a teenager into listening than a car.*

He sighed, resigned to a tense ride home. "Right. Let's get out of the lot first." He steered the car into the Cash Only line exiting the airport and handed his parking ticket and a five-dollar bill through the window to a sleepy youngster who yawned so hugely that Conrad thought he might inhale the bill. In slow motion, the kid laboriously counted out four ones as change, folded the bills in half, and handed them over.

Conrad pulled out onto Tucson Boulevard and headed north. "What do you want to know, Jamie?"

"I want to know *why*," Jamie said. "Oh, almost forgot. Happy *Veterans* Day, Dad."

Conrad's hands tightened on the steering wheel, but he responded calmly. "Thanks, son. Guess I knew this was coming."

"You were in the Army. You beat up a guy and then went AWOL. There was one newspaper article about the guy being in a coma and you going missing, but I guess the Army hushed up a lot of the details."

"Stupid of me to think I could hide it all from you," Conrad admitted. "I just couldn't bear...." He shook his head and gripped the steering wheel harder. "Okay." He began to speak and then stopped, considering where to start and how to make Jamie understand the events that had brought his dad to flee the Army.

The first leg of the trip home was relatively distraction free as traffic was light. "Okay," Conrad said again. *Get a grip. He may hate me for what I did, but I can't keep it a secret any longer.*

"You know I was a corporal in the Military Police, right?" he said at last.

Jamie nodded. "Yeah, though I thought you had to be an officer to be an MP."

"No, I wasn't the only grunt to be one. Anyway, there was this bar, The Lowdown, right outside the gates of the base at Leavenworth. The guys used to go there all the time, especially on weekends. I must have pulled guys out of there at least a dozen times."

Conrad stopped speaking for a few moments. He stared ahead, focusing on merging into the interstate traffic. Looking over his shoulder at the oncoming cars and trucks, he carefully timed his entry into the seventy-five mph stream. "Speed limit's sixty-five, you bozos," Conrad murmured irritably. Jamie was quiet, awaiting the rest of his father's narrative.

"I'll get off at Miracle Mile," Conrad said. "Easier to talk once I'm on La Canada." Jamie remained silent as his father navigated the high-speed race that so many drivers on I-10 always seemed eager to win. Conrad turned left at the light on to La Canada; the quieter street allowed him respite to relive the scene in The Lowdown.

"This particular night," he resumed, "there was a fight and my buddy Jackie and I got called to break it up. It was a real mess—bunch of vets just back from

Iraq back in '91 got into a little argument with some locals. Guys were using fists as well as chairs, bottles —whatever they could get their hands on. It was like some Western movie saloon fight, except the chairs weren't balsa wood and the bottles were real. Everyone was drunk as skunks. Jackie got sucker punched and he went down hard."

Jamie was hunched forward in his seat, hugging himself as if preparing to ward off a physical blow. He rocked back and forth, an old childhood tic that Conrad knew meant he was anxious.

This is upsetting him. But I've got to finish. "So, then it was just me for a while. Finally, I got one of the townies up and cuffed his hands in front of him. I grabbed him by the shoulders, pushed him up against the wall and told him to stay put." Again, Conrad stopped, but this time as they hit a red light, he looked over at Jamie. "His name was Jerry Whitehall. Gerald Whitehall. Young guy just out of high school, I think. Worked in his dad's hardware store."

"But that's the guy..." Jamie didn't raise his eyes.

"I was accused of putting into a coma, yeah. What happened was, after I left him, he kind of slid down the wall and lay on his back and passed out. I didn't hit him," Conrad said firmly. "I never hit him." The traffic started up again. "Anyway, Jackie finally got up, but it took another, I don't know how long, maybe fifteen, twenty minutes for us to get everyone sorted out. Noisy as hell—the bartender yelling, women still screaming at us to leave the guys alone. Neither one of us had time to check on Whitehall." *If only I had seen him in time.* "So, Whitehall choked on his own vomit and by the time we got him on his side, it was too late."

"I don't get it," Jamie said. "The newspaper said if he died, you would be charged with manslaughter."

"Gross negligence," Conrad explained. "They said I had been trained enough to know that leaving an unconscious drunk on his back could lead to death by asphyxiation. I should have put him on his side so if he vomited it wouldn't kill him."

Jamie sat staring out the window thinking it over. The small houses arrayed along the street streamed past with a few eaves already outlined with Christmas lights. "But did he die? I couldn't find any obituary."

"No, thank god. He was in a coma for a few days— I don't know how long—and then a few weeks later, one of my buddies got word to me that he had recovered."

"Then why'd you go AWOL?"

"That was stupid, really stupid," Conrad admitted. "I panicked. I was so sure Whitehall would die. He was a popular kid—football hero—and his dad was important in town. People were mad. A lot of the locals already hated having the base there. And there were threats to close that bar because of all the fights. I knew the brass'd throw the book at me, just to prove the Army could be tough on their own. One of my buddies offered to smuggle me off the base and...I agreed. If Whitehall died, I was looking at ten to fifteen years in Leavenworth prison." *And that's what O'Day was hinting at, during that dinner party in September.* "But going AWOL, especially during wartime, wasn't exactly smart, even if the guy didn't die."

"Let me tell you something, Jamie," Conrad said intently. A stop light at Naranja allowed Conrad to insist, "Jamie, please look at me." After a long pause, Jamie finally did for a few moments. "Every single bad decision I've made in my life was because of impatience or fear. Or both. Please remember that, Jamie. Fear—unless, you know, it's an emergency like you have to get out of a burning building or something—fear is the enemy of good decisions." Jamie dropped his head again as if it hurt physically to look his dad in the eye.

The light changed. When Jamie didn't say anything, Conrad held up his left hand. "Remember how I lost part of this finger?"

Jamie glanced at the truncated finger and nodded. "Yeah, you told me. More than once," he added in irritation. Conrad waited and with an audible sigh, Jamie obliged. "You were ten years old, and you held on to a Fourth of July rocket too long," he recited as if by rote. He paused a moment and then mumbled, "Sounds to me as if you weren't afraid *enough*!"

Conrad shook his head. His ever-logical son. "But why do you think I was holding the rocket to begin with?" As Conrad expected, Jamie ignored the question; he hated being forced to guess at an answer. "Because" Conrad continued, "I was afraid of looking like a wimp to a bunch of so-called friends who were daring me to set it off from my hand instead of while it was mounted on a stick stuck in the ground."

"Stupid," Jamie said.

"Yep."

Jamie was not to be distracted from his interrogation about Conrad's going AWOL. "But how'd you do it? Change your identity?"

"That's where I was lucky. At least it seemed so at the time. There was this corporal I had brought in on fraud charges. Frankie was a real piece of work—fraud was the least of his likely offenses. He was probably selling Army stuff on the black market as well. Anyway, he fought like hell when I grabbed him, so he could have been slapped with resisting, attacking me—a lot worse stuff, a lot more jail time. But he was a little runt, just gave me a couple scratches. I wound up holding him up off his feet like a squirming cat." Taking one hand off the wheel for a few seconds, Conrad held his massive fist in the air as if clutching some object well off the floor. "I felt kind of sorry for him and never brought up any of those charges. I think that kind of surprised him.

"When I got thrown into lockup, he was working there on some type of release program. He kind of 'forgot' to lock some doors and I got out. If I'd been in Leavenworth prison, I'd never have escaped. But I was just in a holding cell. They hadn't even gotten all the paperwork done to move me somewhere more secure. He also slipped me some names in Kansas City—guys who could sell me a new identity. So that's what I did."

"Does Mom know all this?"

"Yep. I told her everything—but not until after I was fairly sure she loved me. Telling her was scarier than anything in my life. Including Iraq. I was so afraid she'd decide she could find someone better. And of course, she could have. Good thing love is blind."

Conrad glanced over at his son and smiled for the first time the entire ride. He knew how Jamie hated talking about "love stuff" and was pleased that his son was resisting his normal impulse to make some dismissive comment. Instead, Jamie looked almost relaxed. The rocking had stopped. Jamie took out his phone, inserted his earbuds, and listened to whatever Jamie listened to for the remainder of the ride. He seemed to be processing his dad's story.

When they pulled into the driveway, Jamie got out and retrieved his backpack. Christine came out to greet them in time to hear Jamie ask his father, "Is there a statute of limitations?"

She threw Conrad a startled look but said nothing.

The three of them walked into the house as Conrad said, "Geezus, Jamie. You're nineteen years old. How do you think of these things? No, not legally. Going AWOL was desertion and during wartime the penalty is death." Christine looked at him and shook her head.

"But no one's been executed for that since 1945," Conrad said reassuringly. "There are still thousands of soldiers out there who went AWOL during the Iraq war about the same time I did in '91."

They all walked into the kitchen where Christine automatically started removing the makings for sandwiches from the refrigerator and laying them out on the counter. Jamie always arrived home hungry.

But this time he didn't seem to notice. His attention was still fully on his father.

"When I escaped," Conrad continued, "the brass was already starting to set up a court-martial. They kind of expected Whitehall to die. Frankie, the guy who took the lead in getting me off the base, said they had assigned some eager-beaver lawyer to act as trial counsel—that's like a prosecutor.

"The guy'd been through the FLEP. That's an Army program that paid for his law school; I guess he really looked forward to showing they got their money's worth. He was interviewing witnesses, preparing for the court-martial and a charge of negligent homicide. Anyway, there's a special AWOL apprehension unit and I'm sure they looked for me at first. I don't really know if they would come after me now, given the five thousand deserters from the Iraq War and that all this happened so long ago. But I'm not anxious to find out." He took a bottle of beer out of the refrigerator. Popping the top, he took a long swig and said, "Well, now you know the whole story."

"Even your grandma and grandpa Sorenson don't know all this," Christine said. "I told them when we got engaged that your dad had PTSD. I insisted that he couldn't talk about the war, and they weren't to ask questions. And they've been really good about it."

She looked at Conrad for confirmation and he nodded. "Yeah, they have."

The two of them sat down on the stools at the end of the counter, but Jamie remained standing.

"Jamie, you must be hungry. How about something to eat. We've got turkey and ham cold cuts. That asiago cheese you like so much," Christine offered.

But Jamie wasn't through with his interrogation. As usual, he avoided looking at either of them and studied his clasped hands as if the questions he wanted to ask were written there. "And your parents,

Dad? Did they really die in a car accident? And how about the house fire you said destroyed all your photos except the album with your baby pictures?"

Conrad glanced at Christine, who shrugged. "Might as well," she said.

"My dad died just after I went AWOL," Conrad said, "and my mom a few months after." *I broke their hearts, both of them. I killed them even if I didn't kill Jerry Whitehall.* "The house I grew up in was mostly destroyed in a fire, but a neighbor rescued a lot of stuff. I got rid of all of it except that one album. Even if someone got hold of that, I figured baby pictures don't give away identities the way school photos do. It seemed kind of harmless to keep it."

"What else have you lied to me about," he asked suddenly. "Like...maybe I'm adopted?"

Both parents laughed. "No such luck for you," Conrad said. He stood up and moved to his son's side. He put out a hand to ruffle the boy's hair but stopped. *Jamie would hate that.*

"We have photos of your birth," Christine said, "but I don't think you're quite old enough..."

"The actual birth? Eww, no thanks. Gross!" He picked up his backpack. "By the way, I'm not coming home for Thanksgiving." Without another word, he walked out down the hall towards his bedroom.

"What?" Christine was taken aback by the cavalier announcement. She started after Jamie, but Conrad gestured to stop.

"Let it go for now," Conrad advised. "I'll explain. Right now, he's digesting what I told him. I couldn't keep it from him any longer," Conrad added, lowering his voice. "He's so smart, and increasingly curious about who he is—and who I am. When he asked if he was adopted...Geezus. How could he even think that? Anyway, he was going to find out most of the truth on his own. I had to give him the rest of it—or most of it, anyway."

"Connie," Christine said, looking over her shoulder towards the hallway, "Are we going to ever tell him the rest? Any chance that he could find out that the hotshot lawyer back then was judge O'Day?"

"I don't see how. It's not as if Jamie would ever talk to him. Dammit, if we hadn't joined that stupid dinner club, maybe we'd never have run into O'Day."

"It's a small community. It would have happened sooner or later. But you can't keep paying the judge forever, Connie. Maybe we should think about moving?"

"That wouldn't do a bit of good. He doesn't need to be physically near to blackmail me. But be patient a bit longer...I have an idea how to get him off my back."

Both of them were startled when Jamie suddenly reappeared in the kitchen doorway.

"Who's blackmailing you?" he demanded.

"Jamie, just forget about it, please. I'm handling it." *How long was he listening?*

11

EARLY DECEMBER

Molly looked at her tennis shoes on the floor, laces loosened, and sighed. *Molly Levin, woman up! This should not be difficult. Let's put all that tai chi you've learned into practice. Pick up right shoe. Raise right leg, balancing on left. Steady, steady—I'm an egret. A great blue heron, balancing effortlessly on one leg. Now slip shoe onto right foot midair. Shoot! Maybe easier with the other shoe.* She shifted weight to balance on her right leg and raised her left foot. *Okay so far. Now for the shoe.* Which she had left on the floor. Start again. *Pick up shoe. Raise left foot. Put shoe on foot. Do not wobble. Do not wobble!* She managed to hook the shoe over the foot, but then she toppled sideways. "Dang it!" Catching herself on the bureau, she glowered at her mirrored reflection. *Who can stand on one foot long enough to put on a shoe midair?*

Unfortunately, the answer was: half her tai chi class.

A glance at her watch showed she had only ten minutes to make it to the bocce courts. Irwin had invited her, and she had tried to beg off, claiming she'd likely make a fool of herself. But Irwin was persuasive, and she finally agreed. Mike was off with the hiking club, and she had the morning free. She sat down and pulled on her shoes, mentally promising that she'd try the standing on one leg torture again tomorrow. Walking hastily to the garage, she thought about taking the golf cart, but the twenty-year-old buggy could barely make it up the hill to the courts. So, a bit guiltily, she climbed into the car.

Irwin smiled broadly and welcomed her. "Wasn't sure you'd make it. I know that bocce wasn't on your radar, but I think you'll have fun. The rules are quite simple. But let's wait till Sal and Margaret arrive to round out our foursome and then we can roll a few balls and discuss strategy."

"Strategy?" Molly asked somewhat alarmed. "Is this a competition or something? Irwin, what did you rope me into?"

"No, no, don't worry. Much as I delight in whipping Sal and his wife, today is just to sample the bocce experience."

While they waited for Irwin's friends, Molly asked him how he was. *Always a dangerous question of the elderly. Might hear more than I wish. But Irwin does not usually go on about ailments.*

"Pretty good," he said. "Finally found a doctor who doesn't talk to me as if I'm an imbecile. You know the secret to his superior intelligence?"

Molly shook her head. "But you're going to tell me."

"He served in the military and was stationed in Japan."

"So sushi and rice wine are the secret?"

Irwin wagged a finger at Molly. "Now this is important, youngster. Turns out that the Japanese revere age. They believe old age should be celebrated and that elders possess wisdom. When I was stationed in Japan back in the day, I decided to climb Mt. Fuji, the sacred mountain. I noticed a crowd of people over by the trailhead, so I moseyed over. Turned out this fella was celebrating his hundredth birthday, and these friends of his were going to help him climb the mountain. Now that's respecting age!"

Molly looked skeptical. "Are you saying all, uh, all old people are deserving of this kind of respect? I could name a few...."

"Okay, not all of them. I could name a few also whose maturity is about level with my great grand-kids. But stop distracting me. I'm getting to the critical part. My doctor pointed me to this Harvard study that showed that elders with positive attitudes about aging actually live longer than the geezers who are always complaining about getting old. So I'm going to help you live longer by telling you all the good things about getting older. You can thank me later when you hit the big nine-oh."

Molly grinned and took a seat on a bench at the end of the courts "You can start any time. Like going bionic? Seems everyone I know has at least a few pieces of metal in their body."

"Yeah. Well, I do too. One of them is a piece of shrapnel in my back. I guess replacing worn-out body parts could qualify. But I'm talking about learning not to sweat the small stuff, reveling in just making it this far on the right side of the grass. And staying active.

Learning new stuff like rolling balls down this green alley here."

"Well, I have to admit, until you invited me, I never considered playing bocce."

"Bocce, schmocce, doesn't really matter. So long as it's something new you've got to wrap your brain, and maybe your body, around. And bocce isn't dangerous. You pickleball players are financing college for the children of all the orthopedic surgeons in town. You'll meet a different set of folks here and...." Molly's ring tone for Mike interrupted Irwin's list. "Go ahead, answer it. It's okay with me. It's annoying as hell, but it's small potatoes." He winked at Molly.

Confirming with a glance that it was from Mike, she decided to call him back as soon as they had played a game. Sal and Margaret arrived, and as Irwin was making the introductions, her phone vibrated again. This time it was a text from Mike.

URGENT CALL ME

PART II

12

DECEMBER 5, DAY 1

Barry Sturges was about to join the other hikers when Tom O'Day screamed "Leggo!" at Mike. The two men were struggling at the edge of a drop-off. Abandoning his pack, Barry raced back just as Tom went over. "Oh my god, what happened?" He gingerly approached the edge of the cliff and peered down. "Is that...is that Tom?" He yelled down at the still form in the dry wash below. "Tom? Tom?" There was no response.

Mike had sunk to the ground. He sat looking at Tom's shirtsleeve still in his grasp. He had heard the sickening crunch when Tom hit the rocks below. *No way he could survive that fall.*

Barry regarded him in disbelief. "Mike? What the hell? Did you just...?" Barry walked again to the edge of the cliff and looked down. This time, he did not call Tom's name. He backed away and confronted Mike. "Mike?" he said again.

Mike just shook his head. "I couldn't hold him. I don't...he just...."

"It looked like you pushed him," Barry said, and took a step away from Mike.

Mike still sat numbly replaying the last few minutes in his head, Barry's voice a distant background noise. *What was Tom reaching for? Why did he look so crazy?* He groaned. *I should have been able to hold him. Did I call for help? I don't remember.*

Barry looked around for the others, but they were out of sight. Finally, he spotted Peter, rounding a curve in the trail ahead. "Peter," he yelled. "Peter, help! Help!"

Peter hesitated and looked back. Barry waved his arms frantically, still yelling. At last Peter seemed to hear the plea and motioned to the hikers behind him to turn around and head back.

By the time Barry found a spot with a single bar on his phone, had reached the 911 operator, and had quickly explained the situation, the rest of the hikers were milling around in confusion on the ridge. Several of them looked over the edge to see Tom's body below. The air buzzed with unanswered questions, some with an edge of near hysteria. "Is he really...?" "How did this happen?" "Should someone go down there?" Anyone who had brought a phone was trying to talk on it.

Mike was sitting on the ground, holding the remains of Tom's shirt, looking dazed. Peter crouched down to speak with him quietly. When a few of the other hikers approached, Peter waved them away.

Ending his call, Barry announced loudly: "The police want us all to stay put until they can get someone up here and—and down there," he said, gesturing to the wash below. All the hikers waited obediently on the trail, still holding out some hope that the fall had not been fatal.

Mike found the same area with some phone reception and called Molly. "Damn, pick up Molly, pick up." When she didn't respond, he sent a text: URGENT CALL ME. His phone rang almost immediately.

"Molly, there's been an indescribably terrible accident. I can't ... Molly? Hello? Damn!" He called again. "Molly, reception's terrible here. I'll call when I..." *One more try.* "Tom O'Day is dead. He, he went off the cliff. I tried to save him, but....Molly, I really can't talk from here. Molly. It will be a while, but I'll fill you in later. As soon as I can."

IT WAS MORE than an hour before a very red-faced, heavily perspiring Sergeant Sarah Partridge appeared. Her partner, Del Washington was also mopping his face, but his long legs had obviously helped him navigate the trail more easily. The county Search and Rescue Team borrowed from the Sheriff's office were on their way. One member of the team was already bushwhacking along the heavily overgrown wash below. Several others followed, laden with a gurney and medical equipment.

While they waited for the search and rescue crew to reach Tom, Sergeant Partridge took everyone's name and contact information. She quickly homed in on Barry and Mike as the only witnesses to Tom's fall and told the others they could go. But they all stayed, in small murmuring huddles of three or four, as if seeking comfort from a storm. It was a shock that a familiar trail could turn so treacherous and that death stalked so close. As they waited, Peter again sat down by Mike. Grateful for the implied support, Mike still could not find his voice. When they heard noises below in the wash, the hikers all cautiously approached the edge and looked over.

Mike didn't need to see the head shake or hear the confirmatory call up to Partridge and Washington to know that Tom was dead. He could still hear in his head the awful sound of Tom's impact on the rocks and knew how unlikely it was that the judge had survived. The other hikers looked about at each other uncertainly, no one feeling comfortable leaving the site. But when Peter started back down the trail, they all filed after him. Partridge told Barry and Mike, "You two head straight for the Cactus Heights police station. Detective Villegas has been alerted. This was an unnatural death, and the police will need your statements about what happened."

"After lunch?" Barry asked hopefully.

"Now, please," Partridge said firmly. "While details are fresh in your mind. The Cactus Heights office has been told that you're coming in immediately after returning to the trailhead."

As the last two hikers starting back, Mike and Barry walked within a few feet of each other. Neither spoke the entire way. The drive back to the library parking lot to drop Barry off at his car was similarly silent.

MIKE SAT for several minutes in his car, preparing mentally for the interviews he and Barry were politely, but very firmly, requested to undergo. He then called Molly.

It took several minutes for Mike to get his voice under control enough to explain to Molly what had happened. Like Mike's fellow hikers, Molly was both shocked and disbelieving. When Mike had answered a few questions, he said hurriedly, "I have to leave right now. The police need to interview Barry and me, as the only witnesses. Barry told me he thought I'd pushed Tom over the edge. I sure as hell hope he doesn't say that to the police!"

"I'm sure he won't," Molly said. "That's so obviously crazy. He knows you. He can't seriously think you'd do something like that."

"Guess I'll find out," Mike said darkly. Then he added with an effort he knew Molly could hear in his voice, "If I need you to bring me a cake with a file in it, I'll let you know."

She tried to respond in kind. "Oh, I'm sure I can come up with a more modern technique for breaking you out of jail! A laser cutter?" They were both silent for a moment, still struggling to comprehend the situation. Then Molly said, "I could come get you, drive you to the station, and wait until you're finished."

Mike barked a short laugh. "Molly, I just need to tell them what happened and trust they'll believe me. Sergeant Partridge was on the scene, and she said that Detective Villegas had been alerted, so I'm hoping he'll be doing the interview. He knows me. I don't know if Detective Rasmussen will be involved, but even The Hulk isn't known for using thumb screws.

I'll come straight to you when they're through with me." His last words echoed ominously in his ears as he drove to the police station. *When they're through with me. Surely Barry wouldn't repeat his ridiculous accusation.*

BARRY WAS ALREADY at the station when Mike arrived. It was almost three hours after Tom's fall. They sat uneasily in the waiting room, avoiding each other's eyes. Barry Sturges was a tall, very thin man with a narrow, pendulous nose. Molly had once described him to Mike: "Dress Barry in pink and get him to stand on one foot and he'd make a terrific flamingo." Remembering that description, Mike smiled slightly. He considered confronting Barry, in hopes of dissuading him from sharing his accusation with the police. *But maybe that would make him even more suspicious.* Adding to Mike's unease, Barry was summoned first.

A half hour later, Barry passed Mike on his way out, his gaze studiously averted. *Uh-oh*, Mike thought as Maria Rodriguez, the receptionist, escorted him to the interview room.

Detective Jose Villegas sat at a small table, impeccably dressed as always in a blue striped dress shirt and sharply creased chinos. He indicated a folding chair across from him and Mike sat facing the detective. Mike was slightly relieved that he would be questioned only by Villegas. His encounters with The Hulk, as he and Molly dubbed Detective Rasmussen, had been far from friendly.

"Let's start at the beginning, please," Villegas said. Mike glanced around the room nervously, very conscious of how different this occasion was from when he had last seen Villegas. Then they had been celebrating the successful conclusion of an assault investigation that Mike and Molly had been instrumental in solving. This time Mike was being accused of the same crime.

Detective Villegas began the questioning. "Mike, tell me about this hiking club. How do you decide who goes on a hike?"

Mike spent the next few minutes explaining the way the club worked, concluding with "So we sign up for particular hikes, depending on our level of fitness and availability."

"I take it that everyone knows who else will be on the hike?"

"Yes," Mike said. "We get a list the day before of who's going."

"All right. Now, today's hike. From what you say, this was considered," Villegas paused to check his notes, "a 'moderately strenuous' hike. That meant only fit club members would sign up, right?" Mike nodded. "Would you look at the list of those on the hike." He handed his tablet to Mike. "Did we miss anyone?"

"It's a big club and I don't know everyone's name, but this looks about right. You'd have to check with the hike leader, Peter Jackson; he'd know if anyone cancelled."

Villegas nodded. "I remember Dr. Jackson from last summer. Now, take me along from the beginning of the hike. You were right behind Mr. O'Day? Was that his choice or yours?"

"Neither really. For various reasons, I got a late start, so I was the last to arrive at the trailhead. The trail was very narrow, so we were hiking single file. I was at the end of the line and Tom was just ahead of me." Mike heaved a heavy sigh. "It started out completely normal. We left about nine, just hiked along, drinking as we went and stopped for snacks about, uh, nine   forty-five or ten?" *I probably should have confirmed the times with Barry before he was interviewed.*

Villegas was his usual impassive self, and after a futile glance at his face to see any indication that the timeline sounded right, Mike continued.

"Tom and I were quite far back. By the time we arrived at the ridge, everyone else had mostly finished and Peter had started up the hike again. We had a couple miles more of climbing before the return trail looped back down to the parking lot, and I wanted to get closer to the front, 'cause I like to walk faster. Tom kept stopping to get at his Gatorade. But when I stood up to go, I saw Tom just sitting there on a rock, kind of in a stupor. His face was beet red. I was surprised, because he's a strong hiker, but suddenly I was worried that maybe he was about to have a heart attack or stroke or something."

"Was he sweating heavily? Maybe burping? Holding his chest? Yawning? Panting?"

Mike looked at Villegas in surprise. "No—none of that." He stopped to picture Tom sitting on that rock. "No," he said again. "In fact," he hesitated as he checked his mental image, "he wasn't sweating at all. I remember noticing that, because I expected that anyone that red would be dripping a waterfall, and I almost pulled out a bandana from my pack to offer it. He had been jabbering practically nonstop the last half-mile or so—sounded angry." Mike took a couple of deep breaths, suddenly feeling panicky as he began to relive the next few minutes. "He stood up, kind of staggered towards the cliff edge, took off his backpack and just hurled it over into the wash! He was looking crazy—his eyes all bulgy. Then he got to the very edge. He was shouting 'There it is!' like he saw something out towards the horizon.

"I just stood there for a minute. Frozen. Couldn't believe he had tossed his pack over. And then he started tearing his shirt off! I saw some buttons fly off. I was really worried by now because he was acting so incredibly weird, I had no idea what he might do next. I mean ripping his damn shirt off? That's when I grabbed his arm and what was left of his shirt. He was so close to the edge. I called his name and yelled at him to 'look out!' I don't think he even heard me. He kept yelling and trying to shake me off." Mike was breathing hard. He grabbed the edge of his chair, white knuckled. "And then his shirt came off in my hands and he...he just went over."

Villegas sat for a moment, Mike's last words echoing in the room. "That's not the way Mr. Sturgis saw it." He looked at notes on his tablet and read some lines off verbatim. "'It looked to me as if they were kind of fighting. Mike kept grabbing Tom's arm and Tom kept yelling for Mike to "leggo, leggo!" And then it looked to me like Mike gave him a shove and he went over.'"

"I can't believe anyone would think that. Why, for god's sake, would I push Tom off that cliff?" Mike said incredulously. "Jose, seriously."

Villegas stiffened a bit at use of his first name, Mike noticed. *Well, he called me "Mike,"* he thought indignantly.

"Why did Mr. O'Day keep yelling for you to let go? Are you saying you were trying to keep him from jumping?"

"Of course I was!" Mike paused, shook his head in frustration. "But he wasn't *jumping*!" Mike was exasperated. *Did they get that idea from Barry?* "He was reaching for something just off the cliff. I can't explain it. It was like he went crazy and he didn't even register that he was at the edge of the cliff. But I most certainly did not shove him. I did my best to keep him back. But he was determined to get whatever it was he saw, and that's why he kept yelling for me to let go of his arm. If I'd been able to grab the other arm, maybe I could have stopped him." Mike paused as a thought struck him. *What if I'd tackled him, instead of going for his arm?* "Maybe," he said slowly, "I should have tried to knock his legs out from under him instead of grabbing him. Didn't even occur to me." He shook his head. "Probably wouldn't have worked anyway. He was too close to the edge."

Villegas referred to his notes again. "Mr. Sturges said he was about 30-40 yards away from the two of you."

"Had to be further than that," Mike said. "He was way ahead of us on the hike." He stopped again to visualize where Barry was standing when he turned back. "I think if we went back there, I could show you where we both were. And, he must have been looking right into the sun."

Villegas nodded. "For now, it's not necessary to head back up there. I asked him about the sun. He said he was wearing sunglasses so the sun wouldn't have bothered him."

Mike was silent, thinking. "Prescription glasses?"

Villegas nodded again. "Good question," he said, eying Mike approvingly. "I asked. They were not prescription."

Mike felt a wave of relief. All Barry could have seen was silhouettes against the sun—and Villegas recognized that. But the relief was short lived.

"However, Mr. Sturges insists he could see the two of you clearly. You struggled, Mr. O'Day was yelling for you to let go of him and at the last second you gave him the shove that sent him over the edge. It's a very serious accusation."

Why is Barry doing this? Can he really believe it? It's not as if we're friends—just acquaintances, but he must understand what trouble he's getting me in.

Villegas studied him, hands clasped in his lap, like the priest he had once been, as if waiting for a confession. "Mike?"

"I don't get it. Why would he say that? It's nuts!" Mike felt mounting anger. "Why the hell would I push a guy I barely know—to his *death*? I was there! I'm telling you exactly what happened!"

"According to Mr. Sturges, you had a very vocal, angry argument with Mr. O'Day."

"What? When?"

This time Villegas had no need of his notes. He watched Mike's face carefully as he repeated what

Barry had said. "Apparently you and Mr. O'Day had a very public argument a couple months ago over the renovation of a major building in Sunrise Acres."

Mike shook his head. "And he thinks that disagreement was enough to make me want to kill the guy?"

"Weren't you both 'mad as hell,' to quote Mr. Sturges? And apparently there was some name-calling?"

"Not by me."

"You didn't accuse O'Day of, quote, 'nepotism or worse'"?

"That's hardly 'name-calling.' It *was* nepotism! Tom was on the original committee in charge of selecting the construction company for a very major, multi-million-dollar renovation of the main Activity Center at Sunrise. Before I joined the committee, he talked the other members into a single-source bid. Argued it would be cheaper and faster. And they bought it. But they didn't know the guy who bid on the contract was his wife's nephew. It was nepotism at the very least—certainly unethical. He was a judge! He should have known better. That contract should never have been single source and it definitely shouldn't have gone to her nephew. Given the way he increased prices on materials after the work started, the HOA got royally screwed! So, yeah, we argued. But that's hardly a reason to...to...." Mike couldn't bring himself to say the word.

"Murder him," Villegas finished for him.

Mike sank back in his chair, the full implications of Barry's accusation hitting him. "Oh my god! That's what he's saying. What kind of monster does he think

I am that I would take a petty argument to that extreme?"

"Does Mr. Sturges have reason to lie, perhaps a grudge against you?"

"Not that I know of. We're not real friendly. Different politics. But certainly not any kind of serious hostility."

"Okay," Villegas said. "We may want to know more about your relations with both men. But right now, let's go back a bit. You said Mr. O'Day was acting crazy. Was he behaving oddly from the very start of the hike?"

"No, not at first. We didn't talk much." *Barry must have told Jose that Tom and I didn't like each other—not just because of the argument. Tom's a womanizing....*Mike realized Villegas was waiting for him to go on. "We paused briefly for water a couple times—well, I was drinking water, he had some sort of sports drink. We did chat a bit at first, just commenting on the view or on how mild the weather was for December—that kind of stuff. He asked me what the trees with the berries were and I told him I thought they were juniper. Perfectly normal conversation. But as we went on, he started acting weird, began talking non-stop, getting more and more agitated, angry. He stopped responding to my questions like I wasn't there. But it was when we got close to the rest stop that he started acting totally nuts."

Villegas started to ask another question, but Mike interrupted. "Except, wait a minute. I remember something else. A little way before we reached our rest stop, he took off his hat and the headband he was wearing underneath and he threw the headband off down the slope into some bram-bles. He kind of waved his hat around, and I thought he was going to toss that too, but he put it back on. I figured the headband was itching or something, but it was totally bizarre that he just threw it away. We never leave trash on the trail like that. One of the club's rules. I called him on it, said, 'Hey, Tom!' but he ignored me. He was gibbering to himself, as I said earlier. I thought at first he was on the phone, but the service out there is really poor, and besides, he didn't have ear buds. So I decided I'd talk with him about the littering when we stopped. But when we did get to the top, I realized there was no way to retrieve the headband, and I decided not to get into it with him. And then everything went to hell, and I totally forgot about it. Didn't Barry tell you anything about that?"

"He said he didn't notice anything odd about Mr. O'Day. That he didn't even look at the two of you until Mr. O'Day yelled for you to 'leggo.'"

"Then how can you consider him a witness? He didn't see what happened leading up to my struggle with Tom."

"Okay, Mike. Say for the moment you aren't a suspect..."

"A suspect!" Mike almost yelled. "What the..."

Villegas held up a hand. "Person of interest."

That's no better, Mike thought. "Witness, okay? I'm just a witness."

Villegas nodded. "Okay, witness."

They sat for a few moments in silence. Then Villegas said, "We'll need to notify the next of kin. Is there a Mrs. O'Day?"

"Yeah, Audrey," Mike said grumpily. Villegas looked at him, clearly waiting for more information.

Mike wrestled with his conscience a bit, still angry. *Why the hell should I help Jose?* But then he said, "Probably won't do you any good to look for her at their house. She lives most of the time in her apartment in Phoenix. She has a gallery or something up there. And," he added quickly before Villegas could ask, "that's all I know. I don't have her address or phone number."

Villegas sat a few moments and then said, "Okay, thanks Mike. We'll locate her. I'll let you know when we need to talk to you again. Maybe tomorrow or in a couple days."

Mike fled gratefully to his car. He sat a few moments, shaking his head in disbelief. *A "suspect"? "Person of interest"? Will "witness" be any better if the Sunrise gossip train gets hold of Barry's accusation? Of* murder! *Bored retirees love a juicy story—especially about one of their own. Unless Barry stops blabbing his version, I'm going to be spending the entire winter explaining what really happened. And knowing him, he's as likely to shut up as a guy who just shot a hole-in-one.*

13

DAY 3

Two days after Judge O'Day fell to his death, Molly's mobile rang at six-thirty in the morning. She was just returning from walking Jessie. Molly checked the phone number. *Area code 602. Phoenix?* She hesitated to answer, but surely it was unlikely to be a solicitation or robocall at this time of day. Sunrise Acres retirees tended to bring the phone numbers from prior residences with them. So, maybe an acquaintance who knew Molly would be up early?

"Hello?"

The voice at the other end was brisk. "Is this Molly Levin?"

"Uh, yes," Molly answered warily. *Clearly not a social call.* "Who's calling, please?"

The woman sounded slightly offended at being asked to identify herself. "Audrey O'Day, Judge O'Day's wife...uh, widow. I'm glad I caught you," she went on a bit hastily, as if she expected Molly to be called away momentarily.

Why would she call so early? A lot of folks aren't even up yet, much less rushing around.

"Ellen Featherstone suggested I call you," she continued. "I want to sell the house and she said you have the market cornered in Sunrise."

To Molly's ears, that comment sounded faintly accusatory—but also flattering. "The judge's house?"

"My house," she corrected. "But yes, where the judge lived. You know the address or can find it easily enough I assume." Without waiting for Molly to respond, she continued rapidly. "I'm in Phoenix. I'm driving back down to Sunrise again this morning. I need you to arrange for cleaning the house and also to, you know, decide what needs to be done to get it ready to go on the market. After all the money we poured into that little place, it shouldn't need much work."

Molly was momentarily offended. *What if I don't want the listing? Or don't have time right now?* But she found herself caught up in the irresistible undertow of a rapidly evolving action plan. "Uh, well, what time will you be here?"

"I can't make it before ten, but why don't you go ahead and look around, make some notes on what needs to get moved out before we have an open house. There's a key under a fake rock in the backyard by the big mesquite tree—sort of behind it. The alarm code is 5432."

The call disconnected. Audrey O'Day was done talking. "What the heck, Jessie?" she asked the dog, who was sitting patiently waiting to have her leash removed. Jessie waved her tail gently, always happy to hear her own name. "Did I agree to do all this?" Jessie cocked her head, looking as if she would have a snappy answer if she just had the right vocal cords. "And why is she in such a hurry? Tom's only been dead a couple of days."

Dead. The stark word seemed to hang in the air. *It seems so out of place in Sunrise. No, "out of place" isn't right. It's not as if I'm thinking about where to arrange the furniture in a room. Just, somehow, incongruous. People here are dying all the time—or being told they are about to. Stage four cancer of the stomach. Brain tumor. Stroke. But plunging off a cliff? That's how rock climbers die—not old people. And yet Audrey seems to have taken this weird death—of her husband!—in stride. Moving on at high speed.*

She pushed the morbid thoughts to the back of her mind. Despite feeling resentful at Mrs. O'Day's high-handed treatment, she couldn't help going into real estate agent mode. "That little place"? *It's the largest of the Sunrise models. Recent upgrades. View of the mountains—maybe a little of the golf course, too. And the market sure is hot right now. Maybe she knows that and that's why she's in a hurry. A bit cold-blooded, but the marriage was over before he died.*

Molly contacted the two-woman team of cleaners she always used for "move-outs." But when she explained what she needed, Margo almost turned her down. "Molly, if it were anyone else, I'd have to say no. We're flat out. But," she hesitated and weakened when Molly said nothing, "if Bev agrees, maybe we could get in on Sunday. But do you think you could do one thing ahead of time? Could you clear out the refrigerators? They might have a second one in the garage. And by Sunday, there could be rotten veggies or even meat or fish. It would make our job a lot easier if you could get rid of all the perishables."

Molly agreed and refreshed Jessie's water and loaded her dish with dry food. Then she called Mike and explained the situation. "If I see I'm not going to be back until midafternoon, would you have time to come let Jessie out for a few minutes?"

"No problem," Mike said. "I can even take her for a walk. But are you sure you want to work with Audrey O'Day?"

Molly had just recounted to Mike her conversation with Audrey, and he was less than enthusiastic.

"Why? I didn't like the way she took for granted that I wanted the listing, and she's obviously used to bossing people around, but a sale is a sale. That house will sell quickly and at a premium price."

"Never mind. I was just thinking about her reputation at pickleball. Not relevant."

"No, tell me. The way people play sports says a lot about them."

"Let's just say I've always thought those two people deserved each other."

"Tom and Audrey?"

"Yep. Everyone knows Tom cheats, uh, cheated at golf. Little kicks to nudge a ball to a better lie when he thinks nobody's looking, that sort of thing. Some guys wouldn't play with him. And a lot of pickleball players were relieved when Audrey decided to leave him and work in Phoenix."

"Huh. We must play in different groups. I've never

played with her. She wasn't very friendly on the phone."

"She's one of those people who sounds sweet, can insult so subtly that you may not notice at first. The steel knife in the velvet glove technique. You don't even feel the cut until you see the blood. You know the kind: 'Good job getting that shot back. I'll bet you were a terrific player ten years ago.'"

"Ouch. There's no good response to that, is there? I roomed with someone like that in college. I couldn't switch roommates fast enough. But I'm forewarned now. I doubt she'd do that to me anyway. We'll be working together to sell her house."

"Yeah, true. And you could just ignore her if she did. But what bothered me more is that she always acted as if the rules applied to everyone but her. She's a true narcissist. There were several fairly major blowups on the courts—one with Monica, for example. I don't think of Monica as someone who gets angry easily. But she sure did one time. I was playing with her against Audrey....Oh hell, I shouldn't be such a gossip."

"Well," Molly said with a laugh, "If you think you can stop mid-story like that, you're nuts! Spill!"

"It was trivial, really. Audrey never liked to partner with weaker players. She was the last one to go on the court and when she saw who her partner was, she walked over to my side and announced that Monica had to switch with her. Apparently, that was the third time she'd done this to Monica, and she flatly refused. After a few minutes standoff, Monica just up and left, leaving the three of us standing there with our, uh, paddles in our hands. Audrey followed her out shouting that she was being a bad sport."

"Huh. Sounds uncomfortable, but not a real blowup."

"No, if that had been the last of it, but Audrey couldn't let it go. Kept telling anyone who would listen that Monica was a bad sport. Most people just laughed about it. It hurt Audrey's reputation a lot more than Monica's because Audrey was known for bossing people around to suit herself. Anyway, the only reason I'm telling you this is that if she conducts business the way she plays pickleball, the deck will be stacked in her favor."

"A bit of a mixed metaphor, Professor Landry," Molly teased, "but I got the point."

ALTHOUGH SHE HAD NOT PROMISED Audrey to start immediately on the task of preparing Tom O'Day's house for sale—*Audrey's house*, she corrected herself —Molly was curious to see the inside. After a quick breakfast of Mike's homemade granola topped with blueberries, Molly drove her golf cart over to her new listing. The ride was chilly, and Molly regretted not taking her car. Audrey's directions were a bit vague about exactly where among the mesquite tree roots was the fake rock concealing the front door key. It took Molly a good ten minutes to locate it. *Good hiding place to put a key,* Molly thought. The precaution was unusual. Sunrise so rarely had any break-ins that many people didn't even bother to lock their doors.

In the front patio, a stone fountain set into one

wall burbled pleasantly, and a bright blue pot harbored a large soft green Monstrose cactus. A few smaller pots in vivid colors, all with cacti, were arranged on the pavers. Twisted brushed nickel bars and a circular metal cutout with outlines of quail decorated the heavy screen door. It opened with the same key as the thick oak front door. Once inside, Molly noted the red light on the alarm control pad to the side of the door signaling that the alarm was set, and nervously entered the code Audrey had given her. She took a deep breath in relief when the light turned green.

It was a cloudy day and Molly, in real estate agent mode, automatically started walking around, turning on lights. She hoped to take a quick look at the layout and décor before Audrey arrived and insisted on guiding her around. Sunrise homeowners could never resist pointing out what they thought made their house unusually desirable and sellable. But their opinions were often idiosyncratic and not what prospective buyers might desire.

Molly opened the door to what she knew would be the guest bedroom in the layout of this particular Sunrise model. When she entered, she was immediately aware of how much cooler that room was than the hall—and the source of the cold was obvious. The north-facing room had a separate French door off the wraparound patio. It was wide open, and a circle of glass had been cut out of the pane right next to the lock. Someone must have reached through the hole and unlocked the door. She knew not to touch the door or the lock, but she stepped close enough to see a circular piece of glass lying on the patio pavers. No shards anywhere. It was a clean cut.

Molly retreated hastily to the hallway and considered the possibilities. Was it at all feasible that Tom (or possibly Shelley) could have done this after being accidentally locked out? Ridiculous notion. Tom certainly had a key and knew where the spare was hidden. And Shelley wouldn't break in. *No legitimate reason for anyone but a thief with a glass cutter to have done this. When did it happen? Last night or...*Suddenly she realized she may have interrupted a burglary. The guest room showed no other signs of disturbance, but it would surely be unwise to assume no one remained in the house. She called 911 and explained the situation. "Could you stay on the line while I walk through the house?" she asked.

"No ma'am," the operator said firmly. "Please leave the house immediately and wait on the curb. I'm sending a police car."

While she waited, Molly called Audrey. The call went straight to voice mail. Molly left a brief message that there had been an apparent break-in at Tom's house. *Darn! I should have said "your house." Oh well, too late. Might Audrey have another telephone number?* As she was trying to think of who might help reach Audrey, she saw flashing lights approach.

The patrol car must have been nearby. It arrived less than five minutes after she had called 911. A tall Black man emerged from the car followed by a middle-aged, sturdily built woman in uniform.

"Sergeant Partridge?" Molly said in surprise.

The policewoman was equally startled. "Ms. Levin?"

The other officer looked back and forth between them. "You know each other?"

"From last summer," Sarah Partridge said. "You remember that assault case here in Sunrise Acres? Ms. Levin identified the assailant. Oh," she said, realizing Molly didn't know her companion, "This is Officer Del Washington. But right now...you reported a break-in? This is your house?"

Molly shook her head. "The owner is—was—Tom O'Day, and he died day before yesterday...."

Washington interrupted. "O'Day? Sarah—Sergeant Partridge—and I were called to the scene of O'Day's jump off that cliff. This is his house? How weird is that?"

Molly hesitated, remembering Mike's strong belief that Tom had not jumped on purpose. But this was no time to debate whether or not his death was a suicide. "Yes. His wife's on her way down from Phoenix right now. She's the one who told me how to get in. No children. No pets. The patio door on the back side of the house is wide open after someone cut a hole in the glass door. But the 911 operator told me not to look through the rest of the house by myself. I've been in the family room and guest room but not the study or master suite. When you enter, they're down the hall to the right."

"Wait here," Sergeant Partridge said.

Washington was already at the front door, which Molly had left slightly ajar. "Cactus Heights Police!" he yelled. "Show yourself—now!"

When there was no response, both officers entered the house, weapons drawn, and repeated the warning.

From where she stood, Molly could see the two heading down the hall to the right. When they returned a few minutes later, weapons now holstered, Molly told them she could not reach Audrey but had left a message.

"Anything missing?" Partridge asked.

"I have no idea. I've never been in the house before. Mrs. O'Day asked me to come in to see what needs to be done to put the house on the market. She should be here within a half hour or so."

"When she looks through the house," Partridge directed, "have her inventory what's missing and come down to fill out a police report. I saw a lot of stuff that a professional gang would have grabbed. That collection of beaded Oaxacan animals, for example. But we looked where the break-in took place. Whoever it was must have gone straight for what they wanted. Either they were sure they couldn't be overheard, or they knew the judge was dead."

"Slick," Washington commented. "I've never seen a job like this. They knew what they were doing. This guy or guys could have cut that glass almost silently. Wanted to make certain no one heard them. There are a couple of round impressions on the cutout. Probably lifted it out and laid it on the ground using suction cups. Even a light sleeper in the other bedroom wouldn't have heard anything."

"Didn't I see an alarm panel?" Partridge said. "Looked like a Home Alert system. Was it on when you got here?"

Molly nodded and explained. "The owner told me where to find a key and gave me the code to disarm the alarm." Partridge noted the name of the alarm company and their telephone number by the keypad. "Who else has the code?"

Molly shrugged. "No idea, sorry. I haven't even met with Mrs. O'Day yet. What are the chances you can find the burglars?" *Probably the first question Audrey will ask me,* Molly thought.

"Not great," Washington said. "Frankly, we don't have the time or manpower, uh," he glanced at Sarah Partridge, "enough officers to spend much time on property crimes."

She scowled at him before telling Molly, "Doesn't mean we won't investigate. We'll give you a case number to pass along to the owner. But until that report gets filed, we don't even know what was taken. If anything. Whatever they took, it wasn't the big obvious items like TVs or rugs. Looks like some high-end Indian pottery, easy to pick up, is still on the shelf."

"But sometimes they're stupid and pawn the stuff they stole right away," Washington added. "That's why we need to know what was taken. Ask her to bring us photos if possible. Really good descriptions if not. It's likely to be jewelry. And let us know right away, so we can send a Property and ID unit to take fingerprints."

Molly's phone rang. She glanced and told them, "It's Mrs. O'Day. Do you want to...?" She offered the phone, but both shook their heads and walked back to the patrol car.

Audrey was obviously irritated. Without greeting, she barked into the phone: "What is it? I'm almost there. Can't it wait?"

So, she didn't listen to my message. After Molly explained the situation, Audrey was silent for a few moments. Then she said, "Have the police wait; I'll be there in ten or fifteen minutes."

"They've already left. They asked you to bring photos or descriptions of what's missing down to the station and file a report. They gave me a case number for you."

Audrey swore. Then she said, "There's not that much of value in the house. At least not stuff that's real portable. I won't be keeping the televisions or sound equipment anyway. Tom kept some personal stuff locked up in his desk. All my jewelry is in my apartment in Phoenix. Some of our artwork is very valuable, some of our rugs, pottery. But the paintings would be hard to fence. I did a quick video the night I was last there, just to be sure I would know if Tom gave any of our good stuff to...away. If he did give things away, it wouldn't be the first time. I can tell from a walk-through what was taken."

She ended the call. Abruptly. Again.

Molly hesitated but decided she would wait for Audrey before entering the house again.

About twenty minutes later, a blue Audi pulled into the driveway and a tall woman slid from behind the wheel. Molly's first thought was that Audrey was more elegant poodle than pit bull. Her brusque manner on the phone had led Molly to expect a fire plug in a severely tailored pants suit with hair in a tight bun. Audrey was slender (*the build people call "willowy,"* Molly thought, somewhat jealously) with carefully styled, shoulder-length red-blonde hair. She wore a short multi boucle blue tweed jacket over a low-cut cream silk blouse and slightly flared black trousers. Her age was hard to estimate. *Fifties?* Her face and figure could still turn heads. The judge had to have been at least fifteen years older. *Mike's played pickleball with her, but he never told me she's so attractive.*

On the ring finger of Audrey's left hand was the largest diamond ring Molly had ever seen. It threw off light like a disco ball. *I'd need a sling for my arm if I carried that around!* Molly immediately felt like apologizing for that catty thought. Instead, she shook hands and gave Audrey a card.

Audrey scrutinized it briefly and assumed an all-business manner. "Okay, let's see what's been taken." She set off for the front door with long purposeful strides. Molly had to trot to catch up.

"Uh, Mrs. O'Day, maybe we'd better use Kleenexes on our hands or gloves to open doors and drawers. In case there are fingerprints we could mess up." She pulled gloves out of her jacket pocket. It had been a chilly drive over in her open golf cart.

Audrey turned in surprise. "We don't know if anything's been taken yet." She hesitated, but then walked back to her car. She was pulling on black leather driving gloves as she returned to the house.

As they entered the foyer and then the kitchen, nothing looked out of place to Audrey. A seventy-five-inch television dominated the family room. Rugs covered most of the travertine floors. Molly surveyed the walls for orphaned picture hooks indicating missing artwork but saw none.

Audrey ran her finger like a caress across the bottom frame of a huge painting. "The thieves obviously didn't know much about art," she said. "Thank god for ignorance."

They walked room to room, and Molly could see

that Audrey's anxious glance went first to the paintings. The only sign of disturbance was the glass door of a cabinet that stood ajar in the hall. The shelves held trinkets, mostly beaded Oaxacan animals, as Officer Partridge had noticed. Audrey smiled. "Guess they didn't want Tom's precious collection." Her tone made it clear that she did not share her late husband's passion. But the top glass shelf was bare. Audrey shook her head and swore under her breath.

"The silver pieces," she said. "They're gone. Four small silver statues, one handmade silver horse and carriage from Indonesia, a water buffalo, a heron, and a miniature silver cow skull mounted on a piece of amethyst. They were small and easy to pick up but hardly worth the effort. I guess they could be melted down, but their real value was that they were handcast and highly unusual pieces of art. We got some of them on our honeymoon in Java and Bali. The skull was made in New Mexico. I imagine they'd be hard to fence."

"Then why would anyone go to all that trouble to get into the house?" Molly asked.

"I don't know. Was the alarm set when you came in?" At Molly's quick *yeah*, Audrey said, "That's odd. That siren is deafening. The neighbors would have heard it. So, it didn't go off. Either it malfunctioned or..."

"Someone knew the code or got around it somehow," Molly finished. "Who has the code?"

Audrey shrugged. "Besides me, and now you? I have no idea. Tom could have given it to somebody. I think he has a cleaning lady and someone who comes in occasionally to cook for him. And there's his new girlfriend. And I do mean 'girl.' He probably gave it to her."

Molly ignored Audrey's last comment. "I wonder why the thieves took so little."

"Probably they got spooked, decided there was a silent alarm or heard something that scared them, and they bailed before taking much," Audrey suggested.

"The police need photos of what was taken."

"I have that video I told you about. I didn't cover everything, but I'm quite sure I did shoot this cabinet. Let me look." Audrey scrolled through videos on her phone. "Yeah, I did. See?" She handed her phone to Molly.

"They are exquisite," Molly said. "And unique. Did you commission these?"

"Just the silver cow's skull," Audrey said. "The others, as I said, we bought on our honeymoon. But Tom had the cow's skull made after we moved to Arizona. For some reason, it amused him, and he said it fit with living in the Southwest. Frankly, I always hated it. So kitschy. I thought it was dumb to take a beautiful piece of amethyst and a lovely medium like silver and make something that ugly."

She turned away from the cabinet. "But I don't see anything else missing here. Let's go through the rest of the house now to check, and while we do that, you can suggest what I sell or donate. I really don't have a lot of room in my apartment in Phoenix, so I'll sell the furniture. Most of this came from our house in Florida. Not really my taste anymore anyway. When Tom and I married, I was so young I thought expensive always meant tasteful." Molly revised her estimate of

Audrey's age down to late forties. And then up again when Audrey added bitterly, "I wasted eighteen years with that man!" She waved her arm at all the furniture in the great room. "Estate sale. I assume you can arrange that?"

"Well…" *What the heck have I gotten myself into. I do not want to oversee an estate sale, even if this really would be one. Not the usual garage masquerading as an estate.*

Audrey noted her hesitation. "For, say, 10% of the profit, after marketing costs?"

"Uh, Audrey, you could get professionals to handle it. I could put you in touch…"

"I'd rather have someone I trust. If I gave you 15%, you could hire help. I can't come down here from Phoenix to set it all up. I stay with Ellen and Ed Featherstone when I need to be here, but I can't impose on them indefinitely. Bad enough I had to come down midweek to hash things out with Tom. And then it turned out he was too *busy* to talk Wednesday." Her tone of voice suggested she doubted he was fully occupied.

"You were here night before last?"

"Not overnight. I told you. I stayed with the Featherstones. I did come over to the house at dinnertime while Tom was out catting around, just to check everything. I didn't want to be in the same house with him after the way he…I've heard about that woman, what's her name…"

"Shelley?"

"Yeah, whatever. Tom seemed besotted with her!" Audrey's laugh seemed labored. "Have you met her? Plain as a broomstick, I've heard. But she's young. Tom likes them young. Oh well, he who laughs last," she said, heading down the hall. "Nothing I want in the bedroom." She tossed the comment back over her shoulder. "Except my clothes, of course. I'll take some of them up to Phoenix this afternoon. And I'll leave my car here and take the Edison. That car at least is worth something—more than mine. Especially given the price of gas these days. I've no idea where a charging station is, but I won't need one to get to Phoenix. I'm sure Tom kept the car charged." She headed into Tom's study, Molly following.

"Wait a sec," Molly said when she noticed a lonely cable stretched across an empty space in the middle of the desk. "Where's his computer? He must have had one. Would it be in a different room?"

"It was a laptop," Audrey said, "Sometimes he would take it out on the patio to work, but he wouldn't have left it out there. He almost always used it right here. And that's the charging cable."

"The burglar must have taken the computer. You need to tell the police. Do you have a photo?"

"I didn't go in Tom's study when I took that video Wednesday night. Everything in there is his stuff, including the computer. It was a new Apple, loaded. Probably worth something. I don't see how a thief would know that, but it's gone."

"Would there be personal financial information on it?"

"Probably, but it was password-protected. I doubt the average thief could get into it. Tom was really paranoid about security. He didn't even trust the cloud." She gestured at the two file drawers in the desk. "His other stuff—memorabilia mostly—he kept in here as hard copies. I guess we'll have to have it all shredded. Some might be confidential."

The royal "we," Molly thought. *Emptying those files is going to be a lot of work and I doubt she's going to help. Can't just dump it without going through it for big paper clips and other stuff that can't be shredded.*

Audrey surveyed the room. "I don't see anything else missing here. Of course, the printer is virtually worthless, so no surprise they didn't steal that. But there's lots of junk in here. We can sell or toss most of it."

Molly looked around at the walls and several large bookcases. "Don't you need to sort through it first? There must be documents, maybe mementos—you know, like that framed one?" She pointed to a photo of Tom in uniform with a military officer—a three-star general, judging from the stars on his shoulder loops. "Does Tom have, uh, any kids or grandkids or other relatives that might like some of these things?"

"Ha! Tom? Kids? That would have cramped his style."

The tone was bitter, but Molly sensed there was more to the story than that breezy denial suggested. From a lower shelf of one of the bookcases Audrey picked up a very small silver-framed formal photo of two people. Molly caught just enough of a glance to identify a youthful Audrey in a wedding dress. Audrey set the photo back, face down. Then she picked it up again and slipped it into a pocket in her jacket.

The gesture touched Molly. She remembered her own wedding day, full of joy and promise. *It's so sad when a relationship goes bad—especially when it's because the husband betrays his marriage vows. I know what that betrayal feels like. Audrey's more hurt than she'll let anyone see.*

Audrey looked a bit embarrassed that Molly had seen her pocket the photo. "No, nobody would really want those things and I guess you can't really sell that junk," she said, motioning to the photos on the wall. "Okay, let's take all the stuff out that's personal and worthless. You take the drawers over there and I'll go through the desk. I'll get a couple of garbage bags. I can come back down for a few hours tomorrow to finish up."

Molly was uncomfortable with her assignment. "Let's put personal papers in this," she suggested as she pulled over a large metal waste basket, "and I'll bring a box over tomorrow for stuff like printer paper and old magazines to recycle. But you may need receipts and cancelled checks."

Audrey groaned. "You're right. Look, could you just pack up all that crap and label the boxes, you know, 'old checks' or whatever?" It wasn't a question. *Beginning to feel like a personal secretary,* Molly thought. *Mike was right about her. I think my commission just went up from four to five percent, and I'd better get our contract written up before I start working.*

"The stuff the accountant will need will be in these drawers." Audrey fished out a small key from the back of Tom's center drawer and unlocked his file drawer. She pulled out files and began piling them in the waste basket they'd designated for personal papers. "Holy crap! What's this?" Audrey had taken out a bulky file folder and dumped its contents on the desk. With small *thunks*, four sealed envelopes fell out. A fifth was open, spilling hundred-dollar bills onto the desk and floor.

Molly was as stunned as Audrey by the flow of money. Audrey picked up a letter opener shaped like a scimitar and slit open the sealed envelopes. More hundred-dollar bills cascaded out. "What on earth..." She looked at Molly incredulously. "The bastard was hiding money from me! There are thousands of dollars here!" She picked up a bunch of the bills and looked at them thoughtfully. "But, honestly, it's still chump change in his overall estate. Why keep so much cash? He'd be able to screw me over a lot more if he changed his will. It wouldn't surprise me if he was planning that, too," she added angrily. "He probably was going to give the Cape Cod condo to that, that..."

"To Shelley?" Molly intervened before Audrey could come up with a satisfactory slur. "Arizona is a community property state. Maybe Massachusetts is also? As long as you're still married, he couldn't..."

"He had a lot of property before we married," Audrey said impatiently. "It's separate. We have a prenup. I can't claim it unless I'm the beneficiary in his will. And I was...I think I still am. I'd better be. But," she said, suddenly comprehending, "I'll bet he's been paying cash for everything he's been spending on her. No paper trail I could use in divorce proceedings."

These must be the hundred-dollar bills Shelley told me about. "What about this?" Molly asked, pointing to a small notation on each envelope. "Every envelope is dated in the corner starting in early November. There's even one for December 4—three days ago."

"Five envelopes," Audrey said. "Who knows how many he already went through. This open one is dated...November 7."

"Where would the cash come from? Bank withdrawals?"

Audrey shook her chin. "There's a thousand dollars in each envelope. You can get only five hundred at a time from the ATM. And besides, we still have a joint checking account. I would have noticed. He must have been doing some work off the books. Probably had some separate bank account I didn't know about. Or else, huh, someone was paying him a thousand dollars a week to do...something."

"You mean like...bribery?"

Audrey shook her head. "He's retired. It's not like he's still seeing cases. Not that I'd put it past him. He really is...was a kind of sleaze bag. But I don't see what anyone could bribe him to do."

"What if it's payment for *not* doing something?" Molly asked.

"HEY, JOSE." Detective Rasmussen mimed a knock on the side of Villegas's cubicle in the Cactus Heights police station. Rasmussen's huge bulk cut off what little sunlight slanted in through the window in the detectives' room. "Gotta minute?"

Villegas's face twitched and the dimple on one side of his mouth appeared briefly at Rasmussen's unaccustomed politeness. Last summer, over Rasmussen's protests, Villegas had invited Molly Levin and Mike Landry to help with the Renee

Holden assault case. It was especially galling to Rasmussen that the civilian interlopers had solved the case, and he and Villegas still occasionally sparred over what Rasmussen regarded as an unforgivable lapse in police protocol. Now the two had an undeclared but unreliable truce. Apparently Rasmussen had declared this a ceasefire moment. "Sure. What's up?"

Rasmussen sat down heavily, the straight-backed metal chair creaking under his weight. "Wasn't O'Day the name of the judge who got pushed off a cliff a few days ago?"

Villegas swung his desk chair around to face Rasmussen. "We still don't know if he got pushed—so far sounds more like he accidentally fell, or maybe jumped, but yeah. His name was Tom O'Day."

"Well, somebody named Audrey O'Day crashed an Edison EV on Oracle Road around three, just north of here where the speed limit goes up to sixty. Maybe a relative?"

"I think that's the wife." Villegas gave his fellow detective his full attention. "Was she hurt?"

"Not enough to be hospitalized. But the car was totaled. Man, that's a lot of money down the drain." Rasmussen shook his head.

"What happened? Drunk? Speed?"

"Naw. Now get this. Mrs. O'Day claims the car just stopped on her. She was telling anyone at the scene who would listen that she lost power completely. Blaming Edison. Said the car started doing stuff on its own, then just stopped dead when she was rounding a corner. Couldn't steer, couldn't brake. Went off the highway, down a swale, then up and plowed through a barbed-wire fence. That slowed her down quite a bit. Air bag deployed, and the car stopped against a bunch of barrel cactus. Except for some minor bruises, mostly from the airbag, she's unharmed. But to say she is pissed is putting it mildly. Furious with Edison. But cold angry, ya know? Not hysterical."

"What does Edison say?"

"The local media are on it now, of course. Here, take a look." He opened a link on his phone, and they huddled over it and read the breaking story.

The Edison spokeswoman said it's impossible for the car to spontaneously shut down. They had already established that O'Day wasn't in auto-drive mode. They suggested she must have had a "medical incident." And O'Day admitted that she had only driven it a couple times before. It was her husband's car.

"Huh," Villegas said. "I never believe..."

"In coincidence," Rasmussen chimed in to finish the phase. "Yeah, I know. You've said it often enough. On the other hand, women drivers..." He raised a skeptical eyebrow.

"...have better safety records than men," Villegas said, ignoring his implication. He sat drumming his fingers on the desk. "Maybe she is at fault, like Edison says. But what if she's telling the truth and it was sabotage?"

"How the hell do you figure that?"

"I heard a podcast on NPR the other day about hacking EV cars," Villegas said. "There were these two guys boasting that because modern cars are basically computers on wheels, they can be hacked. In fact, there's a YouTube video from a few years ago showing these same two men controlling a Jeep Cherokee remotely. Scary stuff. They started small. Turned on the AC and loud music that couldn't be changed by the driver and built up to turning the car totally off—on a highway. I thought the driver was crazy to allow them to do that just to prove a point. What if someone really did turn off Mrs. O'Day's ignition in the middle of traffic? And if it was her husband's car...."

"He was supposed to be driving. But wait a minute. The guy's dead. That kinda shoots your sabotage theory down."

"Unless she really was the intended driver. Or whoever hacked the car didn't know the husband was dead. He died just two days ago."

"Sounds far-fetched to me. Are you sure you weren't tuned into the sci-fi channel?"

"Everything's a computer these days. Our refrigerator at home conked out on us, and when we finally got a repairman to look at it, he said there were five circuit boards in the thing. To identify and replace the one that was failing would cost a minimum of fifteen hundred dollars! And you know what the workaround was? Every time it shuts down, we run outside, flip the circuit breaker off, wait five minutes and turn it back on."

"Yeah. But hacking a car? A brand-new electric vehicle?"

Villegas grinned. "If we've come to the point of having to reboot refrigerators, *possibile est*."

Rasmussen got up. "Always with the Latin," he muttered. Then he added, "You know how annoying that habit of yours is? You want to spout Latin, you should've stayed a priest." He stomped out, shaking his head.

I have to stop doing that, Villegas chided himself. *And I will—when he stops making cracks about gays or Latinos.*

14

DAY 4

Molly sat at her kitchen table looking out at a sudden rain squall that drenched the street in front of her house. *Living in the desert leaves all of us—plants, animals, humans— with an insatiable longing for moisture,* she thought. A few unprepared dog walkers were being dragged towards home by variously sized wet canines, some of them shaking and dousing their owners. A sudden gust threw a sheet of water at the window and distorted the figures outside into wavering outlines. *As welcome as the rain is, grey skies still invite dark thoughts. About how much time is left to me. Regrets about small unkindnesses I'm guilty of, opportunities I have missed, people gone from my life.*

She shook herself like one of the sodden dogs outside. *Enough!* She said to herself sternly. *Get up and do something.* She took out her phone. *Maybe call Mike? But I can't go running to him every time depression threatens.* She remembered something her much beloved grandmother had told her more than once: "If you are feeling down, do something kind for someone else. It'll perk you up and help someone who needs it more than you do."

Good advice. She knew her grandmother spoke from experience. *Lord knows, she had not lived an easy life. Widowed so young....Widowed. Like me. Like Audrey. But is she grieving? Shelley is likely to miss Tom more.*

That thought led her to realize that she hadn't seen Shelley since Tom's death. *I should have called her before now. And I've been sitting here feeling glum. How would I feel if Mike had gotten dragged over the edge of that cliff?*

She dialed Shelley's number before she had planned what to say. The phone rang a long time and rolled over to Shelley's cheery "Thanks for calling. Please leave a message." Molly was uncomfortable when the beep sounded. She hated being forced to leave a sensitive message with an automaton, but she spoke briefly:

"Hi Shelley. It's Molly. Just wondering how you are doing. I'm sorry I haven't been in touch sooner. Please call if you are up for a cup of tea—or coffee —with me."

Less than five minutes later, Shelley called her back. "Thanks, Molly. I confess I've been feeling sorry for myself. Tom was really the best friend I had here, and...anyway, I'd love a cup of coffee—or even your darned Earl Grey tea!"

"Come on over. I can manage coffee. But I don't keep cream in the house, so I guess it's BYOC if you'd like some in your java."

When Shelley arrived, she clutched a carton of half-and-half. Molly gave her a hug. Then she selected from her miscellaneous collection of hand-made mugs one that Shelley had once admired. Bought in that quirky little town in New Mexico, Madrid, it was square, decorated with a coyote. As they sat down at the kitchen table, Molly noticed Shelley's eyes were red. Molly casually slid a box of tissues within reach.

Shelley nodded, acknowledging Molly's gesture, but made no move to use a tissue. "I will miss him a lot," she said calmly. "I wasn't really in love with him —at least not the way he said he was with me—but I was very fond of him." She pulled the mug closer and added some cream. But instead of stirring her coffee, she held up the spoon Molly had set on the table and jabbed it in the air. "Where are his friends? His golfing buddies, the hiking club? You're the only one who seems to have noticed he died. I'm working with several women from Sunrise, and no one has even mentioned his death to me. I'm sure they know we were seeing each other. I don't get it." Before Molly could respond, Shelley banged the spoon down on the table. "Do you realize Audrey hasn't even planned a service for him? At least as far as I know. Has she?" Molly shook her head. "So—*nothing*? I know he didn't get along with everyone, but he was a remarkable man. Certainly a generous one." Shelley set her mug down, unstirred. "Nothing to mark the end of his life. What kind of wife does that? I kept expecting..." Her voice drifted off.

"Some kind of memorial," Molly completed. *Audrey was probably too angry with him.*

Shelley seemed to read Molly's thoughts. "Was it because of me?" she asked plaintively.

Probably. "Oh, no, I don't think so," Molly said. "They'd been estranged for some time, you know."

"Well, *someone* should do *something* for him. I even wondered if I should." Shelley chuckled. "Think what his Sunrise buddies would think about that!" Her face grew serious. "He was a terrific guy; we had an awful lot of fun together. I thought even Brian would have liked him." As always when she mentioned her brother, Shelley's face became a study in sorrow.

She's grieving as much for Brian as for Tom, Molly realized. Recalling that Shelley had once lamented Brian had not had a chance to explore careers, Molly ventured a question. "It sounds as if life threw Brian a curve ball. What happened?"

Shelley's response was an angry outburst. "It wasn't fair, Molly. Police stopped him when he ran a red light. Then he was arrested because he had a little bit of drugs on him. Okay, so he shouldn't have had them, but he should never have gone to prison. The police, the prosecutor—they all tried to force him to give up the name of the guy he got drugs from. They were convinced his dealer was a big distributor. He had been Brian's college history teacher, for god's sake! From what Brian told me, Professor Benson bought stuff for himself, and Brian bought a little from him. It wasn't like Benson supplied all the kids in college. Brian loved him. Really loved him. Guess he was a kind of father figure, you know? Lord knows, Brian needed one. Our father was..." Her voice drifted off and she stared unseeing at the tabletop.

"Inadequate?" Molly hazarded.

Shelley snorted. "Well, that's one way of putting it. Dad loved my mother at first, I'll give him that. He did. He did," she repeated as if to convince herself. "But I don't think he ever wanted children. Certainly not two of them. We were Mom's idea. Then when he left, she just kind of quietly fell apart, stayed in bed a lot, watching TV, smoking. She left Brian in dirty diapers. She was not there for us. Maybe if Dad hadn't walked out on us...."

Maybe Tom was a kind of father figure for her too, Molly realized. *That would explain a lot.*

"What ifs, right?" Shelley said with a weak unhappy smile. "Story of my life. And Brian's, too. What if..." She got up, put her empty coffee cup in the sink and stood silhouetted against the window that faced the desert wash beside Molly's house. "Stupid to wonder..." She turned back to Molly. "Anyway, Brian was too stubborn or loyal to name his teacher, and he made me promise I wouldn't. And our wonderful justice system threw the book at him."

What do I say to that? "Was he imprisoned?"

"Oh, yeah," Shelley said bitterly. She stood.

"For a long time?"

Shelley looked at her with a strange expression Molly couldn't interpret. Almost like she was amused. *What could possibly be funny about that question?*

Shelley grabbed the jacket she had slung over the back of her chair and picked up the cream carton from the table. "No, not long," she said enigmatically. And with a quick "Thanks for the coffee," she headed for the door.

15

DAY 5

As he walked down the hall, Villegas hoped Captain Dubrow was in her office. She waved him in as she finished a conversation. "Yes," she said to someone on the phone. She gestured Villegas toward one of her ultramodern, ultra-uncomfortable metal and leather chairs.

In recent months, as the initial resentment of her transfer in from Tucson had died down in the face of her proven competence, Captain Dubrow had begun to dress more informally. The best indicator of her acceptance within the police corps, however, was the health of the ficus tree by the chairs facing her desk. The frequent surreptitious doses of coffee or soda that had nearly killed it when she first arrived had tailed off until now the tree looked positively thriving .

Today, she was dressed in official captain mode: gold badge and gold stripes on the sleeves set off by the dark navy jacket, hair back in a tight bun, man's white shirt, and a navy tie. *When will women in leadership positions here be able to lose the male dress?* Villegas wondered. *Probably before Rasmussen will feel comfortable meeting my husband.*

"Okay, agreed," the captain said decisively into the phone. With that, she hung up and turned her cool grey eyes on him.

Without preamble, Villegas announced: "We have opened an investigation into the recent death of Judge Tom O'Day.

"I thought his death was an accident—fell off a cliff, right?"

"Yes. But Terry and I agree that there are some...anomalies that bear investigating."

Dubrow smiled. "You and Terry," she said. "That's a welcome development." Villegas knew she was referring to the uncomfortable, sometimes toxic working relationship between the two detectives.

"We tend to have different perspectives on things," Villegas said cautiously. "But we both feel an official investigation is warranted." Dubrow waved a "go on" at him.

"First, O'Day's house was broken into—either the night before the fatal hike, or the night after he died. Second..."

Dubrow held up a hand to interrupt. "*Either*? When was it reported?"

"Two days after he died. But whoever broke in did so into a guest room at the opposite end of the house from the master bedroom and was very careful to make no noise. They used a glass cutter and probably suction cups to remove the glass. O'Day left early the morning of his hike, so it's conceivable that it occurred while he was sleeping and heard nothing."

"No security system?"

"Surprisingly for Sunrise, yes, O'Day had one."

"But it didn't go off?"

"Sergeant Partridge is checking with the security system company to find out if their log shows when the guest room door was opened. She probably has that information by now. Frankly we haven't spent a lot of time on the burglary yet. Very little was stolen. We've been focusing on O'Day's death."

"Sounds as if it's possible that the theft occurred after his death," Dubrow observed. "Someone who found out he was dead and saw it as an opportunity. That's more likely than that it happened during the night on Wednesday. It would be a bit odd for him to overlook a break-in and burglary that morning, even if he didn't hear it." She was twirling a mechanical pencil in her fingers—a habit Villegas knew usually signaled skepticism.

"Only a laptop computer and a few trinkets from a cabinet in the hall outside the guest room were stolen. The laptop was in the judge's study, down the hall from his bedroom by the guest room, and according to his wife, the guest room is rarely used. He wouldn't necessarily have noticed anything out of order. He had that early morning hike to get to. We'd have to assume he didn't try to use his computer that morning. Therefore, we can't rule out the possibility that it happened the night before he died. The alarm company log should help us if he set it that night." Dubrow continued to look dubious, but Villegas went on down his list.

"Second, the person nearest to O'Day on the hike insists that the victim was acting very strangely leading up to the time that he went off the cliff.

Talking to himself continuously, taking clothing off, hallucinating."

"Heat stroke?"

"The search and rescue crew suggested that. Thursday morning was warmer than normal, but heat stroke cases are rare this time of year. And assuming he was not just confused but actively hallucinating, energized rather than tired, heat stroke doesn't fit the symptoms. The two witnesses to his fall disagree on what happened. Mike Landry, who was nearest to O'Day, says the judge was talking loud and crazy, as if to someone or something off in the distance. Landry says O'Day reached out over the edge for an imaginary object or person and fell, despite Landry's attempts to hold him back. The other witness, Barry Sturges, says from his standpoint about fifty yards away, the two men struggled, and Landry pushed O'Day over."

"Mike Landry. I know the name. Is he the one..."

Villegas nodded. "He and Molly Levin are the two civilians who...um...helped us a few months ago with that assault case in Sunrise Acres."

"Isn't that where the mayor's mother lives? I didn't realize senior citizens led such dangerous lives," Dubrow observed dryly. "Two police actions in Sunrise in the same year."

Villegas nodded but then continued with his list. "Third, Mrs. O'Day just crashed her husband's Edison on the way back from Cactus Heights to her place in Phoenix. She claims the car was hacked, that it simply turned off while she was rounding a corner on Oracle. She lost control and totaled the car. She was not seriously injured."

When the captain didn't appear to see the connection, Villegas emphasized, "It was Judge O'Day's car. She wouldn't have been driving it if he hadn't died two days before."

The pencil twirling halted abruptly. "Is she delusional? Hacking a car sounds nuts."

"Well, several years ago, a couple of hackers proved they could take over a car if it's connected to the Internet. And Edisons are." He paused a moment for Dubrow to process that thought before continuing, "And fourth..."

"There's *more*?"

"Well, we find it a bit suspicious that Mrs. O'Day strenuously fought an autopsy—although we proceeded with it."

"Religious reasons?"

"No, she just said it was unnecessary and delayed 'closure.' Her argument was that there is no question about cause of death, which is true. He died on impact. But..."

"But," the captain tried to summarize, "he could have been pushed, he could have been hallucinating...." The pencil started its rounds again. "Did the second witness, Barry whatever, confirm that O'Day was hallucinating?"

"Sturges maintains that he didn't see anything up to the point when Landry was grabbing O'Day's arm, and O'Day was yelling to 'let go!' But he probably wasn't within earshot before then."

"Does Mr. Landry have any motive to kill O'Day?"

"Apparently, there was no love lost between them. There's a big renovation project going on in Sunrise Acres and Landry accused the judge of steering the contract to his wife's nephew. According to Sturges, the two men had a heated, and very public, argument about it. Landry all but accused O'Day of fraud."

"Seems as if that might give O'Day a reason to push Landry over the side, rather than the other way around."

"Yes, and I don't see Mike Landry as a murderer. I got to know Molly Levin and him earlier this year. He's an academic. More brain than brawn. If he wanted to maim or kill someone, he'd find a less physical—or public—way."

"But you've got to..."

"Take the accusation seriously. Yes. We are. But Terry has never forgiven Mike and his girlfriend for their amateur detective work last summer. Terry gets a charge out of seeing Mike as a suspect. Even if I were inclined to dismiss Sturges's account, Terry won't let go as long as he's having fun."

Dubrow pursed her lips as if she'd eaten something sour. *She didn't like that crack about Terry,* Villegas realized. *Be careful or you'll get tossed off the case.* But Dubrow apparently decided to let it go. "So, you think the break-in, the fall off the cliff, the wife's objections to an autopsy, her car accident—they're all related?"

"Unlikely they're all coincidental. Don't you agree? They happened within a space of one or two days—all involving, directly or indirectly, Tom O'Day."

"Quite a few assumptions there: that O'Day wasn't pushed but was high on something and tried to fly off a cliff, that the wife didn't want an autopsy for some nefarious reason, that the car was in fact hacked, and that the intended driver was Tom O'Day."

"Or that Audrey O'Day faked the accident," Villegas added.

Dubrow chuckled. "This is one of those rare days that I'm glad I'm in management." She stood in dismissal. "I'll be following how you handle this case very carefully. Good luck, Detective." She grinned— wickedly, in Villegas's opinion.

He headed for the door, then whirled around. Dubrow was just reaching for a file on top of a precariously leaning pile on a corner of her desk.

"One more thing," he said.

She looked annoyed. "Yes?"

"I don't know the relevance yet, but O'Day was romancing a much younger woman. It's possible that was a threat to the marriage. I'm interviewing Audrey O'Day later today."

"Good grief! It's beginning to sound like a soap opera! Better figure out what happened before the media get hold of it. They'd love it. And the Dynamic Duo wouldn't."

The Dynamic Duo, Villegas knew, referred to the police commissioner and his bosom buddy, the mayor. But he wasn't sure who was Batman and who was Robin.

"Thank you for taking the time to meet with me." Villegas ushered Audrey into his cubicle and gestured towards a metal chair.

Audrey gave a tight smile. "Didn't know it was optional. But I was going to come in tomorrow anyway. I want to review the police report on my crash."

"Yes, I want to hear about that. It's fortunate you weren't seriously injured," he added and looked at the large bruise on her forehead and side of her cheek.

She eyed him skeptically, both eyebrows slightly raised as if she doubted his sincerity. The hint of a smile on her lips made him wonder about hers.

"But first," he said, ignoring the unspoken challenge between them, "I hope you can help us with a couple other issues. We have your husband's cell phone. Do you know the password?"

Rather than answer, Audrey attacked. "Why wasn't the phone returned to me? For that matter, I don't have his backpack or his watch or ring or anything."

"All his personal effects will be returned to you when our investigation is concluded."

"I still don't know what there is to investigate. He fell. He died."

"But surely you want to know *why* he fell."

She looked at him steadily. *Wish I knew what was going on in that beautiful head,* Villegas thought. *She's trying to decide how to respond.*

"ROSCO," she said suddenly. "Name of our first dog. Try that. Of course, Tom may have changed it. But we used that a lot for relatively unimportant sites. He usually puts his passwords in all caps."

After checking the spelling, Villegas said, "Thank you. That'll be very helpful. Oh, and one more detail. You have an alarm system in the house. Did Mr. O'Day usually turn it on at night?"

"Religiously—as part of getting ready for bed. In fact, he set it whenever he left the house for more than an hour or two. We have some extremely valuable paintings. Shortly after we married, our house was broken into, and all my best jewelry stolen. Since then, anywhere we lived, we've had a security system."

"Kind of unusual for Sunrise Acres," Villegas noted.

"Yeah, people here are too casual about security. A lot of them don't even lock their doors at night. But this break-in shows Sunrise isn't as safe as advertised."

Villegas nodded. "We try to advise caution, but burglaries are quite rare. We'll be getting information from Home Alert. That's your alarm company, right?"

At her nod, he continued. "They should be able to tell us when the break-in occurred if your husband activated the system."

"Well, I know that it had to have been sometime after Wednesday night." She thought a moment. "Or maybe Thursday morning after Tom left for his...for his hike. I set the alarm Wednesday night when I left the house about seven. I assume that when he got home later, he would have set it again before going to bed. Our little silver sculptures were there when I left that night. Saturday morning, when Molly Levin and I went to the house, they were gone. My husband's laptop computer was taken—a nice one. New."

"Isn't it possible that your husband had moved the computer and silver pieces, that they were gone before your Wednesday night visit? How do we know that the pieces were stolen?"

Audrey pulled out her phone. She selected one of several videos and handed the phone to Villegas.

"What am I looking for?"

"Just keep looking. You'll see as the video pans

down the hallway outside our guest room. See the cabinet and the sculptures in it? I took this video Wednesday night. It's date stamped. I didn't go into Tom's study, so I don't have a photo of the computer—but he certainly didn't take it on his hike!"

"Did you attach this video to the report you filed on the burglary?"

She shook her head. "Not the whole video—just some screen shots."

"May I have one of our detectives copy this video?"

At her nod, he called Weatherby, and Audrey handed her the phone with the admonition, "Don't copy anything but that one video." Then she appeared to think about the implications of her own caution and pulled the phone back. "I'll send it to you. Give me a phone number or email address."

Weatherby pulled out her phone. "How about if you airdrop it to my phone? That way, you can choose exactly what you are giving us permission to copy. Do you know how to airdrop?"

"Oh no, I'm sure I'll need help from someone younger." Audrey pursed her lips with annoyance, shook her head, and deftly hit a few buttons.

"Got it. Thanks," Weatherby said ignoring the sarcasm.

As Weatherby turned to leave, Villegas handed her a slip of paper. "Mrs. O'Day has provided us with the password to her husband's phone."

"Possible password," Audrey corrected him. "I could be wrong."

"I'll give it a try," Weatherby said. She nodded at Audrey. "Thank you." She shot Villegas a significant glance that told him she would be back if the password didn't work.

"May I ask why you were videotaping your household possessions on that particular night?"

She sat with her eyes fixed on the corner of the cubicle for a few moments before responding. "Personal reasons." Villegas thought she intended to say nothing more, but then she added, "Molly Levin said you wanted photos of what was stolen. Now you have them. Except for Tom's laptop. I don't have a photo of that. As I said, I didn't videotape his study. But I can send you a description; I know the model."

"Could it have been taken to get access to financial records or information that would be valuable for identity thieves?"

"All our financial records were triple password protected and required voice or facial recognition. Tom was paranoid about security. His social security number, passwords, everything important he stored in his laptop, heavily protected. Frankly, I doubt even I could break into the machine."

"That's reassuring," Villegas said. "Now please tell me about your car crash."

"I told the cop or deputy or whoever showed up right after it happened that it wasn't my fault. He insisted on talking to me right then and there, when I was still stunned. The air bag gave me this gorgeous black eye." She gestured to her forehead where the large bruise down the side of her face was turning from black to purple. "Anyway, he took notes, but I don't think he believed me. I want to be sure the report is accurate. I'll need it. I'm suing Edison's ass. Already have a lawyer on the case. I could have been killed! First the radio started blasting when I didn't even have it turned on. Rap! I hate rap—and I'll tell you it was so sudden and so loud that I did swerve in my lane a bit. But then the damned car just turned off. If I hadn't been in the slow lane, I would have been killed. No brakes. And have you ever tried to control a car when the power steering is totally dead? It was absolutely terrifying."

"A new car, I understand."

"The new sports model—my husband's latest toy. All the bells and whistles. Self-driving if you want that option. Yeah, right! As if that were safer than an experienced human driver!"

"Any idea how the car could just turn off?"

"I talked to someone at Edison corporate. She said it couldn't happen. But I know it did. One minute I'm driving as usual, then the radio thing, and next—no control at all. No brakes! No steering!" Her voice rose in anger.

"What did you do?"

"I was at a curve, and the car just went straight. I was trying not to panic, pumped the brakes like mad —lot of good that did. Stomped on the parking brake, but I was already off the road. I held on for dear life as the car went down a swale, then up towards some bushes. No trees, thank god. Or saguaros. Ended up plowing through a wire fence and into a bunch of barrel cactuses."

"How does Edison explain what happened?"

"They just deny it could happen. They put the blame on me. First, they said it could be 'operator error,' as if I absent-mindedly turned off the motor. Next, they suggested a 'medical incident.' Yeah, right,

like I managed to turn the car off while I simultane-
ously had a stroke or something. But I'll be able to
prove that didn't happen. Either there's a massive bug
in their software or someone hacked into the car's
operating system. I've read that it's possible. Either
way, they almost killed me. I'm going to make them
pay."

"This was your husband's car, right?"

"Yeah, and whoever caused the crash must have
expected him to be behind the wheel. They couldn't
have known I would be driving. But if you're
suggesting I didn't know how to drive it...."

Villegas held up a placating hand. "Not at all. We
just found it...curious that you had an accident with
his car so soon after he died. And after your house
was burglarized. An odd series of coincidences. One
could surmise that his death and these two incidents
were related. Wouldn't you agree?"

She looked at him, eyes narrowed in shrewd
appraisal. "So, you do believe me that the car was
sabotaged."

Villegas assumed the blank expression his
husband called his "Mt. Rushmore face." After a
moment's silence he asked, "What does your lawyer
think about your chances against such a large
corporation?"

"He doesn't think we'll win outright," she admitted. "Apparently, it's nearly impossible to prove the
car's software was tampered with. But there would be
evidence that the motor was turned off. Every second
of these cars' operations is recorded and stored in the
cloud. But we haven't been able to get a straight
answer whether they can tell if the signal to turn it off

came from inside the car—which of course they'd love, because they could say I did it myself—or from outside, which is what had to have happened.

"I may need your help to track down the car and get the black box that records everything—assuming it wasn't destroyed when I hit the far side of the swale. That's when the airbag went off, so I guess I hit plenty hard, and that was just seconds after the engine turned off. Why they would be so stupid as to put the black box under the driver's seat next to the batteries is beyond me. Maybe they thought the batteries would protect it. Still, Edison certainly doesn't want bad publicity. This is a new line of cars. We expect they'll settle." She smiled. "For plenty." *She looks like a cat just finishing up a bowl of cream.* "I mean, Geezus, I could have been killed. And the cop who looked the car over said that with all the damage to the undercarriage and front end, it's probably a total loss." She looked pointedly at her watch and picked up the Dior purse she'd carefully set on the chair. "Now I really have to go. I believe I've answered all your questions."

"Not quite. Please, just a few more minutes. As you know, we have opened an investigation into your husband's death."

"I know you did an entirely unnecessary autopsy day before yesterday and found *nothing.*"

"That decision was not entirely up to us. Whenever a death occurs under unusual circumstances, the medical examiner is duty bound to determine what happened. Which brings me to why we're seeking your help. I am curious. Why did you think the autopsy was unnecessary? The ME tells us you objected quite strenuously."

"As was my right. After all, there was no doubt what killed him. He fell off a cliff! I saw no reason to cut him open and analyze his organs just to confirm that his head was bashed in."

She's being deliberately crude. Why? To shock me or make me feel guilty? Villegas did not rise to the bait.

"Yes, of course that is *how* he died. But I hoped you could shed some light on *why* he could have fallen to his death. Had he experienced prior symptoms? Dizziness? Disorientation?"

"I don't know how I can possibly help you," she said stiffly. "We haven't been spending a lot of time together. And I wasn't there when he...when it...when he died. In fact, I was in Phoenix." Her voice wavered slightly on the last words. "And no. Aside from a heart condition that he handles with meds, sometimes a sleeping pill for insomnia, he has always been quite healthy. I don't think he would have gone on that hike otherwise."

Villegas began to reach for the box of tissues he kept handy on his desk, but Audrey's eyes were dry. Her moment of apparent sadness had passed. "I'm sorry to have to ask you so many questions. But as you stated, you were in Sunrise Acres the night before he fell, correct?"

"Yes, staying with friends. And I went to our house to take the video. Then I returned to my friends' house. They can tell you that I left early the next morning, about five-thirty. I had an eight-thirty meeting in Phoenix Thursday morning and wanted plenty of time in case of problems on I-10."

Villegas nodded. "Yes, wise of you. But why hadn't

you stayed the night in your own home with your husband?"

Audrey looked startled and then angry. "I hardly think that is relevant, Detective." Her scathing tone left unsaid: "And none of your business."

"I'm sorry if my questions seem impertinent," Villegas said calmly. "We're trying to understand your husband's state of mind when he set out on that hike. Is it possible that the two of you had argued, for example, or he was despondent?"

Now it was Villegas's turn to be startled, as Audrey glared at him and then suddenly broke into a laugh of genuine amusement. "You think...you think," she said gasping for breath between bursts of laughter. "You think he was...he was distraught...he was worried about his marriage and threw himself over a cliff in despair? Oh my god, that's hilarious! If you only knew..."

She sobered up quickly when Villegas asked, "Knew what?" Looking at her face, Villegas thought *she regrets saying that.* He could see her assess several possible answers and reject them.

"My husband," she said at last, "was not the type to commit suicide over love lost. Or anything else."

Villegas sat silently, knowing his inquisitive expression would probably elicit more. She tolerated the silence longer than most people would have. But finally, she burst out, "Oh, you'll find out anyway. We were separated. That's why I was staying with friends."

As she reached again for her purse, Villegas debated with himself. *Ask about heirs? Might take a while to find out from public records.* "One last question, please."

Audrey gave a theatrical sigh. "Last one," she repeated firmly.

"Who are your husband's heirs? Just you, or are there others?"

She stood to her full height, towering over him as he sat. "That's an insulting question. Are you implying I had reason to wish him dead?"

Villegas rose and faced her. "We'll find out eventually. Why not cooperate with us? It was your objection to the autopsy that most influenced the decision to open an investigation." His voice hardened. "We can make that investigation as unobtrusive—or as obtrusive—as warranted."

Audrey looked at him for several long moments, perhaps gauging how much of a threat this was. She turned and walked to the door that led into the hall, and Villegas thought he'd lost her. But she turned back. "No children. First wife remarried, and she's no longer in the picture. As far as I know, I am the sole heir."

"As far as you know?" Villegas repeated in surprise.

"I haven't seen his latest will. Yet." She opened the door and disappeared down the hall.

Well, there's a mystery! Why doesn't she know who's in that will? And what caused the estrangement with her husband? The other woman? But if the wife's his only heir, that means she had a strong motive for wanting to keep it that way. But how could she have caused him to fall? And what about the car crash that she wants us to believe was aimed at killing him? I'm still not convinced she couldn't have staged that "accident" just to convince us someone tried to kill her husband. Distract us from focusing on her. Time to take a ride up the highway.

LATER THAT AFTERNOON, Villegas popped his head over Rasmussen's cubicle wall. "Terry, I'm going to look at the scene of Mrs. O'Day's car accident. I'll let you know what I find—unless you want to ride along."

Rasmussen shook his head and gestured to a pile of folders on his desk. "But what do you think you can figure out just from looking at where the car went off the road?"

"Terry, there are only a few possibilities for how that car got turned off, and none of them seems very plausible. First, it could have been an accident. Edison claims Mrs. O'Day must have momentarily blacked out or meant to turn something else on and hit the ignition instead. She, of course, vigorously denies this is what happened. Second possibility: a master hacker took control of the car and caused the crash. Denise dug into that story about the guys who controlled a Jeep Cherokee remotely back in 2015. They did it to prove it could be done as a warning to car manufacturers. O'Day's Edison was the newest model. I'll bet auto companies have been falling all over themselves hardening the software against hacking. Edison strongly denies that their cars can be hacked. The third possibility doesn't make a lot of sense either: that Mrs. O'Day would endanger her life by deliberately driving her car off the road just so we'd cross her off the suspect list. She could easily have come away from that crash with more than a couple bruises. So, I'm going to take a drive up Oracle to the crash site and poke around a little."

"I'm still betting that she panicked somehow and turned the motor off and made up that bullshit about the car radio turning itself on and off. You won't be able to tell any of that from looking at the crash site. But knock yourself out." Rasmussen waved a dismissive hand in the air and turned to his computer.

As Villegas drove up Oracle Road, he assumed for the moment that Audrey O'Day wanted to crash the car without seriously injuring herself. She had been driving in the right-hand slow lane. *The speed limit is sixty, but if I pump the brakes to signal to people behind me that I'm slowing, I could safely get down to thirty-five or forty.* He scrutinized the shoulder for less dangerous places to go off the road. For several miles before reaching the crash site, he saw none—too many trees or culverts over a wash or steep drop-offs.

The crash site was not being treated as a crime scene, so there was no yellow tape. But Villegas knew from the police report where the crash had taken place. He parked the cruiser on the shoulder, just before the highway veered gently to the left, and turned on his flashing lights. There was no way to tell how fast she had been going. There were no skid marks—the result, as she claimed, of her brakes and steering being inoperative.

The detective donned a bright orange vest and began walking along the shoulder. About a hundred yards ahead, in the middle of the curve in the highway, he could see the destroyed barbed wire fence.

Hope the rancher fixes that. We don't need his cows wandering onto the highway. The tangled mess of barbed wire and metal fence posts lay on the other side of a wide, sandy swale. Villegas paced off some distances. The swale descended gently for thirty or forty feet, leveled off for another thirty or so, then rose again more abruptly before meeting the fence. He stepped cautiously over the barbed wire and followed the tracks of the car and tow truck through sand and brush until the trail ended at the remains of a group of large barrel cacti.

If I were to select a spot on this highway to make a soft landing, this would be it. The gravelly shoulder would initially slow the car, which would then plunge down a gentle swale filled with sand and scrub, then up the other side, slowing all the time. The barbed wire fence would drop the speed some more, then the final impact would be against the cacti. If her story is true, she was extremely fortunate she left the highway here. And if she planned it? Lucky either way. She still could have been killed or seriously injured. But at least no possibility of an explosion with an electric vehicle.

This was all speculative, of course. *Maybe the hacking story was just to save face. Maybe she dozed off and panicked or intended to turn off the radio but hit the ignition by mistake. But if so, why didn't she brake hard?*

Villegas had to drive beyond the crash site more than a mile before he could reverse direction and return to Cactus Heights. *If I'd been planning a fake crash, I would have driven out here more than once to identify the ideal spot. Did she do that?*

Too many questions. Too few answers. She had a strong motive to get rid of her husband—but opportunity and means? Not clear. Maybe it was just good karma—for her—that he went off that cliff. And I don't see how faking a car accident would benefit her, unless she expects us to find clear evidence that his death was not accidental and wants to be sure she's not a suspect.

16

DAY 6

From the moment Mike arrived at the police station he felt he was in hostile territory. Earlier that year, Molly and Mike had worked closely and amicably with Detective Villegas. Back then, the receptionist had greeted them with easy, friendly recognition. Now Maria was stiffly formal and insisted he give his full name as she signed him in with a certain amount of bureaucratic flourish. Mike tried to convince himself that the cold penetrating his jacket was simply frosty December weather trapped in the stucco building. *But it feels like a different building. And for sure, it's a different situation when you are the accused rather than the accuser.*

He sat uneasily on the bench against the entryway wall and noted that its appearance had not improved since the last time he and Molly had waited for an audience with Detective Villegas. The bench was still a grubby green and wobbled to one side as if nervous suspects had rocked on it too many times. Mike checked his watch every few seconds. After what seemed like an entire morning, but was in fact only ten minutes, Maria called him to go in. The door to the hallway clicked open. To Mike's relief, it was Villegas who motioned him inside. But the relief was short-lived. Villegas escorted him silently to an interview room where Detective Rasmussen sat like a man mountain on a grey folding chair. Mike looked questioningly at Villegas, who finally spoke.

"We have opened an investigation into Tom O'Day's death. Detective Rasmussen is involved in a different case, so I am taking the lead on this one," Villegas said as he sat down next to the other detective and gestured for Mike to take the chair opposite. Mike stumbled over the chair leg and dropped awkwardly onto the thin red vinyl cushion. The chair looked like a refugee from a seedy '50s diner.

For the first time Mike could remember, the police presence—even of these men he knew personally— seemed menacing rather than reassuring. *This must be the way Peter always feels with police,* he thought, recalling his Black friend's arrest for assault during a protest march in Tucson. Although Peter had been exonerated, it was just one in a long line of fraught encounters with police dating back to his childhood. As a white man, Mike had never experienced that kind of prejudice.

After establishing the time and the names of those present for the sake of the recording, Rasmussen started the questioning. "Tell us about your altercation with Tom O'Day. According to Mr. Sturges, you and the judge nearly came to blows."

"That's a vast overstatement," Mike said as he made an effort to keep his voice steady. "As I told Jose, uh, Detective Villegas, Tom and I had argued, yes. And both of us raised our voices, but it was more of a debate than a fight. Tom took advantage of some naiveté among members of the renovation committee directing a major overhaul of the Sunrise Acres Activity Center. By the time I joined the committee, construction was underway."

"So, why take on the fight? Sounds as if it was too late to question how the general contractor was selected." It was Villegas who spoke.

This is going to be an interrogation—and in stereo. And speaking of naiveté, here I thought Jose was my friend.

"I wanted to educate the committee to the flaws in the process and to put Tom on notice that his shenanigans were obvious. And that the nephew had better perform." Hearing his own words, Mike felt uncomfortable. *That sounded pretentious.* The corners of Rasmussen's mouth turned up. *Is that a smile of amusement or a sneer of contempt?*

"What was in it for you," Rasmussen asked, "besides your noble desire to educate the committee?"

Definitely a sneer. "There was nothing 'in it' for me," Mike said, emphasizing the two words sarcastically. *Damn, I wish Molly were here. She would have explained it much better.*

"What's puzzling us," Villegas took over, "is why you would feel so passionately about something that did not affect you personally."

"As a member of the community," Mike said,

choosing his words carefully now, but unable to halt a small quaver in his voice, "and more importantly, of the finance committee, it was my job to protect our investment. If the contractor ran over budget, all of us could be subject to a special assessment. Sunrise Acres retirees hate special assessments. Many people really can't afford them."

Rasmussen continued. "But you accused Tom O'Day—a *judge*—of fraud."

"No, I said—I believe my exact words were, 'You deceived the committee.'" Mike was beginning to feel pushed into a corner.

Rasmussen shook his head, looking exasperated. "This isn't a college lecture, Mr. Landry. The exact words aren't important. You thought he was a crook. Now, isn't it possible that when you were up on that cliff and he was right up on the edge, that the temptation to give him a little nudge was irresistible? Just a tiny shove and the crook went to his reward?"

Mike was so angry that he felt acid rising in his throat. "That's ridiculous!" He half stood, his voice rising in pitch and volume. "I was trying my best to keep him from going over. I told you. He was acting crazy."

A sudden thought hit him, and he sat down heavily. "Wait a minute. Have you done any tests to see what was making him hallucinate and act weird? There had to have been *something* in his blood that explains why he was acting so nutty."

Rasmussen exchanged a look with Villegas, who shrugged. Apparently, it was a signal for Rasmussen to go ahead. "It's routine to perform an autopsy in suspicious deaths. And the ME reported that there was *nothing* in his urine or blood that would corroborate your account. Don't forget, no one else saw the behavior you described. Mr. Sturges even contradicted you."

"Nothing? But that's impossible! There had to be something in Tom's system that made him hallucinate. Barry at least had to have heard him yelling about something out in space that he was trying to get to."

"Mr. Sturges reported that he heard Mr. O'Day yelling for you to let go. Nothing else."

Mike thought quickly.

Which of Tom's actions could not be refuted?

"Well, what about Tom's throwing his backpack over the side? And earlier he threw his sweatband away—did I mention that? I couldn't have made these things up. The backpack was down there where he...where his body was. That's hardly the action of a rational man."

But Rasmussen waved it away. "Again, we have only your word for how the backpack ended up at the base of the cliff. Maybe you threw it down there to make your story more credible."

"What? You think I managed to wrestle his backpack off him and throw it myself? You think he'd just let me do that?"

"Maybe," Rasmussen persisted, "he'd set the backpack down. You were all taking a break at the top, right?"

"And I ripped his headband off him earlier? Maybe you should try to find that!"

"Haystack. Needle. Big desert. Little headband."

Incredulous, Mike turned to Villegas. "Jose, you can't seriously believe that I intended to push a guy to his death." Villegas stared at him with his usual inscrutable expression and Mike could see he could not expect help from that direction. "Oh. My. God. You do think that!"

"We're just trying to understand what happened," Villegas said mildly. "Assuming that your account is accurate, we expected some trace of opioids or barbiturates or cocaine or methamphetamines in his urine or blood. But there was nothing."

"How many drugs did you test for?"

Villegas shook his head. "We're a small outfit here. The best we can do is use our standard toxicity kit of assays for common causes of getting high. We can't look for an infinite number of different drugs. We just don't have the equipment for it, and even if we had our own gas chromatography equipment, we would have to know what we were looking for to justify the expense."

"So, you just decide I was lying? Have you found out what the red stuff was in O'Day's bottle?"

Rasmussen, that smirk again, raised his hands and shrugged. Villegas gave a quick, almost imperceptible, shake of his head. Before Rasmussen could say more, Villegas said, "This is an investigation. We're keeping our minds open to all possibilities."

"It doesn't sound like he," gesturing at a scowling Rasmussen, "is keeping an open mind. Why on earth would I make up such a detailed story?"

Rasmussen gave a small snort of disbelief. "That's

kind of obvious, isn't it? You had motive. You had
opportunity. You had means. Simplest explanation
works well for me. You needed some good reason for
O'Day to be struggling with you at the edge of a cliff,
so you made some shit up. Ah, and then there's the
small detail that a witness said you pushed him."

Mike's breathing became quick and shallow, and
his anger finally erupted. He stood, his voice rising.
"Might have pushed him. *Might* have. And I didn't!
There's got to be some reason for Tom's behavior
besides," he glared at Rasmussen, "my wanting to
cover up a murder. That's just..." He started to say
"stupid," but caught himself.

*Breathe, Mike, breathe. No good can come from antag-
onizing the detectives further.* "Am I under arrest?" Both
detectives shook their heads. Without another word,
Mike walked out of the room and started down the
hall. He hoped his gait did not betray his fear and
anxiety. He paused briefly and turned, as behind him
he faintly heard Villegas address Rasmussen. "Terry,
you know no prosecutor in the world would indict
him on the basis of the evidence we have." Mike
heard the low rumble of Rasmussen's response, but
he couldn't make out any words.

WHEN MIKE ARRIVED at Molly's to report on the
interview, he was still fuming about Rasmussen's
suspicion of him as Tom O'Day's murderer, and
started talking the moment he stepped inside Molly's
house, "I feel trapped in a nightmare. They tag-
teamed me. Jose and The Hulk. Rasmussen seems to

think I'm some sort of vengeful assassin because of my run-in with Tom about the Activity Center. And Villegas just sat there and let him go at me. The notion that I would push Tom over the cliff is so absurd, it should be laughable. And they didn't pay any attention to what I told them about Tom's craziness, about his hallucinating. Worse, Molly, you won't believe this. The police had Tom autopsied. Said it was routine in 'suspicious deaths.'" Mike plopped down on Molly's couch. Jessie immediately came over and nudged his hand. Well trained, Mike absently scratched behind her ears.

"But that's good, isn't it?" Molly set down the Becky Masterman book she had been reading and looked around for her bookmark.

"Yeah, it should have been. But to Rasmussen's delight, the toxicology didn't show any drugs in his blood or urine. But they only looked for about five types. So, now The Hulk accused me of making up the symptoms to cover killing Tom."

"They can't be serious! Where was Jose? He wouldn't think that."

"Like I said, he was in the room and hardly said a thing, certainly nothing in my defense. I'm still a 'person of interest'—if not a suspect. Barry isn't backing me up because he didn't see Tom acting nuts. All he saw was us struggling, and he told the police he thinks I gave Tom a shove. He heard Tom yelling for me to let go—that's all."

"But what possible motive could you have?"

"Damn Barry again. The cops—both of them— kept coming back to the argument I had with Tom over the renovation contract."

"They can't honestly think that would be a motive for deliberately pushing someone to his death!"

"I don't think Jose does, but Rasmussen seems to enjoy putting me in the hot seat."

"I'm sure they'll find a more likely suspect. Or realize it was some sort of bizarre accident and not a murder, for Pete's sake."

"Maybe," Mike said gloomily. "If they try. But Rasmussen has grabbed on to me like a dog with a bone and may not want to give it up."

Molly went over and kissed his cheek. "How about if we go let off some steam at pickleball. You can pretend you're playing against Rasmussen. That should motivate you!"

"Or terrify me. He'd cover half the court without even moving."

She pulled him up and shoved him in the direction of the bedroom where his clothes filled an allotted drawer in her dresser. "Come on, get ready. It'll do us both good. Take our minds off Tom."

Five minutes later, Mike had donned shorts and his "A day without pickleball won't kill you, but why take the risk" T-shirt, and they headed out.

"You're going to be sorry if we go in my golf cart," Molly told Mike.

"Better than taking my car. It's such a short distance. Or we could walk. What's the matter with your cart?"

"I think it's suffering from old age. It's really slow. And that's with only me in it. That's why I don't use it much."

"Oh, it can't be too bad."

"It's so slow that if I raced Mrs. Briggs down the block, she'd win."

"Well, maybe she's really fast."

"Mike, Mrs. Briggs uses a walker."

Mike chuckled obligingly. "Okay—somehow driving a car a distance we could walk is more embarrassing than driving a golf cart. But car it is. Got your paddle? Gloves? Water?"

Usually some of the players waiting their turn greeted friends as they arrived. This afternoon, no one spoke as Mike and Molly walked to the waiting area. Mike didn't think about it until he and Molly put their paddles in the wooden rack that preserved, from right to left, the order of people's arrivals or their completion of a turn on the courts.

As rules dictated, Molly and Mike put their paddles behind those of players waiting to play and took their seats. After a few minutes of unaccustomed silence, a court came open and they stood to move their paddles towards the front of the line. At that moment, Barry Sturges's long arm reached out from the middle of a cluster of players, plucked his paddle rather ostentatiously from the front of the rack and moved it back far enough in the lineup that he would not be playing with them. Molly didn't realize who it was until he turned around.

Mike felt a surge of anger. It was like a slap in the face.

Barry could not be more obvious telegraphing his disdain. I suppose he's told everyone here about his accusation. Mike could feel his face flushing.

Molly noticed and said very quietly as they

walked on to the court. "Calm down. Don't let him get your goat. He's an ass."

But as Mike entered the court, he looked over his shoulder and saw Barry talking to a group of players waiting in front of the paddle rack. At one point, all of them turned to look at the court. At him. Totally distracted, Mike stepped forward prematurely and let a serve that landed well inside the court go by. The obvious mistake handed their opponents a point.

Molly looked at him but said nothing. The rest of the game was little better. Mike muffed shots that he usually made easily, hit balls clearly destined for out of bounds, and delivered serves with half the usual precision. He and Molly lost eleven to four. As they walked dejectedly off the court, Mike said, "I think I'll head home."

Molly grabbed his arm. "Don't you dare! We will not be chased off by one bully and a bunch of wimps."

Mike was encouraged by Molly's "we." He sat down on one of the chairs lined up along the walkway outside the courts. He avoided looking at anyone and didn't initiate any conversations. But to his astonishment and considerable embarrassment, when Barry next came off the court, Molly walked up to him. "I'm sure you aren't spreading baseless rumors, are you, Barry?" She smiled sweetly at him.

Barry looked very disconcerted at this frontal attack, but he rallied quickly, "Not baseless," he said. "I was there."

Molly took a step forward, paddle on her hip. "Yeah, fifty yards away with the sun in your eyes. I'd be very careful about accusations, Barry. You'll be asking for forgiveness when the true story comes out, and don't expect it from us or our many friends. Remember what happened here last summer?"

The hubbub around them quieted as the waiting players began to listen. A budding confrontation promised to be entertaining. Molly raised her voice. After all, some people were rather hard of hearing.

She took one more step forward, inches from Barry's face. "Remember when Renee Holden was attacked here in Sunrise? Who solved that case, Barry? Who helped the police? It was Mike. And he's doing it again."

She whirled around and walked away from him and sat down next to Mike on the brick wall that ran behind the chairs. Several voices were asking. "What's she talking about? Who's Renee Holden? Who solved what case?" A babble of responses began.

"Newcomers and Snowbirds," Molly said with quiet satisfaction to Mike. "Not here last summer. By the time they learn all about Renee's assault, they will have forgotten what Barry's been saying."

"But I'm not helping the police," Mike whispered. "Except by giving The Incredible Hulk a target for shooting practice."

"You will," she said confidently. "Meanwhile, we've given folks a good reason for you to be down at the station."

Mike couldn't help a soft chuckle. "And put Barry on the defensive. Hope your little ploy distracts gossip away from me."

Molly puffed up her cheeks and blew him a friendly raspberry. "It'll work. I'm a main engine of the Sunrise gossip train." She glanced at the paddle rack and spoke in a normal tone. "Hey, we're up. Remember to stay back on long serves until you see where they're going to land, okay?"

As they walked on the court, Mike shook his head. "I don't know, Molly. These days, it seems as if people are predisposed to think the worst of each other. I doubt I've heard the last from Barry Sturges."

17

DAY 7

Detective Villegas sat at his desk studying the alarm company's activity log. Sergeant Partridge had photocopied a couple days of activity and highlighted Wednesday, December 4, the night before Tom O'Day's death, and the early morning of December 5. She included suggestions of possible activities:

- Alarm shut off Wednesday, December 4, 6:08 p.m. (Audrey O'Day? enters, front door, to take video)
- Alarm activated 7:11 p.m. (Audrey O'Day? leaves, front door)
- Alarm shut off 8:40 p.m. (Tom O'Day? enters, front door)
- Alarm activated 10:04 p.m. (O'Day goes to bed?)
- Alarm shut off Thursday, December 5: 2:45 a.m. Back patio door opened/closed. (Burglar? deactivates alarm)

- Alarm activated: 3:20 a.m. Back patio door opened/closed (Burglar? resets alarm)
- Alarm shut off: 6:27 a.m. (O'Day goes outside for his newspaper?)
- Alarm activated December 5: 8:40 a.m. (Door to garage opened, O'Day leaves for hike?)
- Alarm shut off Saturday, December 7: 9:32 a.m. (Molly Levin deactivates alarm)

Villegas set the log aside as Terry Rasmussen strode into his cubicle, sans pleasantries, turned a metal chair around to face Villegas, straddled it, and asked, "So, what did you find out in your little field trip to the O'Day crash site?"

Villegas was too accustomed to Rasmussen's belittling slights and digs to show any annoyance. "It's possible she could have faked it. Where Audrey O'Day went off the road was the only spot for five miles that was relatively level and with no major barriers. So, either she was incredibly lucky, or she scouted it out ahead of time, lowered her speed, and deliberately took the risk that she wouldn't be seriously injured."

Rasmussen thought it over. "She hit hard enough that the airbag deployed, right?"

"And the car was totaled. She still has some impressive bruises. If she did fake it, why do it then? We hadn't even begun an investigation when she crashed. It was only a couple days after her husband's death."

"Depends on how smart she is," Rasmussen said. "She could be one move ahead of us. Suppose she thinks we're going to find something odd about his death. Wants to get herself labeled as a fellow victim along with her husband so we'll never even look at her as a possible suspect."

"Then it was an idiotic move to object to an autopsy. That made her look suspicious. And how very convenient that she videoed those silver pieces the night before they were stolen."

"Yeah," Rasmussen scoffed. "Must have a helluva clear crystal ball."

"Take a look at this security system log." Villegas handed him Partridge's printout and notes.

Rasmussen skimmed it and sat back with a gusty sigh. "Jeesh! So, whoever broke in had the Home Alert code." In an atrocious approximation of a British accent, he added "By Jove, Watson, I do believe that's what we might call a clue!"

"Sure narrows the field. But who had the code?"

"And according to Patridge and Washington's report, the only things stolen were a few trinkets and a computer. If they had the code, why not wait until O'Day was out of the house and go in for some serious loot?"

"I know," Villegas said slowly. "Mrs. O'Day said that's all that was taken, but we have only her word to go by. Maybe our burglar did more or took more than she wants us to know about."

"Like what?"

"I have no idea. Maybe took something that she or the judge had brought illegally into the country from their travels, and she couldn't admit it? Or maybe took some documents that would incriminate one of them?"

Rasmussen laughed. "Good imagination, Jose! How about some classified government documents or blueprints for a bomb?"

"Okay, okay. Far-fetched. But I agree with you that it seems weird that someone broke in, stayed about a half hour, and took a computer and a few little sculptures that only have sentimental value for the O'Days. And managed to stay quiet enough to not wake the judge before sneaking out."

"Did you push O'Day about what she said was missing?"

"No," Villegas admitted. "But that was before I saw the Home Alert log."

"Assuming she's unlikely to admit that there's more missing, let's get back to who had the security system code. Is it conceivable that the judge got up in the middle of the night, turned off the system for some mysterious reason, and turned it back on before going back to bed?"

"I guess it's possible. But the interior doors of the house aren't alarmed. He would have to shut off the alarm only if he wanted to go outside the house. Unlikely he'd want to go for a walk at that time of night. And even if he did, that wouldn't explain the glass cut out in the door. Whoever turned off the code either didn't have a key or wanted us to assume they didn't have one."

"Didn't Molly Levin use a key to get in the day she reported the break-in?" Rasmussen recalled.

"Yes, but apparently the key was well hidden. Mrs. O'Day told her where to find it."

"Mrs. O'Day has a key *and* knows the code." Rasmussen said.

"If something important is missing, something we don't know about, but that she wants to blame on a mysterious burglar, she could have cut the glass out herself."

"Back to the code. Who else has it?"

"Mrs. O'Day says the judge could have given it to house cleaners or other workers. But they'd also need to have a key or know where one was hidden." Both detectives sat a few moments in thought before Villegas said, "There's another person who almost certainly knows the code: Shelley Goossens. She's the 'other woman' that Mike Landry told us about. And I need to update you on my interview with her yesterday afternoon. Denise tracked her down right after our interview with Landry."

Villegas decided to skip the details. Rasmussen would be annoyed that he had suggested Denise Weatherby call Molly Levin for the contact info. Denise had left two bright orange sticky notes in the middle of his computer screen. On the top one, she had written: "Shelley Goossens contact info per Molly Levin." The telephone number and address were recorded in Weatherby's small, neat handwriting. The second note, in an uncharacteristic scrawl had read: "FYI, Levin <u>PISSED</u> at you!" (PISSED was underlined three times). "Almost refused to help when I called. B/c Mike Landry???"

Villegas smiled at the memory. Molly was undoubtedly angry that Mike was considered a person of interest. *Bet she gave Denise an earful! Maybe I should have made the call.*

He recognized a certain amount of schadenfreude

in his relief that he had had the foresight to have Weatherby place the call.

He pulled up the notes from his interview with Shelley.

"Not recorded?" Rasmussen asked.

Villegas shook his head. "I talked with her in my cubicle yesterday afternoon. I'll give you the high-lights. To begin with, she's younger than Audrey O'Day. I'd guess at least twenty years younger than the judge. Early forties."

"I saw Mrs. O'Day when you had her in the other day. She's a looker. So, this Shelley Goossens must be a real babe."

"Maybe that's not the only crit..." *Don't say it,* he admonished himself. *You'll just sound sanctimonious. And probably a woman's physical attractiveness* is *the most important criterion for men looking for romance.* "Well," he said. "I don't think I'd describe her that way."

Rasmussen grinned. "No, guess you wouldn't," leaning ever so slightly on "you."

Villegas ignored him. "Ms. Goossens is quite attractive, though." He recalled the way she glided into his cubicle and sat relaxed with hands loosely clasped in her lap. She wore tailored white slacks and an expensive-looking beige and white silk top. Unusual dress for Cactus Heights. But he was careful to avoid mentioning that observation. Rasmussen would make some crack about the way gay men notice clothing. "Not only is she comparatively young, but she's vital, full of energy."

"Yadda yadda. So, what'd you find out?"

"I spent some time disabusing her of the notion

that we were certain Mike Landry had pushed O'Day to his death. The gossip line at Sunrise Acres has been buzzing. You'll be happy to hear that she denied strenuously that O'Day would ever take drugs. For his age, he didn't take many meds. She only remembered one for his heart and some kind of a statin—couldn't eat grapefruit—and sometimes Ambien to help him sleep. But interesting—she's the only one we've talked to who seemed to think it possible O'Day committed suicide."

"Huh? What'd she say?"

"It was delicately worded but see what you think." Villegas read from his notes. "'Tom was having trouble with getting older. You know, not being as vigorous as he used to be.' Then, when I asked if she meant he was depressed, she said she didn't think it was that serious. That he was..." Villegas looked at his notes again, "'a little insecure. With me. Talked about how he should have met me sooner and that his life was all downhill from here on.' She seemed to think these were normal issues with aging or at least typical for men."

Rasmussen laughed. "If all the guys in Sunrise Acres with wilting willies jumped off cliffs, the washes would be overflowing with bodies."

"I asked her directly if she was implying O'Day committed suicide, and she wouldn't go there. And as far as a heart attack, she again mentioned the heart med and the statin."

"Sounds like she knows a lot of intimate details. Was she living with him?"

"She says no. And when I brought up the break-in at his house, she thought I was accusing her of the burglary and told me she knows where the key to the house is hidden outside, so she could let herself in any time she wanted. And she admitted she also knows the code."

"Does she have an alibi for that Wednesday night?"

"No. She and the judge went out to dinner, and he drove her home she says about eight thirty."

Rasmussen raised an eyebrow and shook his head. "Home at eight thirty?"

"For most Sunrise Acres residents, it's lights out by nine. She says he had that big morning hike planned. Anyway, she was at her place the rest of the night after their date. No roommate. No one to corroborate."

Rasmussen seemed to be in a reverie.

Probably wondering what kind of guy takes a "babe" home at eight thirty, Villegas thought with amusement.

The big detective roused himself: "It's looking more and more like that break-in was totally coincidental."

"And the car crash?"

Rasmussen shrugged. "What if the crash was deliberate, maybe to get insurance for all we know, and the break-in was some lowlife who knew the guy was dead and the house empty?"

"It couldn't have been someone, 'lowlife' or otherwise, who broke in knowing the judge was dead. The security logs for the alarm system show that the break-in almost certainly occurred in the middle of the night Thursday morning, when the judge was home, in bed, very much alive, and presumably sound asleep. I guess it's conceivable that some random thief could have broken in, but this intruder would have had to know about the judge's sleeping habits, the layout of the house, and a bunch of other stuff. Doesn't seem likely. Oh, and would also need to know the security codes to turn the system off and on again."

"Okay, no lowlife. Or at least, a lowlife O'Day knew. But I don't see the connection to his death. The burglar didn't push O'Day off the cliff. The burglary still could be coincidental. Maybe the thief knew that the computer was valuable or that there was financial info on it that could be sold and took the silver trinkets because...." Rasmussen ran out of steam apparently unable to conceive of anyone having a rational yen for silver trinkets. "How about fingerprints? Anything there?"

Villegas shook his head. "Just the ones you'd expect. Both O'Days, Molly Levin's from a couple places when she first went in. She put on gloves after she realized there'd been a break-in. And some of Ms. Goossens—we took her prints yesterday for comparison purposes. Lots of hers in the kitchen and living areas."

Rasmussen waggled his eyebrows suggestively and grinned. "Gotta be some in the master bedroom."

The opportunity to tease Rasmussen was irresistible. "Just on top of the bed headboard and the ceiling," Villegas said straight-faced. He could hardly contain his amusement, looking at Rasmussen's puzzled face as he frowned, trying to visualize the gymnastics that could explain such a bizarre fingerprints placement. *Better confess before he strains his mental muscles.*

"Just joking," Villegas said. "None of her prints were in the master bedroom."

If possible, Rasmussen looked even more bemused. "Huh?"

Villegas moved on quickly. "The only other prints the ID unit found turned out to belong to one—" glancing at his notes— "Sophia Mendez. She's worked for the White Gloves housecleaners for twelve years. They do background checks on all their employees. Can't discount her, of course, but she seems a very unlikely suspect."

Still ruminating on the insult of being taken in, even momentarily, by Villegas's unaccustomed humor, Rasmussen returned to a theme he knew irritated Villegas. "Helluva lot less likely than Landry. Look, forget the burglary. We need to concentrate on O'Day's dance off the cliff. Seems to me there are two possibilities. Landry was telling the truth about O'Day acting crazy and it was either heat stroke or maybe it was suicide, and O'Day was arguing with himself all the way up the trail about whether to do it or not. *Or* maybe Landry couldn't resist giving him a little help over the edge and it was homicide. And I think I know which one you believe."

"Terry, c'mon. Do you really believe this retired English professor would be so worked up about a disagreement over the hiring of a contractor months earlier that he would lure the judge to the edge of a precipice, throw his backpack over, rip off part of his shirt, murder him, then make up a story that the guy was hallucinating?"

"I'm not saying it was premeditated, Jose." Rasmussen sounded almost conciliatory. "All it took was a little push. Maybe Landry just couldn't resist the opportunity. And remember the tox report—no drugs in the blood or urine, so all his talk about the guy hallucinating could have been bullshit."

"Well, let's consider the *possibility*," leaning into the word, "that Landry is telling the truth, but Sturges either has some reason to accuse him of deliberately pushing O'Day, or Sturges just misinterpreted the whole scene from fifty yards away, looking into the sun. He hadn't been near enough to hear O'Day's ramblings, saw Landry pulling on O'Day's shirt, and thought he was pushing instead of trying to save him. Probably seemed likely at the time, especially with O'Day yelling at Landry to 'leggo.'"

"Jose, you can take this any way you want, but in my opinion, you should remove yourself from this case. You are too biased, too close to Landry, to lead it." He stood up, leaving in place the chair he had turned around to straddle and stalked off.

Villegas stared at Rasmussen's retreating back. *He wants to take over lead on this case. Could he persuade the captain to take me off it?*

"MOLLY, before we discuss your website design, I need to ask you something." Shelley and Molly were at Molly's house to start work on Molly's personal website. Shelley seated herself at the kitchen table.

"Okay, sure. Shoot." Molly turned on the hot water kettle and reached into the cupboard for a couple of mugs. She froze, hands in the shelving, at Shelley's question.

"Did you tell the police—Detective Vargas—about Tom and me?"

Molly put two mugs on the counter and turned a very red face to Shelley. "I'm sorry, Shelley. The police called asking for your contact information. I hope it was okay. I couldn't really lie and say I didn't know you. Was it Detective Villegas? He's tough but fair. I hope he didn't give you a hard time."

"Villegas, yes, that's it. No, not really, but he knew about my relationship with Tom. I wondered how much you had told them. Detective Villegas was basically interested in Tom's mental state, any drugs or meds he was taking, that sort of thing." She smiled. "Don't worry, Molly, I don't hold it against you."

"Were you able to give them anything? I mean, I know this still has to be raw for you. What do you think happened up there? Mike says Tom was acting totally weird, hallucinating, yelling, and Mike couldn't stop him from falling."

"Honestly, I've never seen him like that, but he has been kind of depressed. Maybe he was taking something besides his heart meds and sleep aids. I don't know. We went out to dinner the night before...it... and he seemed normal, maybe a little peeved that I wasn't sharing his bed, but that's nothing new."

"Okay, well we both have plenty going on right now, what with what happened to Tom, and Mike being questioned as if he's some kind of murderer," Molly said indignantly. "Maybe it's good to have something to distract us a little. Can we talk about my business website?"

"Good idea. I'm sorry it's taken so long for me to get back to you. All your fault," she said with a smile.

"No good deed goes unpunished, I'm afraid. A couple of those friends you introduced me to have kept me hopping! But now, tell me what you're looking for. I haven't created a real estate website before, so give me your thoughts."

Molly moved the salt and pepper set and the bright red and yellow woven runner off the table. "Let's spread out."

They set up on the table, Molly with her folder and iPad, Shelley with her laptop.

"I don't really need a website for advertising," Molly said as she sat down. "My clients come by word of mouth, and I don't do much business beyond Cactus Heights. But younger clients seem disconcerted when they can't find me on the Internet, as if I am too old-fashioned to help them. And this is my office!" She gestured around the small room, brightly lit from a large window overlooking the street, and a smaller one at the side with a view of the desert. A kitchen counter ran in front of the larger window, and the sill held several African violets and a pot each of tarragon and mint.

"That mint plant looks like it's headed for the door," Shelley observed.

"I know. I'm going to transplant it into a larger pot before it escapes entirely."

"Well, it's a pleasant office. I wish I had such a nice workspace. And no one cares if you work from home. We can keep the website simple, just enough to establish your presence, explain your services, and update your recent sales."

"My services have recently—and unintentionally —expanded," Molly said wryly. "Audrey O'Day put me in charge of an estate sale before we put her house on the market. Not my favorite activity."

Shelley looked startled but recovered quickly. "You don't want to offer that service then," she said. "But give me some idea of what you do offer to potential clients. Especially if you do anything different from other agents. You know, what's your value proposition?" Seeing Molly's furrowed brow, she explained "What advantage do you have over other agents?" Shelley fired up her laptop and prepared to type.

Molly thought for a few minutes. "I guess I would claim I know Sunrise Acres better than most other agents. I live in the community, and I've been here a long time. I also do the tours for prospective residents, so I have a good feel for what people are looking for. When potential buyers come to look at the community, they tend to think that because the houses look a lot alike on the outside, there's no variety. But there are eight different models. I know them all and where the best views are—mountains or golf course. And we have a range of units, some very modest and others, like the O'Days', quite high end. I also do some business in Cactus Heights, outside Sunrise. This is kind of tricky—I'm definitely a Sunrise Acres specialist, but I don't want to emphasize that so much that I turn off 'outside' clients. Do you think you can work with that?"

Shelley nodded and started typing. An hour later, after quizzing Molly more, she closed the lid of her laptop. "I have enough to draft the site for you. I can show you in a couple days. I can suggest some graphics if you want to include them. Maybe you have some photos of recent sales?"

"Definitely. Wow, you are quick! Now, you did all the work but still, I'm ready for a cup of tea. Would you like one, or I can make you a cup of coffee?" Molly asked. She gestured to the stainless steel machine crouching like a miniature manufacturing plant on the granite counter. She gave a little sigh. "It's Mike's, and he'd be able to offer you cappuccino, but all I know how to make is a simple straight cup—and even that's a challenge. Sorry, I don't have any cream. Do you want it black or is milk okay?"

"Milk will be fine," Shelley said. "So, how is Mike? I enjoyed meeting him at that Prepare and Share dinner you hosted back in September. You seem to work well as a team."

After checking that there was water in Mike's machine, Molly pushed a couple buttons that she hoped would result in adequate coffee. She stood watching it anxiously as it went through the noisy process of grinding the beans and spewing coffee into the mug she'd placed under the spout. When the machine subsided into a few final gusty sighs, she turned to Shelley. "Noisy as a 747 taking off," she said apologetically. She put the mug down along with a small pitcher of whole milk and brought her own tea before responding to Shelley's observation.

"He's good," she said finally. "We're working some things out. At our ages, relationships always come with some baggage. You remember my daughter Melanie came out to visit in late September. I think half the reason she came was to check him out."

"Did it matter that he's not Jewish?"

"Heavens no! Melanie and I are both nonobser-vant. My parents are another story, but they've mostly resigned themselves to my life choices. Like marrying Max. Turns out they were right about him, but who knew?"

Shelley shook her head. "Believe me, I know what you mean. My marriage was a disaster from the 'I do.' He wasn't a bad guy—just frightfully young. I'd hardly finished raising Brian when I turned around and married another kid to raise!"

"Then is Goossens your maiden name or married?"

"Married. At least I got a name in the middle of the alphabet. I know it's kinda trivial, but my maiden name was Wigner. I hated being the absolute last in any oral quiz. The kids before me in the alphabet got all the easy questions, but the teachers ran out of those by the time they got to me! You know they say your name is your destiny."

"Well, it sure is if you're Jewish," Molly said. "My last name was the only good thing Max left me."

"Middle of the alphabet?"

Molly laughed. "No, I never thought of that. But my family name is Shapiro. The name triggered so many antisemitic prejudices that my dad changed it to Shafer when I was in college. Levin is a Jewish name too, of course, but maybe less obviously so. Or maybe people are less biased. But when I was growing up..."

It was Shelley's turn to laugh. "Okay, you win the 'whose name was harder to live with' contest. Tell me about your folks. Are they likely to approve of Mike?"

"They don't travel anymore, so they may never meet him unless we visit them. But I think they'd like him. Dad's a retired college prof like Mike, and I think he'd even appreciate Mike's occasional lapses into pedantry. You know, Shakespeare quotes, correcting bad grammar on TV shows. And he was terrific with the grandkids. I think they were sorrier to leave Mike behind than me! He took Clara to a play field and practiced soccer with her. She came back all rosy cheeked and full of enthusiasm. She told her mom, 'That was the most fun *ever*!'

"But then, she tossed a grenade. As only a child can. She asked her mom, 'Is Mike our new grandpa?'"

Shelley chuckled. "What did Melanie say?"

"She looked at me to see what to say, but I was absolutely speechless. Mike rescued us. He sat down on one of my big chairs, pulled Clara to him and said, 'How about if I'm your oldest new friend—and you call me Mike?' Clara looked a bit dubious, but then she said, '*Best* friend!' Mike said something like 'I'm honored,' and gave her a hug." Molly laughed. "The rest of us started breathing again."

"Sounds like Mike passed Melanie's test."

"Flying colors," Molly said. "But she's not a very tough judge. I've been alone for so many years, I think she's just glad to see me having some...some companionship."

Shelley didn't respond immediately. Clearly Molly's narrative raised some related memory.

"My little brother was tough on anyone I dated," Shelley said. "I think he was trying to be Dad—you know, the kind in movies who would grill a daughter's date. It was funny, really, this little squirt giving me—and sometimes the date—the third degree." She smiled, then gave a small shudder; her mouth pursed, and she rubbed her forehead as if she had a headache. She picked up her laptop and grabbed her sweater off the back of the kitchen chair.

"Shelley, are you okay? What's the matter? Do you have to leave?" Molly asked.

"I'm sorry, Molly. I do have to go. Didn't mean to get so personal. Very unprofessional! You are just too good a listener."

"I hope I can be more than a client to you, Shelley. Please. It's so good to connect with someone younger. All my friends are at least my age. That's the only drawback to Sunrise Acres. We're all old! I hope you will still come over now that Tom is gone."

"Oh, I will. Thanks to you, I'm getting some clients here. But I can finish work anywhere. I have a four-month lease on my apartment, but I'm not sure whether to put down roots here now that Tom...."

"You went to college here, right?" Molly asked. "Don't you still have friends around Tucson?"

"I don't know. The two or three I was closest to have moved away. Maybe others I didn't hang around with much are still here, but it would take a lot of effort to locate them. And what if they didn't want to get reacquainted? Tom's death has sure left me feeling alone. I probably should go back to Chicago."

"I know it's not the same," Molly said, "but you do have a few friends here, me included, and you would meet more."

"Of course, you're a friend, Molly, a good one. It's just that everything here will remind me of what Tom had planned. I stayed here because I don't have any family to speak of, and Tom really cared for me. He told me he was going to prove he was serious."

"Do you know what he meant?"

"Another gift, I think. He made a point of telling me about some condo on the east coast—Cape Cod I believe—and that he had an appointment with his lawyer. I tried to head him off, to tell him that it was way, way too premature, but he just said things like 'you'll see' and 'I can't take it with me,' and....Anyway, he was kind of emotional about wanting to prove that he loved me. He actually said that, Molly. That he loved me, that this time was different. I wish he hadn't."

"Difficult for you," Molly said.

"Oh man, and how!" To Molly's surprise, Shelley stepped forward and gave her a hug. "Thanks for being a friend." Then she quickly turned, picked up her laptop, and left.

Well, that was dramatic! But I get the feeling there's more that Shelley wanted to share. Maybe when I get to know her better.

"JOSE, I've gone through Judge O'Day's phone." Detective Denise Weatherby stuck her head around the corner of the cubicle. "I've checked all the calls and appointments. Do you have time now to hear the highlights?"

"Anything interesting?"

"One appointment might even qualify as fascinating!" She grinned. "Most of the notations are for a dentist or his doctor. A haircut now and then, and—Terry would love this—a pedicure!"

"I hope that's not the fascinating one."

"Nope. He had an appointment for the Monday

after he died with Justin Moore, Esquire, down in Tucson."

"His lawyer."

"Yep. Specializes in wills, estates, and trusts. I weaseled my way in to speak with Mr. Moore and tried to persuade him that he could tell us the agenda for the appointment, given that Mr. O'Day is deceased. But the most he'd admit was that there *was* an appointment. Mrs. O'Day, the 'grief-stricken widow'" (Weatherby adding air quotes) "had informed him about her husband's death the day after it occurred. Mr. Moore did slip just a tiny bit— but the lawyerly equivalent of a face-plant on a banana peel. When I said the contents of Mr. O'Day's will could be material evidence in our investigation of his death, Mr. Moore said, and I quote, 'could be.' The words were no sooner out of his mouth when he looked stricken, clammed up, and suggested I get a court order before we could speak again."

"Nice work, Denise. Could you..."

"I have an appointment to see Judge Lila late this afternoon about a subpoena," she interrupted. "I assume we not only want the agenda but any copies of O'Day's will or trust."

"Or drafts," Villegas added. "In case O'Day intended to make changes but hadn't done it yet. Too bad the burglar that broke into his house made off with his laptop. Might have had some drafts on it."

"Well, Mr. Justin Moore, *Esquire* should have what we need."

"Anything else?" Villegas smiled at Weatherby's emphasis on "esquire." After a rather nasty divorce, she had a very low opinion of lawyers.

"Not really," she said. "O'Day called one cell phone with a Chicago area code several times every day starting mid-September right through to the evening before his death. You can guess whose number, wink-wink. Other calls to restaurants, one to the local library, two to a jewelry store in Phoenix, a couple to Lawyer Moore. I tracked down the ones within Sunrise Acres and made a list of those names, although a few phones are the same number for both people at a residence. Landlines," she explained contemptuously. "Some of those local calls were one-offs, but there were a few he called more than once. Peter Jackson, we know he was leading the hike where O'Day died. Some other guys he called several times, maybe golf partners—Featherstone, Konsinski, Greeley. That's about it. Do you want me to interview them?"

"Not yet. The subpoena is more important. It may take more work on your part to convince Judge Lila to issue one. Let me know if she baulks. And we already have several POIs to investigate before we go after all of O'Day's acquaintances," Villegas added. "How about emails?"

"Plenty. Probably hundreds of unread messages, mostly junk looks like, and lots in his 'sent' file. I'll work on those next. I've got them sorted by recipient already, so I'll start with the ones to Moore. Maybe O'Day spilled some beans to his lawyer."

"Or hinted about the contents of his will to the girlfriend," Villegas sighed. "*Dum spiro spero.* Ah, sorry," he added, as Denise frowned her incomprehension. "Hope springs eternal."

WHEN MOLLY'S PHONE RANG, she was pleased to see it was Mike. She had forgotten to eat lunch and was getting hungry. *Hope he's got something yummy on the stove.* But Mike was agitated.

"Molly, I've been stewing all day about what Barry did at pickleball last night. I say 'hello' to someone in Sunrise and I swear they look at me as if I'm Jared Loughner."

"Who?"

"You know, the jerk who shot all those people in a Tucson parking lot, including Congresswoman Giffords. I think some people in Sunrise are carefully avoiding me and others think it's kind of cool to have a suspected murderer in the neighborhood. Nice little thrill running up their spines. I'm kind of expecting requests to autograph their gun holster or hunting knife or something."

"Mike, this will all blow over when the police get through their investigation."

"You know, Molly, I don't get the feeling they're making any progress. Rasmussen's stuck running a little movie in an endless loop, and it's starring me. I don't think I'll get out of that role until we find out what kind of hallucinogen Tom was on. He was completely lucid when we started the hike."

"So," Molly said slowly, "you really think he ate or drink something and..."

"It was in his drink. I'd bet my life on it. He was his usual obnoxious self when we started out, and he got more and more squirrelly as we hiked. The only thing he ingested was that sports drink."

"Maybe some medication that just kicked in? I cleared out his medicine cabinet and there were a few prescription bottles. The only ones I remember were the sleep aids and Inderal—that's a heart med, isn't it?"

"Yeah, my dad took that one. It's a beta blocker. I'd have to check to see if it can cause crazy behavior, but I doubt it. It's always possible, I guess, that he took some other meds before or during the hike. We should check out what medications could make him hallucinate like that. I'd think they'd have a strong warning about that kind of possible side-effect."

"I can do a little research and try to find out. But if they didn't find anything in the autopsy...."

"Jose said they don't have the equipment locally to look for more. Apparently, there's a standard toxicology kit and it only tests for certain chemicals—including some common meds, pot, cocaine, stuff like that. And now Audrey is going to have the body cremated."

"Already?"

"Well, no point in waiting now that the autopsy is done. She told Jose that she can't take any more time off from work."

"I'm sorry, Mike, but I don't see what we can..."

"I'm going to find his water bottle. He was drinking some red stuff. Looked like one of those sports drinks that's supposed to replace electrolytes. I really doubt Search and Rescue would bother looking for his water bottle in all the confusion around retrieving Tom's body."

"But if it's glass..."

"We don't allow anyone to carry anything glass on

the hikes, other than in binoculars or sunglasses. We don't want to leave broken glass on the trail. Tom must have filled his plastic water bottle with the drink."

"Still, the bottle could be anywhere, assuming no one at the scene picked it up."

"I don't think so. I have a clear mental picture of Tom's throwing the pack off just before he fell. The bottle was in the net side pocket. It probably fell out when he threw it or when it hit the ground. I'll bet that bottle is near where he landed."

"But it might have fallen out when they were carrying him out after the accident."

"In which case," Mike said, a triumphant note in his voice, "we'll find it along the wash."

"We?"

"C'mon, Molly. I've got to clear my name, and I know you can't resist a mystery. I really think there was something in that drink. Let's find it. If it's pure sports drink, okay, I'll agree Tom must have had some meds or had heat stroke or something. But if there are hallucinogens in it..."

"Then," Molly concluded, "someone was hoping Tom would have that accident."

"Or maybe a heart attack."

18

DAY 8

"Mike, are you sure this is a good idea? I keep thinking something nasty is going to slither out from behind a rock." The two of them were edging their way through dense undergrowth to the bottom of the wash. Most venomous creatures were hibernating this time of year, but there were still hazards. Hikers always had to be wary of plants with "prickles," meaning ninety percent of all the vegetation—cacti, trees, and bushes —that covered the bank. A number of the southern Arizona flora could embed spines in the limbs of the unwary with painful results. Segments of the so-called "jumping cholla" could separate at the slightest touch and dig in their barbs like deliberate aggression. As Mike and Molly approached the bottom of the wash, she began to regret agreeing to the search "Are we there yet?" she whined in her best imitation of a three-year-old.

Mike laughed. "Come on, Molly, suck it up! Those search and rescue guys were down here in a flash."

"Yeah, twenty-something youngsters. And we don't even know for sure that it's down here."

"You sound like my boys when they were little and we tried to drag them off to a concert or some other activity involving cultcha."

The wash was overhung in places by creosote bushes and a few native palo verde trees that thrived on the seasonal rains. Here and there were clumps of grass, still a bit green from the summer monsoon rains, and dead morning glory vines. It was hard to imagine that the wash had been a raging torrent just a few months earlier. Molly and Mike had started out just before sunup and were glad they had dressed in layers. The subfreezing dawn gave way to rapidly rising temperatures, and they were soon stripped to their light down vests.

"We need to look for a bottle with red liquid in it," Mike said. "I remember thinking that the color probably meant the flavor was cherry or strawberry. I don't know for sure that it's here, but where else would it be? We'll know when we get to the place where he fell. It hasn't rained the last week or so and the ground's sandy, so we should see lots of footprints. I don't think it's much..."

They saw it at the same time. At the edge of the wash, the sand and small rocks were churned up as they had anticipated. But rust-colored stains on a half-buried stone outcropping caught them both by surprise.

Molly turned away from the rocks, hand over her mouth. "Oh lord! I didn't expect...of course there would be."

Mike paled. "This makes it so real," he said softly.

He stooped and put his hand on the stain. "Oh Molly, why couldn't I have stopped him? I heard him hit, and that was bad enough. I'll never get that sound out of my head. Never. But this, this is just as bad." He straightened and said determinedly. "We have to find that bottle. Let's do this systematically. Search around these rocks in circles, tight at first and then further out."

After widening their circle three times with no sighting, they were getting discouraged. "Maybe somebody—the police or Search and Rescue—picked it up. I could have sworn we'd have found it by now. Wait! I'm an idiot!"

"Mike, what is it?"

"Remember, I said Tom threw his backpack down here before he fell. As I recall, he gave it a good heave. We're looking too close to where his...where he landed. We need to look further out."

They trudged across the sandy wash and in a moment, Molly pointed to a small bit of red barely visible in the middle of a stand of grass. "There!"

As they both stood over the spot, Mike said, "Let's take some pictures first." They both got out their phones and photographed what they could see through the grass. Then Molly held the grass aside and Mike got closer photographs. Finally, he put on the single-use gloves he had brought and picked up the bottle. About a half cup of red liquid remained.

"Shouldn't we get the police out here?" Molly asked suddenly.

"I don't think they're interested. As far as they're concerned, this bottle is absolutely irrelevant to Tom's death. They think I either pushed him over or it was suicide or an accidental fall. I don't know if I'll even be able to get them to analyze this stuff."

"Maybe Brandon Liao will do it? We can appeal to his ego. After all, he's the director of the police forensic lab. He shouldn't have to get permission. And he knows us from Renee's assault case."

"I think I may have used up our credit for helping the police on that one. Detective Rasmussen was ready to grab me by the scruff of my neck and toss me out on my rear after the interview the other day."

Molly laughed at the image. "He could probably do it."

"It's your turn to convince the police. Let's tackle Dr. Liao and you turn on the charm. I think he likes you."

Very few civilians in Cactus Heights knew where to find Dr. Brandon Liao, who headed the Cactus Heights P.D. Forensics Lab in a small stucco building behind the police station. Originally, it was a modest residence facing the street. But the front entrance hadn't been used in years, as evidenced by a sturdy forest of Indian fig cacti blocking the walkway like so many bodyguards. Molly and Mike went to the side door and hesitated. "Should we knock?" Mike asked.

Molly didn't answer and simply opened the door. Liao was standing before a desk so covered with papers of various sizes and colors that the whole mess appeared to be suspended in air. He looked up in astonishment. "Ms. Levin, Mr. Landry! How did you....?"

"Hi, Dr. Liao," Molly said with breezy assurance. "So sorry to barge in on you, but we have a really important forensic puzzle related to a current case, and we were just discussing how impressed we were with your expertise earlier this year."

Mike coughed and covered his mouth to disguise his amusement at Molly's brazen flattery.

Liao's face wavered between something close to anger at the invasion of his lair and curiosity. "Do the case detectives know you are here?"

"Not yet," Molly said. "But we have some evidence that you will want to take to them."

Liao continued to look conflicted. "Evidence? For an ongoing investigation? You can't just burst in here and hand it to me, whatever it is."

"Dr. Liao, please let us explain and then we'll do whatever you say. We know how busy you are, and we apologize for not calling first, but it's the only way we could think of to persuade you to..."

Liao held up his hand to stop her. He no longer seemed angry, but he was still shaking his head. "Um, let me get one of the detectives in here." He fished around on the desktop and revealed that under one prominent lump was a phone.

"Please, before you do that, may we explain?" Molly pleaded.

Liao hesitated.

"It's really, really important," she added. He stopped but left his hand on the phone as a tacit threat.

Molly started by describing the fatal hike, but Liao interrupted. "The O'Day case. Yeah, I know." He turned to Mike. "Aren't you a witness? You shouldn't be talking to me. If you have more information...." He lifted the phone to his ear.

"Wait, please. They're paying no attention to what I saw, totally discounting Tom's weird behavior. And I know that the toxicology report after the autopsy didn't show anything that could account for the judge's behavior, but..." Mike then described Tom's symptoms, and as he did, Liao slowly withdrew his hand from the phone and began listening intently, interrupting a couple of times for Mike to clarify what he had witnessed in Tom's behavior.

"And then today we revisited the wash. And we found...this." Mike then produced the bottle with its residue of red liquid encased in a plastic gallon Ziplock bag. They showed the scientist the sequence of photos they had taken on Molly's phone of the bottle in the clump of weeds and grass where they had found it.

"So," Liao summarized, "you believe something in that bottle caused the hallucinations and other symptoms you describe. Something we would *not* have found in the toxicology panel."

Molly and Mike both eagerly agreed. "Yes!"

"What chemical do you suspect?"

Mike shrugged. "We don't know. We just know what that drink did to Tom O'Day. And the toxicity tests only looked for a few common medications, like barbiturates or opiates or cocaine, right? What if the stuff in that bottle is something different—something unusual? The detectives have decided that either Tom had heat stroke, or I was lying about the symptoms and pushed him off the cliff! We gotta prove that I wasn't making it all up."

"I'm sorry," Liao said. "Even if you knew exactly what to look for—which you don't—I don't have the equipment and I couldn't possibly convince a lab in Tucson to use their gas chromatography equipment to analyze that stuff. The protein in that drink would gum up their equipment. No way to justify a fishing expedition. And if the investigation proceeds, you are putting yourselves in legal jeopardy by holding on to that bottle."

"But neither of the detectives is interested in what Tom was drinking. They didn't even *try* to find the bottle. We did. If we give it to them, they'll just toss it."

"And even if they did find some hallucinogen," Liao said thoughtfully, "they could easily claim you put it in there yourself." As the two began to protest, he held up both hands. "I know, I know, you tried to prove the chain of custody with your photos and by sealing the Ziplock, but you aren't officers of the law. And tampering with evidence is a serious crime."

"Evidence? No one but us thinks it's evidence," Mike objected. "As far as the detectives are concerned, Tom's drink is irrelevant." He looked desperately at Molly. "How about if we just leave. If someone decides that this bottle is evidence, we'll bring it in immediately. Until then..."

"...we'll try to find a way to get it analyzed," Molly finished. With a quick goodbye, they hastily left, before Liao could demand they surrender the bottle.

"Think he'll rat us out?" Mike asked Molly as they reached his car.

She shrugged. "Probably. Sounds to me as if you couldn't be in much more trouble. And now I'm in the soup with you. Let's think. Who do we know who might help us get the stuff analyzed?"

"You've always said that we could find most any kind of retired expert in Sunrise. We could look in the directory—you know, where it lists the former professions of the residents."

"Hey, wasn't Irwin a chemical engineer?"

"Naw, he taught physics. Something to do with plasmas, I think. But good idea, Molly. And he's lived here so long, if anyone would know someone who could analyze this stuff, he would."

"Do you know anyone who could help us?" Molly and Mike were sitting in Irwin's patio, enjoying the mild December afternoon as they explained their dilemma.

"Does anyone seriously believe you pushed O'Day?" Irwin asked Mike.

"Honestly, I don't know," Mike said. "One of the detectives seems determined to make me out to be a murderer. I'm fairly sure he doesn't think he has enough evidence to take to the DA, but he enjoys seeing me squirm."

"People in Sunrise can be awful gossips," Molly explained. "All our acquaintances seem to know Mike's been pulled in as a 'person of interest.'"

"And I may be imagining it, but it sure feels as if I'm getting some hostile stares these days," Mike said. "We really need to find someone who could analyze Tom's drink and get me off the hook once and for all."

"Well, I don't know anyone off the top of my head. But," seeing their despondent faces, Irwin added, "a fellow scientist I once worked with at NASA told me, 'Smart people know other smart people.' I know a smart chemical engineer who might know someone to help us." His eyes twinkled. "Networking, you know. If you can believe it, one of my granddaughters actually teaches college undergrads how to 'grow their personal networks.' Fancy name for picking friends who are useful to you. How the heck she can get paid for being an expert on the topic is beyond me." He shook his head. "I don't get it. If it's just a matter of being friendly, who needs to take a course in that? The stuff they teach in college these days! I don't pick my friends to be helpful. If they happen to be, well that's just gravy." Molly and Mike exchanged a desperate glance, unsure if Irwin was getting side-tracked.

But to their relief, he excused himself and went back into the house, all the while continuing to mumble about "nonsense" and "paid for teaching common sense." He returned holding a small book with a brightly flowered cover. Molly smothered a smile at the incongruity of that highly feminine booklet in his weathered hands. He shuffled through it, grunted with satisfaction as he found a number, and took out his phone.

After a few minutes of chatting with the person on the other end of the line, he posed his question. "Say, Al, do you know anyone who could help analyze a mysterious liquid? Naw, not for me. For a good friend." After listening to an apparent barrage of questions, he said, "Hey, how about if I get my buddy

on the phone to explain. I don't have all the details."
He handed the phone to Mike.

Where the heck do I start? Mike thought. It took a
full ten minutes before he felt confident that he had
explained the difficulty of analyzing this particular
drink through the usual gas chromatography and
what expertise they sought.

*I don't have to get into the whole bit about being an
accused murderer,* he thought ruefully. But Molly and
Irwin could tell that he was getting excited, and Mike
gestured wildly to Molly for something to write on.
She dug into her purse and produced an old receipt
and a pen. He scribbled a name and telephone
number down and thanked Al profusely.

"Al says this guy he knows, Evan, is a retired
forensic toxicologist, and he still maintains a small lab
in his garage. According to Al, Evan knows how to do
something called thin layer chromatography—an
older technology, no actual chromatograph apparatus
involved, so no gumming up equipment with our
sports drink. He lives over in the foothills. Al says he's
a real nice guy—likes to help people. I'm going to call
and see if we can see him."

"Offer lunch, maybe?" Molly suggested.

Mike nodded. "Good idea. It would give us a
chance to explain the whole situation. Thanks so
much, Irwin."

"My pleasure. And BOL," he added with a grin.

Molly looked at Mike for translation, but he
shrugged and opened his phone to call Evan. After
that conversation concluded with an agreement to
meet for lunch the following day, Molly and Mike
headed back to her house.

"Did you ever figure out what Irwin meant by 'BOL'"? Molly asked as they climbed into Mike's car.

"Nope and I forgot to ask."

"Let me google it. Hm, I don't think this is what Irwin meant: 'Bill of lading.'"

They took turns guessing.

"Burn Old Laundry?" Molly ventured. "Better Off Liposuctioning?"

"Good one, Molly. How about Bad Odors Linger? Bet On Louie? Butt Out, Loser?" That one cracked them up. They got sillier and sillier and when they reached her door, their vision was blurry from tears of laughter.

19

DAY 9

"How will we recognize Mr. Torberg?" Molly asked as they drove the last few miles on the interstate before their turnoff. Mike had agreed with the expert on thin layer chromatography to meet at Bombolé, a Honduran-Indian fusion restaurant in downtown Tucson.

"He's more likely to figure out who we are," Mike said. "I guess we could have carried a pink umbrella or something, but too late."

The restaurant turned out to be small with just a few wooden tables and bright red plastic chairs for seating. It obviously catered more to takeout than dine-in. Molly spied a small, elderly (anyone who looked ten years older, she considered elderly) man at a window table. He was dressed in a snappy brown and mustard colored checked sports coat and a tie patterned with erratic polka dots that, on closer inspection, turned out to be food stains. Mike was right. When Molly approached, the man stood up politely. "Evan Torberg," he said extending a hand.

After introductions, they stood and surveyed the handwritten menu on a chalkboard behind the counter. Evan ordered a Bombo Combo and after a perusal of the offerings, Mike hesitantly followed suit. Molly ordered a single tamale. As they awaited the food preparation, Mike once again explained what had happened. Evan was particularly interested in Tom's symptoms. "Talked a lot to himself?"

"At first, I thought maybe he was talking to me but when I tried to answer, he talked over me. After a while, he was jabbering practically nonstop. And he seemed to be talking to someone else. I think I caught the name Gladys a couple times."

Evan nodded and asked, "Are you familiar with thin-layer chromatography?"

"Ah, I was an English professor. Sorry."

"No apologies necessary. To keep things simple, this is an old technique. The big labs almost exclusively employ gas chromatography, but TLC is inexpensive, reliable, and fast. It can come in handy when you have some idea of what you're looking for, and from what you've said, there may well be some hallucinogen or collection of hallucinogens in the sample. I can apply a bit of your sample to the TLC apparatus, which essentially comprises two special plates that when exposed to the sample will separate out the compounds based on their solubility. The distance each compound travels up the plates will enable me to identify each one."

"I take it this process is less exact than traditional gas chromatography," Molly said.

"Yes, it's less exact and, frankly, takes a lot of experience and what some people call 'tacit know-how.'"

"Meaning?" Mike asked.

"That it's a combination of art and science. You get tacit knowledge by doing something over and over again, and you learn how to recognize patterns. There's no precise formula. It's like chicken sexing."

He laughed at Mike and Molly's expressions. "I guess you've never heard of that. See, when a chick hatches, its genitalia aren't really developed. Yet, cocks are destined to be meat, and hens will be raised to produce eggs. It's inefficient to wait until the chicks are partially grown to determine which is which, so chicken sexers learn to intuit and separate the sexes when they are young. There was even a school in Japan to teach people how to make split-second decisions in sorting newly hatched chicks." He mimicked throwing a chick one direction and then holding up another for a quick peek to throw in the opposite direction. "Chicken sexers learn through experience, guided by experts. Anyway," he finished a bit lamely. "That's an example of tacit knowing."

"Huh!" Mike said. "Wonder how much a chicken sexer earns."

"Thinking of adding to your retirement accounts?" Molly asked. "If you have to go to Japan to learn how, I'm in!"

Evan watched them, looking amused. "It takes a couple years to learn the skill, apparently," he said.

"Maybe I'll take up something a bit easier," Mike said. Then he brought them back to the purpose of their visit. "How long will it take you to do the test?" he asked Evan.

"Not long at all. You got time now?"

Two hours later, Mike and Molly walked out of Evan's garage with a written report. "But don't bother giving it to the detectives," he cautioned them. "Takes a lab rat to decipher."

"So, how do we get Liao to look at this?" Molly wondered as they climbed into Mike's car.

"We've got his cell number. We'll scan the report and email it with a big "TOLD YOU SO" in caps in the subject line."

"Um, maybe something a tad more...tactful?" Molly ventured.

Mike chuckled. "Just kidding. I'll reserve that line for Rasmussen. No, I think we can just title it 'proof of poison.' That'll intrigue him enough."

20

DAY 10

"Can't play pickleball this morning," Molly told Mike. "Audrey is coming down to her house to take some of her artwork to Phoenix, and for some reason known only to her and her Maker, I have to be there. I tried to argue that I should have Sunday off, but she says it's the only day she has someone she trusts covering the gallery."

"And she still won't let you hire someone to help prepare the estate sale?"

"I don't think she appreciates how much stuff there is still to go through. I didn't, for sure. Every single drawer and closet in this house is stuffed to overflowing. And the garage—ugh. Took me most of two days to go through everything in there. It would be faster if I could make all the decisions myself, but of course I can't. For someone who was in such a hurry to get the house on the market, she's remarkably reluctant to spend time down here helping me sort. I have piles of things set aside for her to decide about. I'm constantly surprised at which items can go into the estate sale and which ones she wants to keep."

"Any way I can help?"

"I don't think so. Some of this stuff is so personal, and only she knows its value. For example, I'd put a little wooden stool, very crudely carved out of some tree stump, in the junk pile, and she was horrified. Turns out she bought it from a native in a remote African village when she was on safari, and she wants to display it in her gallery. Primitive art, I guess. Anyway, I'm headed over there to meet her in a half hour. Good luck with pickleball. Come home with your shield or on it."

It took Mike a moment to get the reference. "Ah, what Spartan women told their men headed out to war. But if I die in pickleball combat, carrying me home on my paddle is going to be a bit difficult! I do appreciate the sentiment, though."

WHEN AUDREY PULLED up in front of the house in her Audi, she was closely followed by a small van with "Gallerie Audrey" scrolled on the side. A short, heavily muscled young man tattooed on every visible piece of skin except his face jumped down from the driver's seat and followed Audrey to the front door. He had a weightlifter's gait with arms held out from his body by bulging biceps.

"Ronny, Molly. Molly, Ronny," Audrey said by way of introducing them to each other. Molly extended her hand. Clearly not expecting the gesture, Ronny hesitated and then, with a slightly embarrassed glance at Audrey, he shook Molly's hand.

"We'll start in here with the Vigotsky," Audrey said to him. "Don't try to take it down by yourself; let me help you."

Ronny looked a bit affronted. "I can handle it, Mrs. O'Day," he said confidently. "But I'll bring in the packing stuff first." He went back outside to the van.

Audrey stood in front of the largest painting. It was of a young girl sitting on a window seat, hands hugging her knees. The light from the window streamed through her hair, giving her a luminous halo. Her face was turned to the viewer, her expression a bit startled as if someone unexpected had just walked into her room.

"Marvelous, isn't it?" she said to Molly. "The way he caught the light. Almost like a Vermeer. I never get tired of looking at it. And her eyes..." Her voice drifted off. She stood as if transfixed. "No one else captures youth the way he does."

Molly felt as if she was seeing an entirely different person. "Audrey is usually all triangles and sharp edges," she explained to Mike later. "All business, rigid with purpose. Brittle. But when she was standing there spellbound by the painting, she was softer, relaxed...kind of hard to explain."

"Look at his brush work," Audrey said. "So precisely placed, those heavy strokes of cadmium lemon yellow in her hair and then the delicate touches of cerulean blue in the shadows around her eyes." She shook her head. "God, to be able to paint like that!"

Unsure if Audrey was talking to her anymore,

Molly backed up a step, but Audrey turned and to Molly's astonishment, gave a genuine smile. "Sorry, I get carried away. Every one of these paintings means so much to me. But this one is pure genius. I won't have room for it in my apartment. I'll have to put it up in the gallery. But I'll never sell it."

"I had heard you own a gallery in Phoenix," Molly said. "Out of curiosity, why not open one closer by, in Tucson?"

"That's what Tom wanted. But I had a chance to lease a place right in Old Town Scottsdale on Main where all the big galleries are. Only a block from the Paul Scott studio—I love his selection of paintings. Location is critical for a new gallery. You know, foot traffic. Lots of tourists."

"How..." Molly started.

But Audrey was intent on making Molly appreciate the quality of her gallery. "Not that I make a lot of sales to tourists. A lot of them go for the Old West stuff. You know, cowboys and Indians," she added a bit disdainfully. "Or looking for a particular palette, regardless of subject matter. Colors to match their décor—just decoration, not art." This time her contempt was clear.

"How did you get into that business?"

Again, the unexpected smile. "Long story," Audrey said. "But short version: I started painting when I was quite young. I even thought of making a career of it, going to art school. But," a rueful shake of her head, "I realized soon that I was a competent mechanic—not a real artist. I could draw well, and people told me I was talented. But I knew better. True artists spill passion—not just paint— on the canvas. I couldn't develop a distinctive style. And to be honest, I wasn't disciplined enough either. So, I majored in art history in college, took a semester abroad in Italy wandering around art museums. I decided I really wanted to run a gallery, to buy and sell the work of truly talented people. And it's been...fulfilling."

Molly was disconcerted. Once again, Audrey belied expectations by sharing this personal, revealing story. *What the heck can I say?* "Well, I'm sure it must take talent to recognize and select the best paintings."

Audrey huffed almost soundlessly. "Huh." Her lips twitched with apparent annoyance.

Molly realized she had hit the wrong note. *Audrey probably thought that was patronizing.* She tried something less personal. "Must be hard to drive back and forth from here."

To her relief, Audrey responded cheerfully. "Yeah. Helluva commute. But I've been almost full time in Scottsdale for almost two years. Tom was furi...uh, disappointed at first that I insisted on going up there so often. He wanted me to be more active in the clubs he had joined in Sunrise. I thought he'd like to be free of me for a few days a week." She laughed, but there was no amusement in the sound. "Didn't know he'd come to love his freedom quite so much!"

Ronny had spread wrapping materials on the floor. When he approached the huge painting, he plunged his arm behind it to grab the hanging wire. Audrey snapped to attention and reverted to the brusque manner Molly had learned to expect.

"Geezus, Ronny. Careful, careful! That's forty thousand dollars you're swinging around. Don't hold it by the hanging wire; it'll flop around. And where are your gloves?" Ronny pulled some gloves from his back pocket and, after donning them, carefully lowered the painting to the floor by the frame. He appeared totally unfazed by her shrillness. *He's probably used to it.*

"Uh, Audrey, do you need to supervise the loading, or may I show you some items I need you to designate for Goodwill or the estate sale?" Molly asked.

Audrey didn't respond. She was bent over the painting, instructing Ronny on how to wrap it. Only after she had seen the Vigotsky safely into the van did she return to the house.

Molly was not happy. *What's the point of me being here if I just stand around?* "Shall I come back later when you're finished loading the artwork? Maybe in an hour or so?"

"No, no. Hang on. There are only three more I'm going to send in the van. I'll take the little ones in the back seat of my car."

Judging by the amount of time expended on one painting, Molly could see Audrey would be at least another hour. *Might as well use the time for more sorting.* The kitchen was next on her list. She set up a card table and began pulling items out of drawers and cabinets, setting them on the table and the huge granite island. *If they're all out in the open, maybe Audrey can go through them quickly.* The kitchen appeared to hold every possible cooking utensil including some whose use Molly could only guess. *Mike would know.* Egg pricker? Cherry pitter? *I wouldn't have pegged either Audrey or Tom as an enthusiastic cook.*

At last Audrey joined her. As Molly had hoped, Audrey surveyed the assortment of tools and utensils and made quick decisions. Molly was hard pressed to sort the items swiftly into piles as she followed directions to "throw out," "sell," "keep—put in my car."

But Audrey suddenly halted when she saw an odd, polished wood stick with a circular metal top shaped like a squat, ornate soup can. It was decorated with colored stones and a few short chains with hollow metal beads at the ends.

"Where on earth did you find *this?*" Audrey asked.

"In that cabinet," Molly pointed to one under the island. "What is it?"

"It's a Buddhist prayer wheel," Audrey explained. "See the religious symbols on the outside? And the top opens so you can put an additional written prayer in it and twirl it." She demonstrated twirling it so that the beads knocked against the sides of the metal cylinder. "It's a Buddhist shortcut to nirvana. You get credit for giving your prayers very fast lots of times, as if you were repeating them out loud. Faster than a Catholic rosary." She looked at it a bit wistfully, Molly thought. "We picked it up on our honeymoon in Asia." Audrey twirled it, smiling at the sound of beads on metal. "I'm amazed Tom kept it."

I wonder if she's reliving some romantic times with Tom. She's full of surprises today.

But then Audrey set the wheel down in the "Toss" pile. "Pity he was such a bastard."

"*MIERDA!*" Villegas exclaimed as he hung up the landline phone on his desk. Then he rounded the corner to Rasmussen's adjacent cubicle. "Terry, Brandon Liao is on his way over here. Says Tom O'Day's death was 'not exactly accidental.'"

"What?" Rasmussen turned away from his computer console. "Why is he involved? And who said it was accidental? The case is still open."

"He said he'd explain when he gets here. I'm meeting him in the Dungeon. You want to join?"

When the two detectives arrived in the windowless, dark, and always slightly musty conference room, the overhead fluorescent lights were flickering like a doomed firefly. The lights sprang to full illumination and both detectives startled as the figure of Laboratory Director Brandon Liao emerged like an apparition at the far end of the table.

"Geezus!" Rasmussen said. "Did you transport yourself here?"

Liao chuckled. "Our science is advancing daily, but on a police budget, it'll be a while before I can avoid walking over." Then his face turned solemn. He shoved a few papers towards the detectives. "Sorry, only one copy."

"Hyoscyamine," Villegas read, scanning down the first page. "Atropine, scopolamine. What are we looking at, Brandon?"

"That's what was in the bottle Tom O'Day was drinking from before he died."

"Where did...?" the detectives spoke in unison.

Liao interrupted to explain who had retrieved the bottle and from where. Rasmussen was the first to react. "What the hell made them think they could waltz over to a crime scene and help themselves to evidence? Jose, this is your fault for letting them play junior G-man on that earlier case. Father Brown and Miss Marple!" At Liao's puzzled look, Rasmussen explained. "Stupid TV shows. Everybody's a super sleuth."

"In fairness, Terry, Molly Levin did crack the case for us last summer," Villegas said. "And technically, where they retrieved the bottle wasn't a crime scene— although it looks like it might be one now. But I don't understand, Brandon. We saw the autopsy report and all the tests were negative. And who is..." He looked at the paper again. "Evan Torberg? Somebody new in the ME's office?"

As Liao explained who the retired toxicologist was and how he had discovered the presence of the chemicals, Rasmussen became increasingly agitated. "This is totally out of line, Brandon. Totally! The autopsy didn't show any of this stuff. For all we know, our local Sherlocks put some poison in the bottle to get Landry off the hook. And why could this Torberg guy find stuff that our toxicology tests didn't? You can't be serious!"

It took a few minutes for Rasmussen's rage to subside to a minor growl. Liao explained why the older system of thin plate chromatography could turn up chemicals that were not targeted in the limited toxicology panel in the Cactus Heights kit.

"But just because Torberg found chemicals in O'Day's drink doesn't mean there was a crime, right? What are these, medications? We know that O'Day was taking something for his heart."

"There are some medications that contain

hyoscyamine," Liao said. "I can think of several used for treating peptic ulcers or other gastrointestinal illnesses—Levbid, Levsin. But at this concentration and in combination with atropine and scopolamine? No. The fact that all three of these chemicals were found in the drink points to one conclusion: Tom O'Day's drink was laced with datura, also known as jimsonweed. Grows all over the Southwest."

"The flower? I knew that was poisonous for cattle, but how would it get into a sports drink?" Villegas asked.

Liao happily slid into lecture mode. "Easy. Someone put it there. With the summer's big rains, the desert filled up with datura plants. Those big white flowers are quite beautiful. They've all died back by now, but there are plenty of seeds on the old plants free for the harvesting. Datura is used in some cultures as herbal medicine or even in witchcraft ceremonies. But shamans or Chinese healers know the right amount to ingest. Ask at the local hospitals and the ER docs will tell you they see a few datura poisoning cases every year—mostly teenagers eating the seeds to get high. As little as 15 grams—15-25 seeds —can be fatal. But you don't have to eat them to hallucinate. You can make a kind of tea out of them, boil it down, cool it, strain it. And you'd have to know how strong to make it. Then add it to the sports drink. EMTs and emergency room doctors have this litany of symptoms they look for:

> Dry as a bone—no saliva, no sweat.
> Red as a beet—dilation of blood vessels.
> Blind as a bat—huge pupils, can't see sharply.
> Nutty as a fruitcake—high, hallucinates.

Naked as a jaybird—sheds clothing, right down to fully naked."

"Cute," Rasmussen said.

"Helps them remember," Liao shrugged. "But those symptoms fit precisely what Mike Landry told me about O'Day's behavior. And unless this guy deliberately wanted to get high as a kite while on a hike, somebody spiked his drink."

"Wouldn't he taste it?"

"You ever try that sports drink gunk? It's like crushed cockroaches in bubble gum. Probably deadly without the datura. And it could certainly cover the bitter taste of the datura."

Liao held up a vial of red liquid. "Either of you wanna try it? A couple sips and Jose might decide to go back into the priesthood."

Rasmussen recoiled as if he'd been offered snake venom. But he wasn't quite ready to give up. "So, it fits what Landry claims. That's a good reason for him to put datura in the bottle—doesn't prove O'Day drank it."

"Terry, what are you saying—that Landry put the datura in the sports drink, then made up the hallucinations and all the other symptoms of datura poisoning, but that O'Day didn't actually drink it?" Villegas was staring at his fellow detective, head tilted, both eyebrows raised.

Rasmussen shrugged. "Just sayin'...."

"Easy to check," Liao interrupted. "Get the Tucson lab to analyze the blood and urine samples that we have in the freezer from the autopsy. Now that we know what we're looking for, they'll agree to do it.

And datura would show up for sure in the urine—it would concentrate there."

"Is it possible he drank it on purpose? Maybe he wanted to get high and just overshot the dosage," Rasmussen speculated.

"There are a lot easier ways to get high," Liao said.

"Now I understand what you meant by 'not exactly accidental,' Brandon," said Villegas.

"Yeah. I mean, falling over the cliff was kind of accidental, but clearly if he'd been in his right mind, he wouldn't have stepped off."

Sergeant Partridge appeared in the doorway, her hand raised as if to knock, but she had stopped to listen to the discussion about the poison.

"But suppose someone did spike the drink. They couldn't know he'd get so potted that he'd walk off a cliff. It's a mighty iffy way to off someone," Rasmussen said.

"However," Liao said, "that much poison in the system can cause a heart attack. Especially if the guy is older, has a tricky ticker, and is going on a strenuous hike. But Landry's description of O'Day's behavior doesn't fit a heart attack. Sorry," Liao said, looking at the detectives' gloomy faces. "I know you were hoping to close the case as an accident, or..."

"Yes," Villegas interrupted, glancing at Rasmussen, "we were about to write it off as heat stroke. Not enough evidence that it was anything but an accident. And we aren't the only ones who don't want to hear about foul play. The mayor is not going to be happy if the investigation swerves towards homicide. Cactus Heights is supposed to be, as the mayor loves to preach, 'the safest little city in Arizona.' Can't have senior citizens getting high from drinking datura-flavored Gatorade and hurling themselves off cliffs. This is turning out to be an *annus horribilis*!"

For once, Rasmussen ignored Villegas's Latin.

"The Chief won't exactly be doing a happy tap dance either," Rasmussen said. "Or Captain Dubrow."

"What an image!" Liao smiled, perhaps visualizing the retired Marine and the only slightly less ramrod straight captain hotfooting it on a stage. "So," he added, "what are you going to do?"

"First off, the captain has to know about this," Villegas said. "Not looking forward to that conversation."

The three men rose from their chairs, ready to leave, when Partridge spoke from the doorway. "Hey, have you seen the latest on the O'Day car crash? Look what's making the rounds online."

She handed her phone to Villegas, who read the headline out loud from the screen: "'Edison employee admits car can be hacked.'"

"Apparently," Partridge said, "this engineer was being interviewed on live TV and the doofus said that Mrs. O'Day's claim that the car was hacked and just turned off while she was driving was 'entirely plausible.'" She raised her fingers in air quotes, then continued. "He got a phone call firing him the minute he walked away from the reporter."

"Huh," Rasmussen said. "I would have bet she accidentally turned it off. But if she didn't, and the judge was supposed to be driving, sure looks as if someone had a hard-on for him."

"Unless the objective was to get rid of both the O'Days," Villegas mused, "But poisoning with datura and hacking an electric car like the Edison are two completely different MOs. Assuming at least for the moment that both those 'accidents' were in fact attempted murders, who the heck are we dealing with here?"

"Someone in Sunrise Acres," Partridge said. The three men turned to her in surprise.

"What makes you so sure?" Villegas said.

"The car hacking could be done from anywhere," Partridge said. "But in order to poison the judge, you'd have to know he was going on that hike."

"Yeah, that's true," Rasmussen agreed. "And while anyone in the Sunrise hiking club could find out who had signed up for that day's hike, 'cause it's posted on the club website, it'd be harder for someone outside the community to get the list of hikers."

"Except that anyone who could hack a car would certainly be capable of getting into a Sunrise website. I can't believe it would be that well protected. The same person would also have little trouble overriding an alarm system and spiking O'Day's drink," Villegas said.

"If it was a genuine break-in," Rasmussen added. "Audrey O'Day could have faked both. She admits she was in Sunrise the night before her husband's death. She would know how to turn the system off. And she's the only suspect we have so far—although I'm not quite ready to exclude Landry. Motive, means, opportunity for both. Check, check, check." He marked an imaginary list in the air.

"Um," Sergeant Partridge said hesitantly. "You probably know this, but apparently Mrs. O'Day is going ahead with a suit against Edison. And she's pushing the insurance company to work with her on the suit."

"What? How'd you find that out?"

"Denise did. You know how good she is finding stuff. Apparently, Mrs. O'Day has continued talking to the press. Sorry I didn't mention it sooner."

"How much was that car worth? Insurance companies don't go after Chevys," Rasmussen said.

Villegas said, "It was a high-end electric—probably eighty to ninety thousand. And it was totaled." He interpreted Rasmussen's expression as surprise. "Yeah, I know, a bit pricey for Sunrise Acres."

"But if Mrs. O'Day is going after Edison, doesn't that mean it's more likely that the car actually was hacked?" Partridge asked. "A lawsuit like that would be expensive especially if the insurance company doesn't join her."

"She could hope to make enough noise that Edison will settle—whether or not they're actually at fault. And that poor sap of an engineer who confirmed that hacking was possible gave her an early Christmas present," Rasmussen said. "So, it could be just another ploy by Audrey O'Day to get off the hook for poisoning her husband."

"Thanks for the info, Sarah," Villegas said. "Terry's right. The lawsuit doesn't prove Mrs. O'Day is innocent. But Tom O'Day was a judge for eight years, and a lawyer for nine or ten before that. There must be quite a few disgruntled defendants or clients out there. I don't want to make the same mistake we did...uh, before," Villegas said as he avoided looking at Rasmussen, "by focusing on the first possible suspect we identify before looking at others."

Rasmussen knew the reference was to the last case he and Villegas had conducted together. His face darkened with anger. But before he could erupt, Villegas went on hurriedly. "If we agree that the suspect is most likely a local, let's cross-reference the names of Sunrise residents with the database of cases brought before Judge O'Day. Maybe there's someone in Sunrise Acres who was unhappy about one of the judge's rulings."

"But wouldn't we have to look at every case he litigated when he was a lawyer before he was a judge too?" Partridge asked.

"It may come to that," Villegas said. "But let's start with more recent history."

"No reason to take Landry off the list yet," Rasmussen said. "His argument with O'Day is *very* recent history."

Villegas walked out. *Give it up, Terry*! he thought— but didn't say.

"Why do you suspect Mr. Landry?" Sarah Partridge asked Rasmussen.

"You can't discount an eyewitness just because you don't like what he says. Jose's a bit...biased. Landry's his golden boy. And an overeducated prick." Rasmussen grinned. "Besides, it really annoys Jose when I push on Landry as a suspect."

21

DAY 11

"Just wanted to give you a heads up." Molly had opened her front door to find Shelley standing on the brightly lettered "Bien venidos" doormat.

"Shelley. Hello. A heads up about what?" Molly asked, warily waving her in. *That phrase rarely means anything good.* An unannounced visit by Shelley seemed ominous. "The way these past two weeks have gone, I'd just as soon bury my head in the sand," she observed drily.

Shelley ignored the attempt at humor and bent to pet Jessie, who had bounded ecstatically towards her. Friendly visitors often meant liberally dispensed doggy treats.

As usual, the two women migrated to the kitchen table. "Coffee?" Molly offered. Jessie followed, ever hopeful. She planted herself by Shelley's feet on the sunset-colored floor tiles and fixed pleading eyes on the visitor.

"I can't stay long." Shelley reluctantly took a seat

and waved off the offer of coffee. Absentmindedly scratching behind Jessie's ears, she announced abruptly, "I've decided to move back to Chicago. I thought I'd stop by the library to let them know how to reach me if they need guidance with the website. But I wanted to tell you first."

"Shelley, what's happened? I didn't realize you'd made a final decision on moving back East."

"My lease on the apartment was only for four months and it's up in January. I had to decide whether to renew for another six months or leave now. Well, no time like the present, right? I don't have a lot of stuff to move, so I'll probably head back in the next couple days."

"Oh, Shelley, I hate to see you leave Cactus Heights so soon. I feel like we've just started to become friends."

"Thanks, Molly, but present company excepted, Tom was my only friend out here. Chicago feels more like home. My aunt Myra still lives there. With Brian gone, Myra's my only relative left and she's elderly and frail."

"Shelley, wait, what do you mean Brian is gone? Is he...?

"He died, yes. Like my mom, my dad, now Tom. And who knows how long Aunt Myra will live. She's in her late eighties." Shelley started weeping, silently.

Molly hesitated, but her curiosity got the better of her. "How did Brian die?"

"I really can't talk about it," Shelley said, her voice choking. "The point is, Aunt Myra is all the family I have."

"I'm so sorry, Shelley. If you stayed out here, I

know you'd make more friends. I could help. You don't need to be so alone." Molly reached over to give Shelley's arm a pat, but the gesture felt inadequate. *How would I feel if I didn't have Melanie and the grand-kids? And Mike?*

There was a long pause as Shelley swallowed hard, obviously struggling with emotion. Then she sat up and threw her shoulders back as if shaking some-thing off.

"Coming out here was kind of a boondoggle anyway. If it weren't for Tom, I probably wouldn't have stayed long." After a few moments staring at the table where sunlight streaked across the wood, she looked up and unexpectedly grinned. "Guess I'll never get that property on Cape Cod now!"

At Molly's slightly shocked look, Shelley added, "Sorry. That sounded terribly crass. But if Tom hadn't died, life would certainly have been different for me. You know that old saying: 'As a help for big problems, money is not. But when problems are little, it'll help a lot.' I can tell you from experience, when there's no money to fix the small problems, they can grow expo-nentially into big ones! Tom gave me my first glimpse into a world so wealthy you don't have to even look at prices on the restaurant menu. Order whatever you want!"

"Tom was well off," Molly observed. "But I doubt he was very rich. People in Sunset Acres generally aren't."

"Honestly, I think he could have afforded to live anywhere he wanted. He told me once that he moved to Sunrise Acres because there were so many sports clubs for older people. Healthy things—like hiking. Ironic, huh?"

22

DAY 12

Decebmer could be chilly in southern Arizona, but this morning was particularly cold.

The clothing of the dog walkers gave a clue to the weather. Mike stood in front of the large family room window with coffee in hand.

"Must be below freezing," Molly said. "Most people look dressed for a trek in Antarctica. Same for a few of the pooches. Let's turn on the fireplace."

Just then a woman in shorts and a light fleece vest walked quickly by, followed by two beagles bundled in sweaters. "Depends on what weather they're used to," Mike said. "She's a Minnesota snowbird, I'll bet."

"Nope, Canada," Molly countered.

"Betcha a dollar."

"You're on."

"Sucker bet. There are a lot more Minnesotans than Canucks who come here to thaw out in our nice mild winters. I'll go ask her, just to make sure."

"Before you make a fool of yourself, you should

know that I sold the Petersons their house here two years ago. They moved from Toronto. Sucker bet. Pay up."

"Crap. Never bet on Sunrise Acres residents with a real estate agent," Mike grumbled, reaching for his wallet.

"Never mind, just put it on your tab. I think you're up to double digits."

"Okay, I'm quitting before I have to dip into my IRA. Time for some breakfast."

While they were enjoying cantaloupe and Mike's freshly baked blueberry muffins, Mike's phone began vibrating, inching its way towards the edge of the breakfast table. He snatched it up and glanced at the newly arrived text. "Oh for god's sake," he said. "Not again! It's from Jose Villegas. I thought we finally got the police off my back. We've already told them everything we know." He looked up at her. "He wants both of us again. Are you game?"

Maria smiled at them when Molly and Mike arrived at the police station and said, "I'll let Detective Villegas know you are here."

They sat down on the now familiar wobbly greenish bench against the wall. "Either the winds have shifted since I was last here," Mike said quietly to Molly, "or else the friendly reception was exclusively for you. Last week Maria greeted me as if I were a serial child abuser."

They sat less than five minutes before Villegas appeared in the doorway and held the door open for them. He greeted them both cordially, and Mike waggled his eyebrows at Molly to draw attention to that behavior. "Definite wind shift," he mumbled to her.

Villegas led them to a rather dingy conference room and motioned them to take chairs around the table. Mike went on the offensive as he sat down. "So, may I assume I'm here as a taxpaying citizen rather than a prime suspect?"

Villegas sent one of his rare smiles in Mike's direction. "Safe assumption," he said. "You'll be pleased to know that we got a report from the Tucson lab confirming that Mr. O'Day's urine contained a very high dose of what could only be datura."

Mike felt as if the detective should give him a high five or some other kind of an "atta boy," but he had to be content with a congratulatory nod from Villegas.

"In fact," Villegas continued, "I asked you here to help us with the investigation into Tom O'Day's death. "We need to identify others, besides his wife, who might have had reason to want him out of the way. Can either of you think of anyone else, perhaps someone who had a more serious argument with him than you did, Mike?"

"What about all the cases he heard as a judge? Must have been a few unhappy losers."

Villegas toyed with a chain of paper clips someone had left on his desk. *He's trying to decide how much he can tell us about the investigation,* Molly thought.

Finally, he said, "We have reason to believe the crime is more likely tied to someone local."

"Doesn't mean a local couldn't have been on the losing side of a case the judge heard," Mike insisted.

Villegas nodded. "Yes, but we cross-referenced the last names of all Sunrise residents with all the county cases the judge heard." Molly and Mike looked at him eagerly. He shook his head. "Nothing," he said.

"What about the renters in Sunrise? Their names aren't in the official directory if that's what you used."

"Good thought, but we were able to get those names also—and of folks who've moved in since the directory was published. We're not at all sure that Tom O'Day's death was connected to his work as a judge. More likely it is someone in Sunrise Acres who really hated him." He turned to Molly, "I understand you've been working with Audrey O'Day to put their house on the market."

Unsure where this comment was leading, Molly just nodded.

"So, maybe you've gotten to know her personally?"

"Um, a bit."

"Has she said anything about her...relationship with her husband? Apparently, they weren't living together at time of his death."

Molly looked very uncomfortable, and Villegas took pity. "I know about the estrangement, and I've spoken with Ms. Goossens. Was the judge serious about his relationship with her?"

When Molly cast a despairing glance at Mike but said nothing, Villegas probed gently. "It could be important, Molly."

"Apparently," Molly said, still reluctant to add details.

"Enough to be a threat to the marriage?"

Molly hesitated, but then sighed and nodded. "The O'Days had been living apart for some time."

Villegas switched topics abruptly. "The break-in," he said addressing Molly. "You discovered it. And there were items missing? According to Sergeant Partridge's report, nothing much valuable besides a new computer. But," he added with a skeptical tone, "Mrs. O'Day happened to take a video of their belongings the night before the break-in."

"I know," Molly said. She shook head. "It sounds a little, um, oddly timed. But apparently Tom had a history of giving stuff away to...to..."

"Lovers?"

"Yeah. Well, girlfriends." Molly took a quick look at Mike, who nodded. She decided to tell the detective what she knew but would not speculate. "Audrey began to realize Tom was serious about Shelley. That's why she took the video. Then when we cleaned out his study, we found these envelopes full of money— thousands, all in hundred-dollar bills—that Tom had stashed away in a locked desk drawer. Shelley told me that he has been paying for their, uh, dates and everything lately with hundred-dollar bills." Molly stopped abruptly. *My god. Should I be giving the police all this private information?*

"What?" Mike was startled. "You didn't tell me about finding that money!"

Molly blushed. "I felt kind of in the middle, you know, between Audrey and Shelley. Didn't think I should tell anyone—even you."

"Did Mrs. O'Day have an explanation for all that money?" Villegas asked.

"No. She was totally surprised by it. But is this truly relevant to the investigation?"

"If, as it appears, the judge was hiding cash from his wife, it could certainly be relevant."

Molly looked imploringly at Mike again. He shrugged.

"Well," Molly said, "Audrey thought he was hiding money from her to spend on Shelley. But Audrey couldn't figure out how he got the money without her knowing. They still share a checking account."

"The cash was in separate envelopes?" Villegas asked.

"Yes, that's what seemed kind of odd."

As usual, Villegas made no comment but held her in a steady gaze.

Molly felt compelled to fill the silence. "Five of them. One was open but the others were sealed and dated. Audrey opened them and each held exactly a thousand dollars."

"What do you mean 'dated'"? The question came from Mike this time.

"Each envelope had a date marked on it. A week apart, I think."

"So, a thousand a week," Mike said. "Consulting income maybe? But paid in cash? Strange."

"Audrey didn't think Tom was doing any work. And Shelley never mentioned anything about case work. It sounded to me as if Tom spent most of his time golfing."

Villegas sat back, a bemused expression crossing his face as he watched the interview continue without him.

"Sealed envelopes! Sounds shady," Mike said.

"Maybe a payoff from Audrey's nephew! The contractor," he added to Villegas. "The one I said was..."

"I don't think so," Molly interrupted. "I told Audrey about your argument with Tom over hiring the nephew. She said the guy was, in her words, 'off-the-scale angry' that he'd taken the job. Said Tom talked him into it, that he had more work than he wanted and was likely to lose money on the Sunrise job, even after increasing the materials prices."

Mike looked at her in astonishment. "You never told me that either!"

"Well, I thought you'd already put the whole thing behind you, and I didn't see any point in bringing it up again."

Villegas appeared to think about that for a few minutes. Then he took them both by surprise by switching to a different line of questioning. "Has Mrs. O'Day said anything to you about her car accident?"

Molly grinned. "And how! She's livid about the crash. Insists the car was hacked and she's suing Edison."

"Supposing for the moment we take her at her word," Villegas said. "The car went off the road because it was hacked, either by a software program implanted in the electronic controls or someone in real time controlled the machine—although that seems unlikely. And again, assuming that the datura cocktail was planted by a local and therefore by the same person who hacked the Edison—I know, lots of assumptions there," he said, looking at their skeptical faces. "Do you know anyone in Sunrise Acres capable of such sophisticated software manipulation? Any software geniuses in your community?"

At the words "software geniuses," Molly looked up sharply, then said quietly to Mike, "Conrad."

"Molly," Mike said in warning, "be careful who you point a finger at. And I think he's a good guy. I'm sure there are other retired computer geeks in Sunrise."

"I'm just answering the question," she said. "Do you know anyone else in Sunrise who is a software genius?"

"I suppose we could ask Irwin, tap into his network," Mike said. "And there's Conrad's kid, I guess. Remember what Christine said at the dinner about their son? That he was some kind of computer whiz?"

"That's even nuttier than suspecting Conrad," Molly objected. "The son's what—seventeen? Eighteen? And he doesn't live in Sunrise most of the time. He's in college out of state."

"Just answering the question," Mike mimicked her but with a small smile to soften the words.

Villegas watched their exchange. "Tell me about Conrad. Last name?"

"Konsinski. But if he had run afoul of the judge in some case, you would have found him on your cross-reference list, right?"

"Maybe not. Tell me more about him. Why do you think he's capable of hacking a car?"

They took turns explaining about Conrad's old business and that while he disclaimed being a software guru himself, he said he hired very smart programmers. "And he'd have had to be awfully good himself to have created such a business. He told me once that it was totally boot-strapped," Mike added.

"Meaning?"

"That he never got investors. I don't know, he may have taken out loans. Probably had to. But the point is, he started the business based mostly on his own skills, gradually built it up, and hired others as he could afford to."

"Any reason to think he disliked either of the O'Days?" Villegas persisted.

Molly hesitated and then said, "Not really. Except that we had a dinner party both Conrad and Tom attended. And there was definitely some tension between them. We never figured out why, but Conrad dragged his wife off before we had dessert. And it was *crème brûlée*," Molly added, as if that proved the strangeness of the behavior.

"Molly's favorite dessert," Mike explained.

Villegas's lips twitched, but he suppressed a smile. "Tell me more about the tension you observed, Molly."

"I thought...maybe I was way off base, but I thought Tom recognized Conrad from somewhere and kind of goaded him. Asked him weird questions about where he was from. And Conrad was clearly uncomfortable."

"What made you think O'Day recognized Mr. Konsinski?"

Mike was restless. "This is all pure speculation, Jose. We really don't know any more than that the two men *seemed* to dislike each other. We may have completely misread the situation."

"But," Molly protested. "It was more than that. Remember? Conrad stopped using his knife."

Villegas looked totally lost. "What has..." he

started.

"I know, sounds crazy, but Conrad is a memorable guy. Not only is he as big or bigger than Detective Rasmussen, but one of the fingers on his left hand is kind of chopped off." She held up her hand and indicated about a knuckle down from the tip on the ring finger. "And when he saw Tom looking at it, he stopped using that hand. Kept it under the table, even when it would have been more normal to use it to hold his meat down with a fork in his left hand and cut it with a knife in his right." She illustrated what she meant. "It was so awkward to use just his right hand. I mean, for beef bourguignon. That's what made me think that Tom knew him from somewhere—and Conrad didn't want him to remember."

"Molly does have an active imagination," Mike said apologetically.

"Don't patronize me!" Molly said angrily.

"Well if anyone else had told me about this," Villegas said, "I might attribute it to a, uh, creative imagination. But given your track record...."

Molly gave Mike a defiant "see there" look.

"Sorry," Mike said. "It was so long ago, and I didn't notice it at the time the way you did." He glanced at Villegas. "*Mea culpa*."

Villegas, as usual, did not react. He was scrolling through notes on his tablet, and when he reached a particular page he stopped with a tiny grunt of satisfaction. "Konsinski," he said softly. Then he looked up at them: "Anyone else come to mind?" They both shook their heads.

"We'll follow up," Villegas assured Molly. "Detective Weatherby is a talented bloodhound. If there's something between the two men, she'll find it."

"Well, I hope she's more successful than I was," Molly said. "I certainly tried, and I couldn't find a trace of Conrad until he started his company. It was as if he'd just been born. I told Mike I thought Conrad might be in witness protection or something. I'm sure Detective Weatherby is a lot better at internet searches than I am. And she'll have access to databases beyond the public ones. But there's nothing obvious or easy to find about Conrad."

"Why were you trying to find out about Mr. Konsinski's past?"

"At first, I was trying to learn more about his company. I had just met Conrad and his wife Christine at the dinner party, and in Sunrise, it's useful to know what skills our retirees have. I thought we might be able to call on the Konsinskis to help one of the clubs I work with on IT issues. I'm an ignoramus about software or computers, so I thought I'd research enough that if I called on them, I could sound halfway intelligent. It started as a five-minute kind of idle search. But then, when I found so little about him on the company website, nothing about his education, for example, I got curious. I mean, he founded the company, and he's listed as a former board member. You'd think...." She gave an embarrassed glance at Mike. "I do tend to get intrigued by..."

"Mysteries," Mike finished.

"Puzzles," she emphasized. "And once I start on one, I don't like to give up. I'm sure there's a logical reason, but it struck me as odd that a company founder and CEO had no Internet presence. I mean,

Google knows everything about everyone. I'm a nobody, but if you do a thorough search on me, you can find where I was born, where I went to school, who I married. I just don't know how you keep people from finding *some* information."

"So, you think he's somehow been able to erase his online presence?"

Molly glanced at Mike before she spoke, but then she said: "Not exactly. I don't think it was ever there. I don't think Conrad Konsinski is his real name."

23

DAY 13

"Jamie told me he's not hungry," Christine told her husband. "He's not coming to dinner."

Conrad sighed and got up from the kitchen table where Christine had laid out chicken enchiladas, guacamole, rice, and beans. "When a teenager's not hungry, there's something wrong for sure. I'll go talk to him."

Jamie was sitting at the small Ikea desk in his room, staring at the phone in his hand. His walls were bare, with the exception of a framed Mondrian print, *Broadway Boogie Woogie,* exactly centered above his desk, which held a laptop computer and nothing else. A cloth laundry hamper stood in the corner of the room with one dirty T-shirt hanging over the edge as if someone had tossed it and not quite made a basket. The spines of Jamie's books—mostly technical manuals and science fiction novels—were carefully aligned in his bookcase. The only element that violated the perfect order was an unmade bed.

"What's going on, Jamie?" Conrad sat down on the

edge of the bed, conscious as always of trying not to crowd his son physically.

Jamie shook his head. But as his father repeated his name, Jamie silently handed him the phone. On the screen was a local news feed with the headline, "Local Woman Sues Edison." The article described Audrey O'Day's passionate anger about her car crash and her description of what had happened—the radio suddenly blared rap and then the car totally shut down. "I could have been killed," she was quoted as saying.

"I'm screwed," Jamie moaned. "I'm totally screwed!" He curled in on himself, arms across his body.

Conrad sat silently for long moments, struggling to figure out the connection between Jamie's despair and the article. The explanation that occurred to him seemed so bizarre, so outrageous, that he hesitated to voice it. When he finally spoke, the words sounded far harsher than he intended.

"What have you done, Jamie?" Conrad felt a band of fear tightening his chest. *I can't be right about this.*

Jamie hunched over even farther. He started rocking back and forth and chanting quietly, "I'm screwed. I'm screwed."

From the kitchen Christine called. "Conrad? Jamie? Dinner's getting cold."

At the sound of her voice, Jamie stopped his chanting. "Don't tell her!" He almost screamed the words.

"Jamie," Conrad said deliberately flattening his tone. "Son, maybe you'd better tell me what you...what you know about this." He gestured at the phone screen.

"It should have come back on, Dad. It was supposed to go off just for three seconds—four at the most. Long enough for him to realize the motor was off and get scared. It would have worked on a Tesla, but I guess the Edison is different. It stayed off. And maybe they'll find what I did. Every few seconds the EDR uploads to the cloud. The Event Data Recorder. They'll find it! They'll know! And it wasn't even *him*! It was his wife!"

Conrad put a calming hand on his son's shoulder, but Jamie twisted violently away and resumed his frantic rocking.

"But why...?" Conrad asked.

"The bastard was blackmailing you, Dad. And he was supposed to be driving."

"Tom O'Day? But Jamie, he was dead."

"Don't you think I know that?" Jamie said angrily. "I did this before he died. I guess it was just the day before. Anyway, the worm was already in." With a flash of pride he added, "Best one ever!" Except, his shoulders drooped as he added, "Guess it wasn't quite as slick as I thought. The power should have come back on. I need to figure out why." He sat up straighter and stared at the ceiling as he began to puzzle over what mistakes he had made in the software.

"Geezus, Jamie! No, you don't need to figure out what went wrong. Do you have any idea how much trouble you are in? This woman is suing Edison. Won't they find your worm or trojan horse or whatever you planted?"

"Yeah." He turned in excitement to his dad. "But they won't know how it got there!"

Conrad contained his temper with difficulty. Still, his voice boomed. "How do you know no one can track it back to you?"

Jamie covered his ears. "I never used any of our devices. They can't trace it back to me! No," he reassured himself. "It's okay. It's okay, Dad. I used an internet café to hack the DMV to get his VIN. Untraceable!" he said, proudly now. "Getting the VIN was the easy part."

Christine stood in the doorway frowning and mutely asking Conrad with a baffled expression what was going on. Conrad shook his head at her and tilted his head to the hall. They both stepped outside Jamie's room and closed the door.

"What is it I'm not supposed to be told?" she demanded.

"Let's not panic," Conrad said in a tight voice. He told Christine about the article and explained what Jamie had done. Christine reacted in horror.

"Why on earth?"

"He figured out O'Day was blackmailing me. Guess he did overhear us that day, remember?"

"That woman in the crash said she was almost killed! I heard an interview with her on the radio."

"I think she exaggerated," Conrad said. "She's trying to make a strong case for her lawsuit against the car manufacturer. But still, if anyone finds out what Jamie did..." He left the unfinished thought hanging.

"What do we do?" Christine's voice rose to a near wail.

"Hope he's right, I guess, that no one could trace the hack to him. When we all calm down a bit—me included—I'll look at his code and the way he covered his tracks to see if it can be traced."

He stood a bit straighter as a reassuring thought struck him. *No one has any reason to suspect him.* Then another, unbidden, thought followed. *Could our son have possibly done something else, something more, to stop the blackmailing?*

VILLEGAS WAS on his hands and knees under the desk in his cubicle trying to untangle cables and electric cords when Detective Denise Weatherby rapped her knuckles smartly on the doorway. Startled, Villegas hit his head on the underside of the pull-out support for the keyboard. He gave a muffled curse and backed out, trying not to transfer his anger with the mess under the desk to Denise.

"Sorry, Jose, but I have two pieces of information about the O'Day case you're going to want to hear."

Villegas pulled himself into his chair and motioned for her to sit.

"First, the boring part," she began. "We've located the so-called black box from Audrey O'Day's car crash. The car was towed to a junkyard down in Tucson instead of a holding lot because the crash was initially considered just an accident. That's why it took a while to find the car. Then at first, Edison didn't allow anyone except their people to look at the black box because the software that reports the operations of the car is proprietary and its workings a carefully guarded secret. But Mrs. O'Day's insurance company pushed and got an independent assessment. That's still going on. The box was crushed during the crash, so no one knows for sure if they can extract any data from it."

"And the second, presumably not boring, piece of information?"

"The background you wanted on Conrad Konsinski."

Villegas tilted his head. "And?"

"Mostly Ms. Levin was right. Conrad Konsinski first appeared online a little over twenty years ago in the late 1990s. Remember the Y2K issue? Everyone thought companies all over the world would come crashing down on New Year's Eve 1999 because most embedded systems and existing computer programs represented four-digit years with only the final two digits. The year 2000 would be indistinguishable from 1900. KCS—it was Konsinski Computer Solutions at the time—offered consulting and service on the issue. After a few years, they changed their focus to cybersecurity, kept the KCS name, but now the 'C' and 'S' stood for Cyber and Security." She looked up from her notes and explained. "Most people hadn't heard the term cybersecurity at the time, even though it had been around for a while." Back to her notes. "His first software product was based on an 'expert system'—a very early form of artificial intelligence. Very sexy at the time." She glanced again at Villegas, and he tried to check his desire that she get to the point.

This love for the nerdy details is what makes her so valuable, he reminded himself.

"All very interesting, Denise, but nothing about Konsinski before he joined the company?"

Weatherby grinned, anticipating the response to the grenade she was about to toss. "Not about the one here in Cactus Heights, no. But I did find a Conrad Konsinski born sixty years ago in a small town in southern Illinois."

Villegas nodded. "Sounds the right age. So, good."

"Except that little Conrad Konsinski of Jerseyville, Illinois died of the flu when he was three years old!"

"What?" Villegas's normally expressionless face was a satisfying mask of astonishment.

Weatherby continued smiling, clearly enjoying the sensation she had caused.

Villegas sat staring at Weatherby as he considered the implications of her discovery. "You're sure there's *nothing* on the Internet between that child's death and Conrad Konsinski's debut in a start-up?"

"Not that I could find. And I really looked. Spent hours on it. I also checked every database available, including FBI files."

"Suppose the obituary for the child is authentic..."

"No reason to think otherwise," Weatherby said.

"Okay, let's think about this. If I wanted to take a new identity, why would I choose such an unusual name? Why not reinvent myself as Bob Jones? There must be a forest of Bob Joneses in the world that I could hide in."

"Yeah, I've been thinking about that. My first thought was that maybe our Mr. Konsinski was in WITSEC. But the government wouldn't need to use a dead kid's identity to put him into witness protection. Whoever helped this guy become Conrad Konsinski didn't know how else to do it. Remember, this was at least thirty years ago before search engines and the era of no secrets. The Internet was in its infancy or at least puberty. Not many electronic data bases. Assuming the kid's name and using it to get a social security number must have seemed quite safe back then. Konsinski, or whoever he is, probably bought a whole new identity package through some black-market operator. He could have faked his resume when he started the tech company. Or more likely, he bootstrapped, built the company employee by employee and client by client without any outside money. Never had to show anyone a resume."

And that's exactly what Mike said he did, Villegas remembered. Weatherby continued, noting his nod at her comments about bootstrapping the company.

"Once the company was established and success-ful, who was going to ask him about his past? Even a board of directors would be unlikely to go into his background at that point."

"Huh. That's very intriguing, Denise. Would you please ask Sarah Partridge to arrange for us to inter-view Mr. Konsinski tomorrow? At a time when Terry's free to join?"

"At home or here?"

Villegas thought for a minute. "Here, I think. Let's say we are investigating Audrey O'Day's claims about her car being hacked, and we're asking his help in determining how easily that can be done."

"And if he doesn't want to come in?"

"Then we'll go to him. But my guess is that he'll cooperate. He'll probably want to know how much we know about him."

"And to find out if he's earned a place in our expanding 'persons of interest' list?"

"Yep. And I think he certainly has."

When Conrad came in from pruning one of the Texas ranger shrubs at the edge of the back patio, Christine knew at once that something was wrong. He glanced around the kitchen making sure Jamie was still in his bedroom before saying quietly, "Just got a call from our Cactus Heights police. I am 'invited' to go down to the station and meet with a detective Jose Villegas tomorrow morning."

"Oh no! Oh my god! So, they know Jamie hacked into Mrs. O'Day's car? What can we do?"

Conrad held up his huge hand like a traffic cop. "Not panic. The sergeant who called said Detective Villegas wants my help as a software expert to help determine how likely it is that a car can be hacked."

"And I'm supposed to feel reassured by that?"

"Assuming the sergeant wasn't totally lying to me, they aren't certain that her car *was* hacked. And my guess is that they don't even know Jamie exists. I think it's a fishing expedition. They're looking at anyone who would be capable of that level of programming. For all I know, I'm only one of numerous people they're pulling in." He tried to believe his own words for her sake.

"What will you do?" Christine asked unsteadily. She sat down hard on a kitchen chair and stared at him anxiously.

"I'm going to take them at their word and go down to the station as the resident Sunrise software guru."

"If they really needed an expert, couldn't they have found someone in law enforcement—maybe the FBI?" Christine asked. "Why you?"

Conrad looked at Christine's anguished face and tried to comfort her, although he was wondering the same. *What's the real reason they are pulling me in?* "I'm going to do my best to seem totally ignorant of anything beyond what I read in the newspapers," he said calmly. "Audrey O'Day claimed the motor of her car was deliberately shut off, leaving her without steering or brakes. That's all I know. Tell them that I used to *hire* software gurus, not that I claim to be one. And," he added, more to himself than to her, "I will be skeptical that hacking is possible. Highly unlikely. After all, car manufacturers are all aware of the Jeep incident in 2015. I'm sure they have taken steps to thwart hacking."

"Do you think they believe they've made it impossible?"

"Damned if I know what they believe. And you and I both know that even if they do think their car is hack-proof, one clever young hacker proved he could still get through all the defenses. But the police have no way of knowing that I know that. And if I'm a good enough liar, they never will."

"Even if they don't find out about Jamie, won't they find out about you? Could they turn you in to the Army for going AWOL?"

"I don't see why they'd dig deep enough to find out my history."

"Jamie did."

"First of all, he's a lot smarter than a small-town cop is likely to be. Second, he was highly motivated to dig. And finally, he used my fingerprints to get the whole story."

"Can't they take your fingerprints?"

"Why would they?" *Unless they do suspect me of hacking the Edison. But physical fingerprints wouldn't prove any connection to that.* "Anyway, I don't have to let them. Try not to assume the worst, Christine."

"What if I went with you?" she said suddenly.

He gave a brief chuckle. "And do what?"

Her face began to redden. "I don't know. Just for moral support." She tried unsuccessfully to stifle a small sob. "We've done so well for so long, Connie, keeping the secret. I can't bear the thought of it all just...you could go to jail! One mistake, so long ago."

"Our whole lives could...unravel," she said softly. Then she stood again and grabbed his arm as potential consequences occurred to her. "And Jamie—what it would do to him. Oh, Connie, this is terrifying."

He wrapped his arms around her. He wanted to promise that what she feared wouldn't happen. But he knew it could.

24

DAY 14

Detective Villegas met Conrad by the reception desk and offered a hand that he watched disappear into a monstrous grip as large as Detective Rasmussen's. "Thanks for coming down."

"Hope I can help," Conrad said easily. "But I have to warn you. I could assist with your computer security, but I know nothing about hacking cars. That's what your sergeant said you wanted to talk with me about."

"Yeah, well for sure you know more than we do," Villegas said. "We're a small outfit here. And we aren't sure what we're dealing with."

They probably don't, Conrad thought. *But he's also saying that for effect. Put me off guard.*

Villegas led the way down the hall to an interview room and stood aside for Conrad to enter.

Detective Terry Rasmussen was already in the room, sitting on one side of the small gray metal table. He introduced himself and gestured to the matching chair across from him. "Have a seat." Villegas sat down beside Rasmussen.

Conrad hesitated, then pulled out the chair indicated and sat down across from the two detectives. Rasmussen glanced at Conrad and straightened up to his full height. *He's not used to interrogating someone his own size,* Conrad thought with some amusement.

"Are you okay with our recording the conversation?" Villegas said. Without waiting for a response, he announced the names of those present, the date, and the time.

Conrad did his best not to look nervous. He crossed his arms and sat back as far as the small chair allowed.

"I expect you know about Audrey O'Day's car accident," Villegas said.

"Just what I read in the papers."

"And you knew her husband, Tom O'Day." Villegas looked at him for confirmation.

"Barely," Conrad said. Villegas looked at him steadily and waited for more but Conrad said nothing.

When the silence had stretched out long enough to be awkward, Rasmussen said, "We understand you two were friends from before living at Sunrise Acres."

What the hell? Conrad kept tight control over his face, but he could feel a small tic developing in his temple. "Whoever told you that was mistaken. But I thought I was here to talk about software, not my acquaintances." He looked at his watch. "Did you have some questions?"

"Yes," Villegas said. "We're wondering how

feasible it is to hack into a car and cause the motor to turn off."

He's going to play the good cop, Conrad thought, sizing up the two men in front of him. In Rasmussen, Conrad recognized a man accustomed to domineering because of his size and muscles. *And he'll play bad cop. Sorry, buddy. Can't intimidate me.* "Honestly, in my opinion? Not." Conrad said flatly.

Both of the policemen looked a bit surprised. "But it has been done," Rasmussen said.

"Yeah, that Jeep Cherokee that was so publicized. I've seen the YouTube video. Impressive how those two guys turned on windshield wipers and the radio, and then turned off the engine—all over the Internet. But after they explained at a public conference how they did it, car manufacturers plugged the holes. I really doubt they could pull it off today. But why are you asking me? You must have better sources—maybe the FBI?"

"We try not to involve other law enforcement," Villegas said. "Our chief...." He allowed his voice to trail off as he shook his head.

"Have you gotten hold of the car's EDR—you know, the Event Data Recorder? What people call the black box? That could give you a lot of information if it's still intact."

"Yeah." Rasmussen said.

Yeah, it would; yeah you have it; or yeah, it's intact? Conrad thought. But he wasn't about to ask.

The two policemen looked at each other. Some signal that Conrad could not read seemed to pass between them.

"Have you ever been in the O'Days' home?"

Conrad was startled at the abrupt change in focus but willed himself to maintain a neutral expression.

"No." *And you won't find any evidence that I was.*

"Never?"

"Never," Conrad said firmly. "Why do you ask?"

"We need to know who was in the house, and we have some unidentified fingerprints."

Suddenly Conrad made the connection. *The break-in everyone's talking about. They think I was involved in that burglary.* He almost smiled with relief. *Let them chase that wild goose.* But his relief was short-lived.

"We'd like to take your prints for elimination purposes."

Now we're getting to why I'm here, Conrad thought. *They want to know who I am. Probably ran into the same roadblocks Jamie did on internet searches.* He looked puzzled and shook his head. "I'm sorry? I told you I was never in the O'Day house. Consider me eliminated. I heard about the break-in. What has that to do with car hacking?" He deliberately looked at his watch. "I think I've given you all the help I can."

Villegas persisted. "I know it's an inconvenience, but fingerprinting these days is electronic—no ink mess. Only takes a minute."

Conrad felt rising panic, but he knew his face was unlikely to show it. "I see no reason to give you permission to fingerprint me. I am down here of my own free will, trying to cooperate, and I resent being treated like a criminal."

"Fingerprinting isn't for criminals these days," Rasmussen said. "Your fingerprints are probably on file a dozen places. You can't even travel internationally without giving them."

Only for Trusted Traveler cards, Conrad thought. "I don't do much international travel. Anyway, if you have no more questions about car hacking, I need to go." *How hard are they going to insist on fingerprinting? The more I object, the harder they will look at me—and my family. Will I have to get a lawyer involved?*

Villegas looked at Rasmussen and shrugged, as if it wasn't worthwhile to try and persuade Conrad to give his fingerprints.

"Well, maybe you wouldn't mind telling us where you were the night of the break-in—just to confirm that the fingerprints in the house couldn't be yours."

Uh-huh, sure. Play along. "Almost certainly home asleep with my wife, but I'd have to check our calendar to be sure. What day of the week was that?"

"Wednesday, December 4."

"Well, we have bocce every Wednesday night, but we're home by a little after nine."

Sergeant Partridge appeared in the door. She set three plastic bottles of cold water down. "Thought you might be thirsty by now," she said to the men. "Our heating system is on the fritz," she explained. "It's turning the whole building into a sauna. I've phoned in a service request," she said to Villegas.

The two detectives each picked up a bottle. "Cheers," Villegas said, unscrewed the top and chugged half the bottle. Rasmussen followed suit.

Yeah, right the HVAC is broken. They've probably set the thermostat at ninety.

"Did Tom O'Day play bocce?" Rasmussen asked.

"Not with us." Conrad picked up the water bottle,

very deliberately unscrewed the top and took a leisurely drink.

Villegas looked a bit sheepish. "I know it's a long shot," he said, "but we're trying to trace Tom O'Day's whereabouts the day and the night before his death."

"Can't you ask his wife?" Conrad asked in disbelief. "Or his girlfriend, Shelley whatever her name is?"

"Well, there are still a few blanks we were hoping you could help us fill in since you were a friend of his."

"I didn't say I was a friend, and I'm not. I met the guy once," Conrad said with a bit of an edge to his voice. "And I haven't the faintest idea where he was or what he was doing." *And that's not what you asked me. What kind of circus is this? If they think I'm going to leave this bottle with my fingerprints on it, they're even dumber than I thought.*

Conrad looked at his watch again, picked up the water bottle, and stood up. "I really need to go. I'm sorry I couldn't help you. Thanks for the water," he said and lifted the bottle in a mock salute. He waited for one of them to open the door to let him out, but they both sat, clearly not intending to move.

Now to get out of here without leaving prints on the doorknob. Squeeze it tight, turn it with more palm than fingers and try to smear whatever residue is left.

He wrenched the door open as if angry and walked down the hall.

"Well," Villegas said with a slight smile, "at least he made one mistake."

～

THE MOMENT CONRAD KONSINSKI was out of sight down the hall, Villegas called police lab director Brandon Liao. "You can send Juan over. Our person of interest took the water bottle with him, but we have another couple possibilities. Tell him to check the chair the guy sat in."

The technician was the same man who had carefully cleaned all the surfaces on the table, chairs, and the interview room door before Conrad was brought in. "No-go with the bottle of water, I hear," Juan said cheerfully. He was a small dark-haired man with a luxuriant moustache. He began working with quick, efficient movements, whistling as he started dusting surfaces. "I'll let you know what I find in a half hour or so."

Rasmussen and Villegas were together in the latter's cubicle discussing the case when Juan called Villegas. "Nothing on the table; a partial on the doorknob—he did a good job smearing his prints on that. But—pay dirt on the top back of the chair where, I assume, he had to pull it out to sit down. I got four good prints. Sending them over now."

"Send them also to Detective Weatherby, please. She's our database wizard."

"Will do. I also got a little touch DNA. Do you want that?"

"Preserve it for sure, but we'll start with the fingerprints. I'm not sure what kind of DNA match we'd be looking for."

Villegas turned to Rasmussen. "Captain Dubrow wants an update tomorrow. I already told her what we know about Audrey O'Day."

"Which is pretty much squat," Rasmussen said

disgustedly. "She has motive for sure with her husband playing hide the salami and..."

"Yes, the girlfriend," Villegas interrupted. *Don't be a prude*, he warned himself. But he was never comfortable with Rasmussen's vulgar similes. "And it sounds as if the judge was getting ready to change his will, so Audrey O'Day needed to act urgently. I'm convinced that she *could* have faked the car malfunction, but that's no proof that she *did*. She's top of my list until we find out more about Conrad Konsinski."

"He sure acted like he's guilty."

"Of something," Villegas agreed. "Let's just say that I am very curious to see if we get any hits on his fingerprints. He may turn out to be a stronger suspect than Audrey O'Day."

"Aren't you forgetting someone?" Rasmussen said. "Your buddy Mike? You can't just ignore the Sturges testimony."

Villegas suppressed a groan. "A defense lawyer could take that testimony apart in two minutes. Sturges was too far away to see clearly and looking into the sun. O'Day's yelling 'leggo' is ambiguous. Now that we know O'Day was poisoned and likely hallucinating, he could have been trying to jump and was trying to shake free of Landry."

"But Landry insisted O'Day was *not* trying to jump."

"QED," Villegas said. "*Quod erat demonstrandum*," he explained helpfully.

Rasmussen frowned and mumbled a curse. He got up to leave but sat back down with a sigh. "More friggin' Latin! Enlighten me, padre," he said with heavy sarcasm.

"The very fact that Landry denied O'Day was trying to jump demonstrates innocence. Landry said O'Day was out of his mind and trying to reach something out in space. Landry and Molly Levin went to a lot of trouble to show that O'Day hallucinated because of the datura he drank. That was a lot harder to explain than attempted suicide. If he was guilty of trying to kill O'Day, Landry could have explained their tussle by saying that O'Day attempted suicide and Landry tried to save him. Period. Would have made Mike a hero instead of a...a..."

"Suspect," Rasmussen finished. "Jose, that convoluted reasoning doesn't get Landry off the hook. Even if O'Day was total nutso and Landry *claimed* he was saving O'Day from suicide, that wouldn't change the Sturges testimony that he saw Landry give the judge a little help over the edge."

"Okay, Terry. Setting aside the fact that he was left holding part of O'Day's shirt, which strongly suggests Landry was pulling, not pushing, and ignoring the relative lack of motive, as a courtesy to you we'll keep him on the list as a person of interest for the moment. But Mrs. O'Day had a better motive, and the way Konsinski acted, he's a more likely suspect. I'll bet you a beer that we take Landry off the list before....No, wait, I have a better bet." Villegas's sly smile summoned his seldom exposed dimples. "Dinner. If I win, you take Gunther and me out, and if you win, you and Barbara come to our house for dinner."

"Wait a damn minute yourself. Who decides when Landry gets taken off the list?"

"Well, I am the lead detective."

"No way! Captain decides. On or off after you meet with her."

"Done." They shook hands.

"Do we have any info on how much the grieving widow stands to inherit? And if the girlfriend—what's her name—Goossens is in the will?" Rasmussen asked.

"Sorry, I thought Denise showed you what we got from O'Day's lawyer. It's all in the case book. But in brief: O'Day was worth over two million, and it all goes to Audrey O'Day."

"Wow, that's quite a motive to off a husband. Maybe you shoulda told me this before we made our bet."

"But it gets better," Villegas said. "The subpoena specifically included the agenda for the judge's scheduled meeting and the draft addendum to his will. Guess who would have gotten a condo on Cape Cod in Massachusetts if the judge hadn't taken his untimely step into oblivion."

"I'll take a wild swing at it: Ms. Goossens."

25

DAY 15

"We've identified another suspect in Tom O'Day's death." Villegas was sitting in the captain's office. Captain Dubrow had made a superficial bow to the season. A Christmas snowman snack bowl sat on her desk, his concave chest and belly each filled with red and green M&Ms. Not entirely sure if the candies were for show or for eating, Villegas resisted the impulse to grab a handful. His resolve was strengthened by remembering that his husband had teased him just yesterday about the appearance of a small paunch beginning to bulge above his belt. *Gunther's fault for cooking so much and so well,* he thought. *But no candy.*

"Conrad Konsinski is a Sunrise Acres resident who once ran a cybersecurity company. If any local is capable of hacking a car, unlikely as that is, he'd be a candidate. I asked Denise Weatherby to see what she could find out about him on the Internet and she came up with something interesting. Apparently, some years ago Konsinski assumed the identity of a three-year-old boy who died of the flu. Yesterday we had Konsinski in for an interview, requested his fingerprints, and he refused. In fact, he seemed determined to avoid leaving his prints on any of the surfaces we had cleaned before his arrival. Fortunately, we were able to obtain some good prints from a chair that he touched. We've submitted the prints to a number of databases and hope to get something back soon."

"So, Konsinski could possibly have caused O'Day's car crash, and he obviously doesn't want his true identity uncovered. Any reason to think he had it in for the judge?" Dubrow said.

"Molly Levin reported that at a dinner party that both O'Day and Konsinski attended back in October, there was obvious tension between the two men, and that Konsinski and his wife left the party abruptly. We're hoping that when we learn more about his past from the prints we'll be able to establish if there's a compelling motive."

"Molly Levin again, huh?"

Villegas ignored the sly grin aimed in his direction. "Her knowledge of Sunrise Acres and its residents has been proving useful," he said primly. "But while we are following up on Konsinski, our primary focus remains on Audrey O'Day."

"Your report suggested she could have faked the whole hacking thing."

"Agreed. Extremely unlikely that car could be hacked. And so far she's the only one with a clear motive to kill the judge. And we just found out that her motive is even stronger than we thought. We got access to the judge's will and the notes from his lawyer about some planned changes. He had an estate of over two million. But in the new version of the will, he was going to leave a pricey property back East to his new girlfriend."

"So a black widow murder, huh? Sure sounds like Mrs. O'Day is your prime suspect."

"But we're going to keep looking at Konsinski."

"Any other suspects?"

Villegas explained the Home Alert log information showing the time of the break-in at the O'Day house. "There's only one other person who for certain had the security system code: Shelley Goossens."

"The other woman?"

Villegas nodded. "But we don't know that the judge didn't give the code to other people."

"Why would Ms. Goossens want the judge out of the way? Wasn't he her sugar daddy?"

Wow: that term really dates her. I didn't think she was that old. Or maybe she just watches ancient movies. "Yeah, it seems she didn't have much motive. In fact, if anything, the judge's death deprived her of that Cape Cod property. But she definitely had the means."

Dubrow sat in thought a moment. "Could the security system be overridden? I remember a case a few years ago in Tucson. We had a string of burglaries and couldn't figure out why the alarms never went off. All the houses had the same security system. Turned out a former employee knew how to disarm them. It wasn't Home Alert. Can't remember the name of the company...ugh, well, it'll come to me. Anyway, have you considered that possibility?"

Villegas felt abashed. *She's got me again. We haven't*

even thought of that. "Haven't looked into that yet. But we'll get on it."

"And what about Mike Landry?" Dubrow asked.

"Well, I wouldn't want him to skip town, but frankly I don't see much of a case against him. One witness who was probably too far away to be certain says Landry pushed O'Day, no known motive, or at least a very flimsy one. His descriptions of O'Day's weird symptoms and hallucinations are consistent with the datura found in the judge's urine. And Landry and Ms. Levin found the bottle with the datura. I'd like to take him off the persons of interest list."

Dubrow looked at him suspiciously. "Why?"

"I want to continue to utilize Landry and his girl-friend Molly Levin as informants in the community. They can find out things a lot easier than we can. They fingered Konsinski for us when he wasn't even on our radar. Landry can't help us and be a suspect at the same time."

Dubrow's computer sounded the arrival of an email. She hastily checked the source with a glance and turned away from Villegas, fingers already poised on the keyboard to pull the message up. "Sure, okay," she said carelessly. "But better tie this case down. I gotta give some people time off for the holidays."

Villegas grinned as he left the office, thinking about his bet with Rasmussen. *Gunther's the foodie. I'll ask him what restaurant we should choose.*

26

DAY 16

"Mike, Mike, can you...I need to show you...oh god, this changes every... can you come over please?"

Mike was pulling out the dead flowers from the large brown and green pots on his patio. Lined up by each pot were the intended replacements—pansies, some ornamental kale, and other hardy winter annuals still in their Home Depot plastic containers. It had taken a moment for him to free his hands from his gardening gloves and answer the phone. Molly's urgent incoherence frightened him. He couldn't interpret the emotion. *Is she excited or scared? Or worried?*

"Molly? Are you okay? What's happened? Where are you?"

"I'm at Audrey's house. It's better if I show you. Do you have time to come now?"

"Of course. Ten minutes?"

He hastily watered the new plants, not knowing how long he would be gone. He washed his hands and bolted for the car.

The house from outside looked as it always did. No obvious reason for concern. When he reached the front door, Molly was standing in the hall waiting for him.

"Down here," she said and led him to what had been Tom's study. The room was a mess. Two massive piles of books lay on the floor.

"Don't worry about those," Molly said, gesturing to the books. "They're Tom's lawbooks and I'm sorting them into those that can be donated to law school libraries and those that are simply too outdated to be useful to anyone. Here's what I need to show you. I was going through Tom's files." She gestured to the two desk file drawers. "There's a lot of confidential information in them that needed to be shredded. But I wanted to recycle the folders as well as the papers inside and of course I had to take any large paperclips out before they could be shredded, so I was sorting....Anyway, these clippings just fell out of one file and the headlines caught my eye."

She had laid out the clippings on one end of the desk. "Take a look." They were from several different newspapers and varied in length. Most were short notices about an arrest for drug possession, but one from *The Wichita Eagle* was considerably longer.

The headline was "Wigner Found Guilty, Sentenced to 18 Months." Mike hastily skimmed the text. One sentence caught his attention. "Brian Wigner refused to identify his drug supplier." And further down, he saw what had agitated Molly. "After imposing what defense attorney Joseph Abernathy described as an 'unusually harsh sentence,' Judge Thomas O'Day told a full courtroom, 'Those who refuse to aid the law, break the law. Brian Wigner is protecting a criminal even more culpable than himself. He may think this is a noble act, but it is despicable.'"

The article went on to quote the judge further: "Drug users must be severely punished to set an example to other youths about the hazards of drug use and the slippery slope, from a small amount of a recreational drug like Ecstasy or marijuana, to addiction and use of extremely dangerous drugs like Fentanyl."

"Who is Brian..." Mike looked again at the clippings "Wigner"?

"Shelley's maiden name is Wigner."

"Holy cow! Is Brian...?"

"Shelley's brother, yes. Shelley was very angry about the prison sentence he was given. And Mike, it gets worse. Look at this!"

She passed a short clipping to him. The headline read: "Prisoner Commits Suicide." The article gave few details beyond the day and time when Brian Wigner was found "unresponsive in his cell" after using strips of a bed sheet to strangle himself.

"Shelley told me Brian had died but not that he killed himself in prison."

"Judge Thomas O'Day." Mike stood staring at the clippings in his hand, still working it through. "But if Tom was the judge at Brian's trial, Shelley must have known Tom from the trial. And vice-versa. Why would either of them want to get romantically involved? They were on opposite sides in what sounds like a traumatic trial and an unfair prison sentence. It makes no sense."

"I wondered the same thing. But I don't think Tom made the connection. The trial was about four years ago. Shelley sat in the courtroom, sure, but she would never have met the judge personally and up close. She showed me a photo of her with her brother right about that time. She had very short dark hair, wore glasses, and was kind of pudgy. I wouldn't have thought it was the same woman if she hadn't told me. And she and Tom met at a U of A reunion, remember? That gave her a chance to find out if he recognized her."

"But Tom must not have changed that much since the trial; surely she knew who *he* was."

"Yeah. She had to know. She told me the whole trial was unfair—bad defense lawyer, aggressive DA, inattentive jury, and a justice system that threw the book at Brian."

"A justice system embodied by Tom O'Day. Why would she go out with him, lead him on, sleep with him?"

Molly shook her head. "I don't think she was sleeping with him. But still, if I was that angry with someone, I don't think I could stand to be in the same room with him, never mind all the dates and phone calls."

Mike smiled at the thought. "No, for sure you wouldn't!"

Molly ignored his comment. "Mike, what on earth am I going to do? Shelley's a friend, but this clearly gives her a motive to poison Tom. I have to tell Jose, don't I?"

"Yeah," Mike said slowly. "I agree you do. But let's think about this for a moment. Motive isn't evidence.

And what about the burglary? Whoever broke in also put the datura in Tom's drink, right? If Shelley was the one to poison Tom, would she have needed to break in? She probably had a key."

"I don't know about that. She mentioned that Tom had hidden a key where anyone could find it, so I'm sure she knew its location. And Tom might very well have given her the Home Alert code."

"So why break-in?"

"Very few things were taken. It could have been staged."

"Take a few trinkets and a computer to make the break-in look like a burglary?" Mike said. "Kind of dumb to take so little if that was the purpose. And why stage a break-in if you could get in and out with a key and leave no sign of tampering with Tom's drink?"

"Yeah," Molly said, as another possibility occurred to her. "Audrey obviously has a key. And she has good reason to dislike Shelley. Maybe she knows about the case and Tom's role in it. She could have left the clippings for me to find, so I'd suspect Shelley of poisoning Tom. What if Audrey was the one to stage the burglary?"

"Man, that's too convoluted for me. Tell Jose about the clippings and let the police figure it out."

"Thanks, Terry, Denise, for coming in," Villegas said. The detectives were gathered in the gloomy Dungeon conference room. Rasmussen claimed a chair midway down the side of the table and shoved back a chair on either side of himself for extra room.

Someone *Maria?* Villegas wondered, had put a small, slightly drooping and dusty fake Christmas tree on the long table at the back of the room that occasionally boasted refreshments to lure staff into meetings. *Nice idea,* Villegas thought, *but that tree looks as discouraged as we all feel about this case.*

"I met with the captain yesterday," Villegas said, "and summarized where we are on the case. She hopes, like the rest of us, that we can close it before Christmas. I focused on the two main suspects, the not-so-bereaved widow, Audrey O'Day, and the computer expert, Conrad Konsinski."

Rasmussen stirred and appeared to be about to protest. Certain that he was about to resurrect Mike Landry yet again as a possible third suspect, Villegas hurriedly went on. "The captain agrees that the evidence against Landry is too slim to pursue him further. He's off the list of persons of interest." Visions of Rasmussen and Gunther breaking bread together flashed through his mind, and Villegas carefully suppressed an urge to look at the huge detective. *Must not gloat!* "I'd like to review what we have on those two.

"Audrey O'Day," he began. "Motive? She and her husband were estranged. He was seeing another woman, Shelley Goossens. Most important, Tom O'Day was about to change his will. Thanks to heroic efforts by Denise," he nodded in her direction, "in getting a subpoena for Tom's lawyer, we know that O'Day planned to include Ms. Goossens in his will. While most of his estate is communal property, the judge owned a condo in Falmouth Massachusetts— that's on Cape Cod—prior to this marriage, and therefore he was free to leave it to Ms. Goossens. Well, not any longer. Denise, what did you find out about the value of that property?"

"I accessed the Falmouth town tax records and checked on Zillow, and the condo is valued in the neighborhood of four hundred thousand. Apparently, Cape Cod is a very popular destination for the moneyed set. And this condo is near the ocean. I looked at the property on Google Earth. Might even have ocean views. You should see it."

Rasmussen sat up when the price was mentioned. "Jeesh. Nice little chunk of change. If the judge had lived long enough to finalize his new will, Audrey O'Day would be out of pocket. A lot! Spouses have been knocked off for less."

"Okay, clear financial motive. Means?"

"Well," Weatherby said, "no problem faking a burglary, assuming she knew how to use a glass cutter. And she obviously knew the alarm code. She'd need to read up on how to make some super-strength datura tea, but that wouldn't have been difficult. Those plants are everywhere in the desert. All you'd have to do is pick up some seeds."

"And," Rasmussen added, "if she was sneaky enough to fake a break-in, she'd be capable of claiming the Edison was hacked."

"Agreed. And remember, that car went off Oracle at the precise spot—the only one in miles—where she could do a controlled crash without getting seriously injured," Villegas added."

"But doesn't that seem like overkill?" Weatherby said. "I mean, why would she go to all that bother? Was she stealing her own stuff and wrecking her car just to make us believe she was innocent? What's that line about protesting too much?"

"But we did home in on her as a suspect right away because of her objections to the autopsy," Villegas said. "Along with Landry," he amended, looking at Rasmussen.

"So, if she's a prime suspect, we must believe she did the break-in and the car crash in *anticipation* of being accused of poisoning her husband, right?" Weatherby said. "Yet we're also saying that it was her opposition to the autopsy that made her suspect. So if she hadn't protested...I don't know, it doesn't add up for me. That she would be clever enough to think ahead on how to clear herself from suspicion and yet be dumb enough to do the one thing that caught our attention. At the time, remember, we still thought O'Day's death could have been an accident."

"But if she *is* our killer," Villegas said, "she might not know that datura doesn't normally show up in an autopsy. *We* didn't know that. She may have assumed that we'd find the poison and then of course she'd be an obvious top suspect. In that case, she'd need to divert suspicion."

Weatherby nodded. "Okay, I'll buy that. Audrey O'Day is still top of the list."

"Let's move on to Conrad Konsinski, real name Joseph Osterhous. Once we got his fingerprints, Denise got to work on—let's call him Konsinski for now. Denise, your show."

"Okay," Weatherby said. She opened her laptop but had most of her notes in her head. She glanced at the computer only a few times during her recital. "The more we find out about Mr. Konsinski, the more suspicious he looks. He first appeared on our radar when Molly Levin identified him as a possible hacker of the O'Days' Edison—assuming it *was* hacked," she added with a glance at Villegas. "But then Molly Levin added a detail from some Sunrise Acres dinner club get-together, that O'Day was giving Konsinski the stink eye." Villegas raised an eyebrow and Weatherby said, "Technical term, Jose." She grinned at him. "Anyhow, O'Day asked Konsinski if he had ever lived in Kansas, which he denied, and the Konsinskis got up and left the party abruptly. Then we got his prints, ran them through the usual screens, and hit paydirt with the military. He was going to be court-martialed after some drunk schmuck almost died when Konsinski—then an Army MP—didn't prop him up the accepted way and he aspirated his vomit."

"Yes, thanks for that, uh, graphic description," Villegas said. "Where was that?"

"It was…" She checked her notes. "Fort Leavenworth. In…hmm, Kansas." She continued, "Well, long story short, he got help escaping, went AWOL, got more help finding a convenient alias, worked on his computer skills and—ta-da!—became a semi-successful entrepreneur and landed in our bailiwick."

"Denise," Villegas said. "Hold on a second. A court-martial? In Kansas where he was an MP at Leavenworth? And at this dinner party *Judge* Tom O'Day seemed to recognize him. Was O'Day at Leavenworth? How quickly can you get back to us with information about O'Day's legal career?"

"I already have it. You asked me to cross-check his cases with current residents at Sunrise Acres. Of course, I didn't get any hits, since Konsinski had changed his name. Anyway, I checked back to when O'Day was an Army lawyer at Fort Leavenworth. It coincided with Konsinski's stint as an MP—and his going AWOL."

"So," Rasmussen, now fully engaged, concluded, "O'Day recognizes Konsinski at this party, maybe helped by Konsinski's size and the missing finger. Maybe O'Day sees a chance to put the screws on him. Add a little blackmail to retirement income. When did those envelopes of C-notes start arriving at O'Day's place?"

Now it was Villegas's turn to check his notes. "According to Ms. Levin, she and Mrs. O'Day discovered five dated envelopes. Of course, there could have been others that O'Day had already gone through. But it looks like they began arriving shortly after the judge and Shelley Goossens attended the dinner party, which was in October, I believe. O'Day could have been blackmailing Konsinski, threatening to turn him over to the Army and...Wait! Wait! Denise, bring up that list of O'Day's phone calls to Sunrise residents during the past three months. You mentioned some people were contacted more than once. I think Konsinski was one of them."

"Got it." Weatherby had quickly brought up the spreadsheet. "Yep, three calls in a one-week span in late October to Conrad Konsinski."

"I knew that name rang a bell. Quite a few calls for someone who, according to Mr. Konsinski, was definitely not a friend," Villegas said. "Those calls probably set up the blackmail."

"And there's nothing to say that Konsinski couldn't

have staged the break-in and by-passed the alarm," Weatherby said. "After all, he's a software wiz."

"And a security guru. And his teenage son is also reputed to be into computers. Useful if he needed some up-to-date consultation from the younger generation," Villegas added. He intended the comment as a bit of humor, but the other two ignored it.

"If he could kill O'Day by crashing his car, why would he need to get into the house and poison his drink?" Weatherby asked.

"Redundancy," Villegas answered. "After all, he couldn't be sure the car crash would be fatal."

"And it wasn't," Rasmussen added. "The datura could have been a back-up plan. From what we know about Conrad Konsinski, he's a careful planner."

"And clever," Villegas added. "Look at how long he's managed to hide from the Army. They have a unit devoted to tracking down deserters."

They sat in silence digesting the information they had on the suspects. Rasmussen had taken out a quarter and was passing it over one knuckle at a time, forward and back. Weatherby was still staring at her notes. After absently watching Rasmussen for a few moments, Villegas started jotting notes on his tablet. They all looked up surprised when Maria Rodriguez entered the room.

"I'm really sorry to break in like this, but I just got a call from Molly Levin. She says she has some, quote, 'critical information' about the case, and she'd like to speak with Detective Villegas. She said she tried your cell phone, but I guess you turned it off for your meeting. She says it's urgent, can't wait. I've got her on hold on the station phone."

Ignoring Rasmussen's disgusted grunt, Villegas said, "Thanks, Maria. Go ahead and transfer it to the phone here."

Villegas switched the phone to speaker, and the other two moved in closer.

"Molly, good morning. Maria says you have something for us. I have detectives Rasmussen and Weatherby with me."

"Jose, I'm at Audrey O'Day's house. As you know, I'm getting the place ready to put on the market for her. I was just now going through her husband's, uh, Tom O'Day's office to see what might be donated or sold. There are two file drawers in his desk and I was getting the paper files ready to go to shredding, pulling out the large metal clips and stuff that couldn't be shredded, and a bunch of newspaper clippings kind of fell out."

Villegas smiled at the wording and asked her to continue.

"Some of the clippings were about a trial of a man, Brian Wigner, accused of unlawful drug possession. Brian is almost certainly Shelley's younger brother. One article reported on Brian's suicide while serving an unusually long prison sentence for a relatively minor drug offense. Shelley had told me about that. But I'm calling you because the judge in the case was The Honorable Thomas O'Day. He went beyond sentencing guidelines because Brian refused to name the person who supplied him with the drugs. Anyway, I thought you ought to know."

"Thanks very much." Villegas looked at the other

two detectives before adding, "We'll need Mrs. O'Day's permission for you to hand those clippings over to us. Would you mind asking her? We'd like to see them for ourselves. This sounds...very interesting for the case. Let Maria know when, uh, if we have Mrs. O'Day's permission to send someone over to pick up the file. I've turned my cell phone back on, so you can reach me. Thanks, Molly." He hung up the phone.

"I very much doubt Mrs. O'Day will object," Rasmussen said. "Gives her rival a juicy motive for poisoning the judge."

"Well," Weatherby observed, "doesn't that depend on how much Ms. Goossens loved her brother? I mean...seems extreme to take that kind of revenge. And this didn't just happen, right? How long ago did the brother commit suicide?"

"Good questions," Villegas said. "I should have asked more." He picked up the telephone on the conference table and asked Maria to get Molly back on the line.

Molly informed them that the clippings about the suicide were only two years old. "And Shelley seemed close to her brother. She basically raised him from birth—he was a lot younger. Her father had left, her mother was depressed and ineffective. Uh, one more thing you might want to know," Molly said hesitantly. "Shelley told me she's about to leave Arizona, go back to Chicago. Within a couple days."

After asking a few more questions, Villegas thanked Molly and disconnected.

"But she was dating Tom O'Day. What the heck?" Weatherby looked shocked.

"I know. Awfully cold-blooded if she poisoned him," Villegas said.

"Well," Weatherby said, musing out loud, "I guess raising her brother could cut both ways. Maybe she was really close to him. Saw the judge as responsible not just for sending him to prison, but for his death as well. Therefore, a strong motive for revenge. On the other hand, if she had to raise him because her mother didn't, maybe she felt her brother was a burden. If he was into drugs, he could have been high maintenance, kept her from living a normal life and she resented him. In that case, she could have seen his suicide as his choice and not O'Day's fault. Maybe even a relief to have him out of her life."

"Hmm," Villegas said, "Then she, what, seduced O'Day out of gratitude? Doesn't make a lot of sense to me."

"So now," Rasmussen said, "instead of one prime suspect—the widow—we have three." He shook his head and grimaced. "Setting aside Landry."

This time Villegas didn't try to hide his smile.

"Audrey O'Day: means, motive, opportunity. Konsinski: ditto, assuming he could hack the alarm system. And now, Goossens: if she was furious enough about her brother's sentence and suicide to want revenge," Rasmussen summarized.

"Agreed." Villegas nodded.

"So where does that leave us?" Weatherby asked a bit plaintively.

"It means we lean on all three of them. And soon."

There was a collective groan as the meeting broke up.

MOLLY CONCLUDED her conversation with Villegas and turned to Mike. "Well, now I've done it. I've handed Shelley over to the police as a suspect in Tom's death. Can't say that I feel good about that."

"I don't see that you had a choice. And it's up to them now to find out if she actually took revenge on Tom for what he did to her brother. Having a motive doesn't mean she acted on it." He looked around at Tom's study. "I don't feel comfortable talking about it here. Let's go back to my house, sit down with a drink, and discuss it."

"Feel like Tom's looking over our shoulders?" Molly teased.

"Sort of," he admitted sheepishly. "Just seems unseemly somehow. Creepy. Anyway, I'm looking forward to a nice glass of wine."

"Okay, but let's stop by and feed Jessie first. And she'll need a few minutes in your backyard if that's okay."

"So long as she continues to, uh, favor the rocks in the corner under the tree, no problem."

It was nearly dark as they drove back to Mike's house. As soon as he was in the door, Mike switched on the lights of the artificial Christmas tree in the corner of the living room. He and Molly had discussed buying a real tree this year, but it would be an impractical choice in the desert. Cut trees were already desiccated by the time they journeyed from the Northwest and ready to shed needles like a molting bird.

By unspoken agreement, the two of them didn't

immediately return to discussing the case and Shelley's role in it. They settled in front of the gas fire with wine, cheese and what Molly referred to as "bird seed crackers" from Trader Joe's. After a few minutes quietly savoring the time together, Molly finally broke the silence.

"It's just hard for me to imagine Shelley deliberately poisoning Tom. She told me she was fond of him, that he was charming and vital."

"To say nothing of a wealthy, adoring date who lavished all sorts of expensive attention on her. Didn't you say he gave her a diamond and ruby bracelet?"

"Diamond and sapphire," Molly corrected absently. "And she was going to return it to him. But what bothers me, Mike, is that I thought she genuinely grieved for him. When we got together a few days after his death, her eyes were red from crying."

"Or from onion juice."

"Really? You think she'd be that...that devious? That calculating? If she was faking, she sure fooled me."

"Think about it. If she was the one who spiked his drink with datura, that would mean she was also the one who faked a break-in to cover her tracks—an elaborate ruse, cutting the glass when she already had a key, shutting off the alarm, stealing just enough to convince the police that there'd been a burglary, locking the door behind her on the way out. She would have to have been a terrific actress, leading him on for months, hiding her contempt and hatred of him. 'Devious' doesn't begin to cover it!"

"I really like her," Molly said sadly. "I hope she

didn't do it. Audrey's motives seem just as strong. If Tom hadn't died, not only could Shelley have been wife number three, but even if Tom hadn't married her, it sounds as if he was planning to give Shelley some very valuable property. Why would Shelley kill him now?"

"I wonder if they've given up on Conrad as a suspect," Mike said. "No way Shelley has the kind of IT chops to hack a car. If it was hacked. I'm not sure anyone has those skills. Edison keeps insisting it's impossible. I know you said Audrey was certain it was. She told anyone who'd listen that the car could have killed her. And she's suing Edison. But if someone—Conrad, say—had already put the datura in Tom's drink, why hack his car? That's, if you'll excuse the expression, overkill."

Molly winced at the joke. "Yeah, and we don't know that Conrad had any compelling reason to kill Tom. Except," she added, "that Tom recognized Conrad at the Prepare and Share dinner, and remember, I couldn't find out anything about Conrad on the Internet," Molly said. "I still think he and Christine could be in WITSEC—and Tom could have outed them."

Mike shook his head. "Weak," he said. "That's not a real motive. The government could handle it—or move them to a new place if need be. And we both know that Tom was a jerk, but why would he do that? What would he get out of it? Besides, poison's usually a woman's weapon."

"Maybe Conrad hoped the police would be sexist enough to think that too!" Molly said indignantly. "Why couldn't he have been the burglar?"

"That's not sexist. It's a statistical fact. Think Lucrezia Borgia, Catherine de Medici. Men usually shoot or stab or bash their victim's head in. Face it, either Audrey did it or Shelley did."

"But why would Shelley poison him when he was promising her all sorts of goodies?"

"Maybe she only wanted to scare him, make him feel miserable or embarrassed or...." Mike shrugged. "Depends on how mad she was at him, I guess."

"I wish I could figure that out for sure. I think if I talked with her...."

"What, you think she'll just confess? Yeah, I really hated his guts, so I killed him"?

"Not in those words, of course. That's a guy thing —'hating guts.' But I'll bet I could get a feeling, some sense of whether she'd be capable of such...deception. She's leaving to go back to Chicago either tomorrow or the next day. I think it would be a nice gesture to go say goodbye, don't you? Maybe help her pack?"

"If she is the murderer, do you think going to her apartment is smart? Maybe I should come too."

"You said women don't bash heads in, remember? I won't drink anything there, except what I bring myself, I promise."

"Are you going to tell her you found the newspaper clippings?" Mike asked a bit anxiously. "Or that you gave them to Jose? That could make her very angry with you."

"I don't know," Molly said slowly. "I just want to talk to her. I can't believe she could be so, so...cold-blooded. As you said yourself, having a motive doesn't mean you act on it. I know her better than anyone else here now that Tom's dead. Maybe I can get some sense of how she's feeling. If she did poison Tom, she's not at all the person I think she is."

Mike shook his head. "I really think you should let the police handle it from here."

Molly laughed. "Somehow I just don't see Shelley opening up to The Hulk, do you?"

27

DAY 17

"**H**i!" Molly said cheerfully as Shelley opened the door to her apartment. Shelley looked astonished.

"Molly! What are you doing here?"

"You said you're leaving soon, right?"

At Shelley's bewildered "Yeah," Molly said, smiling, "Well, aren't you going to invite me in? I've brought a farewell breakfast. Hope you haven't eaten yet. Coffee—skinny soy latte for you and two of our favorite pastries. I took a chance on you being here because I figured you'd be packing. Shelley?"

"Uh, sure. Sorry. Please, come in and, uh, excuse the mess. I've been..."

"...packing. Of course." Molly finished for her. "That's why I'm here. I've had a lot of practice."

It was a small one-bedroom apartment, scantily furnished. *Graduate student décor,* Molly thought. *She didn't add any furniture while she was here.* A few generic abstract paintings decorated otherwise barren walls. *Motel 6 art gallery. I could have lent her some framed photos of desert landscapes if I'd known she could use them.* Various sized boxes, most sprouting packing materials out the tops, were scattered around the floor and on a small table in the family room-cum-dining room. Molly could see through to the bedroom, where mounds of clothing covered a double bed.

"What can I do? Maybe fold clothes or pack breakables?"

"Uh, I don't have that much left to pack," Shelley said, gesturing towards the bedroom. "Mostly clothes. Same stuff I drove out here with, so I know the car can hold it all." Looking around for a place to set her coffee and the small box of pastries, she took a partially packed box off the dining room table and set it on the floor. Then she pulled out two chairs, gesturing to Molly to take one.

I really shouldn't have come, Molly realized. *She doesn't seem that thrilled to see me and if this is all she has to pack, we're not going to have much time to chat. I'm not going to find anything out.* "I'm sorry, Shelley. Maybe I should just leave you to it?"

"No, no," Shelley said. "If you can stand the mess, please stay and let's have our drinks. It was a very friendly gesture to come—and how sweet of you to remember my taste in coffee. I can't think of anyone else who would do that."

"I won't stay long," Molly assured her. "But tell me, where will you stay in Chicago? With the aunt you mentioned?"

"Oh no. She'd hate that. So would I. My apartment's just five minutes away from hers."

"You found an apartment already? That was lucky."

Shelley looked uncomfortable. "Uh, I didn't give my old one up when I came here. I thought I'd hold on to it until I decided if I wanted to stay in Arizona."

Kind of expensive, Molly thought. *Especially for someone who said she had no money.* But she said nothing, just made the kind of small grunt that could be read as "I'm listening."

"What's really lucky," Shelley went on brightly, "is that my Chicago network has already turned up some new jobs for me."

"Tell me about them. And were you able to finish Lauren's project?" They chatted a few more minutes as Shelley described a website for an insurance agency and another for a girls' club.

Then, getting up from the chair, Shelley held out her hand for Molly's empty take-out cup and dropped it with her own in a trash bin. "Well," Shelley said.

It was clear to Molly that the farewell meeting was over. The moment to confront Shelley with her discovery of the newspaper clippings that Tom had kept had passed.

Molly got off the chair and offered a hug. But as she put her arms around Shelley, she froze as she looked past Shelley's arm at the open box on the floor.

Shelley pulled back from the embrace. Molly had dropped her arms but was still standing frozen in place. "Molly? What is it?"

Now what do I do? "Uh, Shelley, where did you get that?" Molly pointed to the box that Shelley moved from the table to the floor. A piece of brown wrapping paper had partially fallen away, revealing a chunk of amethyst. Attached to it, still nestled in the wrapping paper, was a silver cow's skull.

Shelley followed Molly's finger and looked startled for a moment. Then she said casually, wrapping the paper back over the little sculpture as she spoke, "Oh, Tom gave that to me. It'll be a nice memento of the Southwest. And of Tom, of course," she added hastily.

She doesn't know about Audrey's video, Molly realized. *She doesn't know what I know—that Tom couldn't have given it to her.* Molly's thoughts careened around in her head as she tried to make sense of what she saw and what Shelley just said. *There couldn't be two identical pieces like that. This has to be the one taken from the O'Days' house the night of the break-in. Could someone else have stolen it and given it to her? But then why would she say that Tom gave it to her?*

Molly reached for the piece to unwrap it again and took her phone out of her pocket to take a photo, but Shelley knocked her hand aside. Then she stood between Molly and the box. "I think it'd be better if you go now, Molly," she said firmly.

Molly couldn't move. She stared at Shelley, not comprehending what was happening, until Shelley said again, calmly but a bit louder than before, "Go home, Molly." Then with quiet emphasis, she added, "I'm leaving here tomorrow, Molly. I'm not coming back. You'll never see me again."

Molly started for the door, but she stopped midway. *She must have an explanation. Maybe she found that silver piece in a pawnshop. But she said Tom gave it to her. Obviously, a lie. Can I just let her go? Say nothing to anyone? That's what she's suggesting. Would she do that if she had an innocent explanation?* She looked down at the phone in her hand and hit the video button.

Then, sliding the phone into her pocket, she turned back to Shelley. *I've got to give her a chance to explain.*

"Shelley, you need to know that Audrey took a video around the house the night before Tom died. Including the cabinet where that silver sculpture of the cow skull stood. The police have the video. It's time stamped."

It took several long moments before she reacted, as Molly's words registered. Then Shelley turned pale and swayed, grabbing the counter for balance. Molly automatically reached out for her, but again Shelley swatted her outstretched hand away. "Oh my god," she said quietly. "Oh my god." A single tear coursed down her cheek "How stupid!" she said, almost to herself, looking at the box where the sculpture reemerged like a silent accusation, as the scrunched packing paper refused to stay in place. Then she gave a wild, hysterical bark of a laugh, startling Molly. "What if I'd thrown the damn thing away? Like the computer? What if? What if? Got me again!" She picked up the sculpture and for a moment Molly thought she might hurl it at her. But instead, Shelley threw it furiously at the wall, where it left a large gash. The silver skull detached from the amethyst and slid across the floor in front of the couch.

Then she sat down abruptly on the floor and put her face in her hands. She sobbed quietly.

Molly crouched down beside her, knees protesting audibly. She hesitated, but then cautiously reached out to put a hand on Shelley's back. "Maybe you'd better tell me," she said. "It'll all come out anyway. The police know about the datura in Tom's bottle. They know whoever took the silver pieces and Tom's computer had the Home Alert security code. They'll piece it all together. They'll know it was you, Shelley."

Shelley raised her head, tears now running down both cheeks. She made no move to wipe them off. "Not if you don't tell them about that damned skull," Shelley said. "It's the only thing that ties me to...to the whole...to Tom's death. The only thing. And it just reminded me of.... Did I tell you that when Brian was little, he was obsessed with bones? That skull was the only thing I ever kept of Tom's. And I didn't kill him, Molly!"

Molly said nothing, just shook her head.

"I have no motive," Shelley insisted. "If Tom hadn't died, I would have gotten a valuable piece of property. Why would I...hurt him?"

Because you blame him for Brian's death, Molly thought.

When Molly said nothing, Shelley burst out angrily, "If you hadn't seen that...that stupid little...." She broke off, visibly controlled herself and said, "Molly it was an accident anyway, right? When I was in college here, my roommates and I experimented with datura seeds. Ground up the seeds and mixed them into Hawaiian Punch. It was a cheap high and after we came down, we were sick as dogs. But we survived. I gave him almost the same amount. Well, maybe a little more."

"You must have known how dangerous it was, especially for someone his age and with a weak heart," Molly insisted.

"Yeah, I guess. But I couldn't be sure..." She glanced at Molly and revised, "I didn't think it would kill him. I just thought he'd get sick, the way we did in college. How could I have known he'd go so nuts that he'd step off a cliff? That was an accident. How is it my fault that he did that?"

Molly looked at Shelley's tear-streaked face and felt a pang of pity. *But she was responsible for his death,* she reminded herself. *He'd be alive today if she hadn't poisoned him.* They stared at each other for a few long moments and finally Molly said, "You really need to tell the police what happened. You're responsible for the 'accident' that killed him."

"And go to jail, like Brian? What kind of justice would that be? Molly, for god's sake. It's not as if I pushed Tom off that cliff."

Molly felt a surge of anger recalling Barry's false accusation and the trouble it caused Mike. "*Nobody* pushed him! That's the point. If you hadn't doped him up, Tom never would have hallucinated, and he never would have died. Besides, you knew he had a weak heart. He could have died from a heart attack on a strenuous hike like that. You knew that!"

"Yeah," Shelley said. Her lips turned up, almost a smile.

At Molly's shocked expression, Shelley began talking rapidly. "Look, can't you see how perfect it worked out? I wasn't there when Tom fell off that cliff, and I don't see how I can be held responsible for that just because I put a little datura in his drink. And if he'd had a heart attack, that would've just been...fate or something. Not my fault. Anyway, even if Tom did have a heart attack, it probably wouldn't have killed him."

What a rationalization for murder! But Molly didn't react outwardly. "Why did you fake the break-in?" she asked as if mildly curious. "You knew where the house key was. Why not just use it?"

"Why do you think I cut out that glass in the door? It had to look like a break-in by someone who *didn't* have a key! I needed to get hold of Tom's laptop. Audrey would have noticed it was gone. I had to make it look stolen. I probably should have taken more stuff, but I couldn't carry a lot. The little silver doodads were handy."

"Why Tom's computer?"

"His files!" Shelley said, her tone suggesting Molly was being thick. "Once he was dead, Audrey or the police might go through his computer and maybe they'd find..."

"Find what? What would be so important or critical that you'd need to...to..."

"Molly, I don't know. Just stuff about me that I wouldn't want to find on Twitter or some other place. I have a business reputation and it might..." Shelley's voice trailed off, leaving the explanation unfinished.

More likely she feared something incriminating rather than something sullying her reputation, Molly thought. But all she said was, "But Tom must have had backup, on the cloud or a hard drive."

"Tom didn't trust sending stuff to the cloud," Shelley said, dismissing the issue with a small breezy wave. "When that password security company, Last-Pass, reported a data leak, Tom was all 'told you so!' He did have a little external hard drive backup next to the laptop, but I took that too, just in case. I'll bet Audrey didn't even notice that was gone, did she?" Shelley finished scornfully.

"What about paper files?" Molly couldn't resist asking.

Shelley laughed. "Who the hell uses paper anymore?"

Or clips newspaper articles, Molly thought. But she said nothing. *Better to see what else Shelley reveals before I tell her about them.* "And were there files on the computer that...connected Tom to Brian?" she asked.

Shelley gave a short laugh. "I have no idea. Couldn't open it. But no one else will either. I smashed it and put the pieces in several different dumpsters, along with the external hard drive."

"But why take the risk of stealing the computer? If you weren't certain there was something incriminating on it, and that was the only purpose...." Molly's voice trailed off as she tried to understand Shelley's reasoning.

Shelley was getting her self-confidence back, almost bragging. "It muddied the waters, that's why. Two birds, one stone. I got Tom's files, and the break-in confused the police. Even if they discovered the datura right away, they had no idea who broke in and put it in his drink—still don't, do they? Could have been anyone."

"Anyone who knew the Home Alert code," Molly said. "That narrowed the number of possible people down a lot."

"Not that much," Shelley said. "Probably lots of people knew the code. Handyman, or housecleaner, or, or...or someone who knew how to override the alarm." She had stopped crying now as she reasserted herself and her voice grew stronger. "In fact, there's absolutely nothing for the police to find that would incriminate me. My fingerprints are all over the house —probably DNA too. So what? Everyone knows I was in and out of that house all the time. They can't prove I did anything. And they don't have a motive. It's not as if I benefit from his death. Why would anyone suspect me?"

"Maybe they wouldn't if you hadn't staged a burglary," Molly observed. "That was overkill. Not only did that focus them on who could control the alarm, but the items you stole are so easily recog...."

Shelley interrupted her. "You keep forgetting. As far as anyone knows, I have *no motive*. Quite the contrary, in fact. If Tom had lived, I could have been rich."

"Yes, I wondered about that. A few weeks more, and you'd have been in his will for that Cape Cod place. Must be worth quite a bit."

"You don't understand, Molly. I didn't know anything about that property when I made my plans." She stopped abruptly, then continued. "That condo was a complete surprise. And, yeah, I considered waiting a while. But if he gave me the property in his will and, uh, something happened to him right away, for sure the police would suspect me. I'd have to wait for months, probably at least a year before I could... And I'd have to stay with him all that time. I couldn't keep putting him off, or he'd break off with me." She gave a small shudder. "There's a limit to what I'm willing to do for money."

"But for revenge?" Molly prompted.

"What do you mean?"

"You wanted Tom to die because of his role in Brian's death."

Shelley stared at her. "What? I never told you how Brian died. I know I didn't."

"You didn't have to. The whole story—the trial, Tom's part in it, Brian's suicide—was all covered in the press."

Shelley's face contorted with anger. "What the hell, Molly? You snooped around about that? You looked it all up?"

"Tom kept newspaper clippings," Molly said quietly. "I found them. By accident."

Shelley looked incredulous. "Physical clippings? What on earth for?"

This may not be the best time to discuss different generational preferences, Molly thought. But still she explained, "People of Tom's—and my—age like paper records. Maybe he was going to make a scrapbook of important cases."

"A scrapbook," Shelley repeated uncomprehendingly. She was silent for a few minutes, thinking through the implications of Molly's revelation.

"Do the police have the clippings?"

Grateful to escape being forced to admit her own role in providing the police with them, Molly said simply, "Yes."

Shelley appeared shaken again; she stared down at her hands. But then she rallied and raised her head to glare at Molly. Unconsciously parroting Mike's earlier comments to Molly, Shelley said, "Even if they do find out about Brian's death, having a motive isn't evidence, doesn't prove I was the one who poison...who put the datura in his drink."

"How will you explain the little sculpture to the

police?" Molly asked. She walked over to where the silver skull lay on the floor and without touching it, pulled the phone out of her pocket and swept the camera eye at it.

As Molly turned to record the amethyst, Shelley leapt up from where she sat. She lunged forward and grabbed at Molly's phone, but she tripped over the box that once held the sculpture and Molly made it to the door.

"Don't," Molly said loudly and turned her back to Shelley. and She tucked the phone behind crossed arms on her chest. "You're not doing yourself any good." She quickly pushed the screen door open and stepped outside, where two neighbors stood. They had clearly been chatting until the loud voices interrupted. They looked at her curiously and at Shelley standing in the doorway, her face streaked with tears. Molly said, "Good morning, folks," in as normal a voice as she could summon.

"Molly!" Shelley almost screamed. "Please! Don't! You said we were friends! You know what I've been through. Please, Molly. Think what you are doing!"

"I am," Molly said. She hurried down the outside stairs to her car.

MOLLY PULLED out of the apartment parking lot and headed for Sunrise Acres. At a stop light, she punched Mike's number from her list of Favorites. He answered, "Hey, love, I'm on my way to the library. Do you want me to see if you have some books on hold, or…"

"Mike!" she said. She tried to say more, but her voice failed her.

"Molly, Molly, are you okay?"

She choked out "Yeah," and then realized she was crying. The light had turned green and the cars behind her were honking. Mike was frantically trying to get through to her, but her adrenaline level was off the scale, and her vision was blurred by her tears. She managed to turn into the post office lot and parked in a customer spot, struggling to regain control.

Mike became increasingly desperate. "Molly, I'm calling 911. Where are you? Are you hurt? Please, Molly—answer me!"

"Just a minute," she said, recovering somewhat now that the car was parked. "I'm not hurt. Don't call 911. I've pulled off the road. Give me a minute and I'll explain." When she had mopped her face with the tissues from the center console, she could speak almost normally. "Actually, Mike, could you hold off on the library? It's about Shelley and I really need to talk to you. Are you at home?"

"I'm just turning into Sunrise Drive," he said. "By the time you get here, I'll be home. Can you give me a hint about what's upset you so? What did Shelley do? I thought she was leaving soon."

"I think it'll be today," Molly said. "That's why I need to talk to you. We need to go to the police. Now!"

VILLEGAS GREETED Mike and Molly with unaccustomed coolness. He escorted them to the conference room. "You said it was urgent. I'm hoping it's good. Saturday is my day off. I'm supposed to meet Gunther."

Molly and Mike looked at each other and Mike gestured to her to start. "Well," Molly said, "It's urgent, but it's not good. At least from my point of view. It's about Tom O'Day's death. We know you already concluded that the person who broke into his house did so to poison his sports drink. And that same person stole his computer and the silver mementos from the cabinet outside the guest room."

Villegas sat unmoving, expressionless, only a twitch of his fingers on one hand betraying impatience at Molly's review of the case. But he nodded politely.

"I found one of the silver sculptures this morning —the most unusual one. The cow skull mounted on a piece of amethyst. I surreptitiously recorded my conversation with the person who had it in her possession, and I would like to play that recording for you." She set her phone on the conference table in front of Villegas, where overlapping circles from wet glasses created Venn diagrams on the wood, and pressed Play.

The video display was black from being in her pocket. Voices came across slightly muffled but from the beginning of the recording, the words were clear. The first voice was Molly's:

"Shelley, you need to know that Audrey took a video around the house the night before Tom died. Including the cabinet where that silver sculpture of the cow skull stood. The police have the video. It's time stamped." Shelley's "Oh my god. Oh my god" were faint. Villegas listened to the whole tape, only a slight widening of his eyes betraying his surprise—or perhaps excitement—as Shelley told her story. "Not if you don't tell them about that damned skull. It's the only thing that ties me...to...to the whole...to Tom's death....Molly, it was an accident anyway, right?...I didn't think it would kill him. I just thought he'd get sick....How could I have known he'd go so nuts that he'd step off a cliff?...If he'd had a heart attack, that would have just been fate."

They could hear Molly ask, "How will you explain the little sculpture to the police?" The video was suddenly showing the apartment, the silver piece and amethyst and then the sounds of a scuffle as the camera view swung wildly around the room.

Then Shelley's loud wail: "Please! Don't!"

The recording continued documenting Molly's flight down the stairs and to the car. The video display went black again. "I set it face down on the seat," Molly explained.

But Villegas could hear the car door closing and the squeal of tires as she peeled out of the apartment building lot. Molly reached over and stopped the recording before they could hear her sob and make a frantic call to Mike. "You don't need to hear the rest. I forgot to turn it off," Molly said apologetically, "until I was parked."

Villegas pulled out his own phone and spoke quietly, "Denise, are you at the station? Okay, I need you to drop whatever you're doing and get down here. I need you to make a copy of a recording on a phone." He listened a moment and then, "I'm sorry. But it's good you're close by. I'm afraid it's quite urgent. And do you know where Terry is? He needs to hear this recording."

"Could Molly get in trouble for recording Shelley without her permission?" Mike asked.

"Not in Arizona," Villegas said. "In twelve states, recording someone without their permission is a crime. Arizona isn't one of those states. However," he continued, "Ms. Goossens's confession on a covert recording might not be admissible as evidence in court. A good lawyer might be able to get it thrown out."

"She'll get away with it?" Molly asked. Her tone suggested she felt ambivalent.

"No, I don't think so." Villegas looked at her curiously. "You were friends, right?"

"Yes, I was a friend of the Shelley I thought I knew. She was always so...not exactly sweet. She could be quite assertive. More...I guess 'damaged' captures her —her brother's suicide, her upbringing....But she shouldn't get away with it."

"You are a direct witness to what seems to me a clear confession. If you testify as to what she told you, it's probable that the recording can be used to back you up. And now that we know she's the one who staged the break-in, we can see what other evidence might tie her to the poisoning. Perhaps someone saw her collecting the seeds. Or maybe there'll be traces of datura in her kitchen."

"And what about the photo of the silver piece," Mike asked. "Doesn't that prove she is in possession of stolen goods?"

Just then Detective Weatherby appeared in the doorway. Molly showed her where the video was on the phone and Denise disappeared, phone in hand. "I'll hand it over to Sergeant Partridge," she said.

"Uh, can you maybe stop recording when you hear my car door close and drive away?" Molly asked. "The rest is just me driving—and panicking," she added, sotto voce.

Villegas glanced impatiently at his watch. "You think she's leaving town today?" he asked Molly. She nodded just as Rasmussen arrived.

Rasmussen frowned when he saw who was in the room. "Well, if it isn't our local crime-stoppers. Solved another case for us?" he asked sarcastically.

"Actually," Mike said with undisguised pleasure, "yes."

"Let's debrief on the way, Terry. Our prime suspect is about to leave town. Weatherby's coming in a patrol car; you and I can go in my car. We're going to need a warrant to search her vehicle and her apartment for stolen goods."

Villegas almost tipped over his chair in his haste to leave the room. Rasmussen followed close behind him, bellowing "Who? Who?"

Detective Weatherby was in the hall just outside the door. She handed Villegas a note as he strode by. "Address," she said.

"Need search warrant," Villegas said.

"On it," Weatherby said, her phone to her ear as she walked. All three detectives disappeared down the hall.

Mike and Molly sat at the table watching the action blow by them. Then they leisurely gathered their possessions.

"That has to have been one of the most satisfying moments in my life," Mike said.

"Solving another case?"

"Well, yes, of course. But the look on Rasmussen's face when I told him we had. That really took the prize."

28

EARLY IN THE NEW YEAR

"That should do it for shirts," Conrad said as he added one more to the suitcase that lay open on the bed.

Christine hovered anxiously, going through a mental checklist of what Conrad would need for a five-month stay at Fort Leavenworth. "Belts? Handkerchiefs? Did you change the address for Express Scripts to send your meds?"

"Christine, I'm not going to jail—or to Afghanistan. If I forget something, I'll go to the PX on base and buy a replacement. Or you can send it to me. And I'll be back for a few days in March. Maybe sooner. Depends on who they'll have working with me, whether or when I can get away."

Jamie came in and threw himself down on the bed, earning a displeased glance from his mother as some carefully folded pants bounced into disarray. "What exactly do they have you doing, anyway, Dad? Will you need my help?"

"God, no!" Conrad said. "Don't even think of 'helping' me with the stuff I'll be working on!" He fixed his son with a grim look. "I mean it, Jamie! I signed an ironclad nondisclosure agreement. I can't tell anyone what I'm doing, or I could go straight to prison. They may even monitor my personal computer. I don't know." Then he softened his tone. "I won't know what's needed until I get into their systems and find out where the potential weak points are. Apparently, the software is an appalling mixture." He smiled at his son. "May even be some ancient Fortran lurking inside. I just hope I remember enough legacy software languages to do the diagnoses."

"Will they lock you up at night?" Jamie asked.

Conrad chuckled. "No, I'll have an apartment on base. The deal is, I work on their cyber security for four or five months with one of the IT guys who has top security clearance—my minder, I guess you'd say. He'll be looking over my shoulder, maybe literally, not only to check everything I do but also to learn how to look for access into the systems. There have been many programmers working over the years. The software is probably riddled with back doors."

"Back doors?" Christine repeated.

Jamie rolled his eyes and exchanged a knowing glance with his father. "Developers put a portal—unguarded—in a system so they can get in to do remote tech support. Also helpful to hackers," he added, smiling innocently at his mother.

Christine's puzzled look remained, the explanation no help to her. "I could do the stuff you're going to be doing," Jamie said somewhat dismissively to his father.

"Yeah, you could probably do a better job than

me. But I'm the one who's got to atone for my mistakes. The Army would have been within their rights to court-martial me. I guess technically I'm still in the Army. I'm very, very lucky that I'm not going to get locked up for a year. And," he added, looking hard at Jamie, "so are you! I don't want to hear about any more hacking." Conrad looked meaningfully at Christine, and she nodded.

Conrad cleared his throat. "And your mother and I have been discussing what you should do to make up for messing with Mrs. O'Day's car."

"I didn't know she'd be driving!" Jamie burst out.

"Jamie, that's irrelevant. You intentionally endangered someone's life. And she was injured. She could have been killed. If the police knew you hacked that car, you'd be looking at lots of time in a juvenile detention center. You can't expect to walk away from doing something like that without any punishment at all."

Jamie sat upright on the bed. "Dad, that's not fair! I did it for you!"

"Let me introduce you to a saying old people use. 'The road to Hell is paved with good intentions.'"

"I suppose that's meant to have some deep meaning," Jamie said sullenly. He climbed off the bed, sat on the floor, and curled his arms around his knees.

"I think you know what it means, Jamie," Christine said gently. "We know you were trying to help your dad, but that doesn't excuse what might have happened to that woman."

"And maybe," Conrad added, "maybe you hacked the car just to show you could?"

Jamie had his head buried in his arms, but they both heard a faint, "Maybe."

"You have a lot of brain power," Christine said. "Please be sure you use it for good, sweetheart."

"Do what you say, not what you do, huh Dad?" Jamie raised his head, his tone belligerent.

Conrad winced. *I deserved that.* "We both made mistakes. And we both have to pay."

Jamie looked pleadingly at his mother, but she just shook her head. "Your dad is right."

"This spring while I'm in Kansas," Conrad said, "you are going to use your computer skills to help other people. Not many kids have enjoyed the advantages you've had to learn programming."

"Help who?"

"The local Autism Research nonprofit organization. Mom has already arranged it. You'll be working on their donation management system unless they ask you to take on something else. You'll do it remotely, but you'll spend at least ten hours a week, for a total of a hundred hours."

"How the heck can I spend that much time helping them and still do my homework?"

"You'll give up Dungeons and Dragons for those months."

"Oh, come on, Mom. I can't leave my guys in the lurch like that. I'm Dungeon Master!"

"They'll have to find someone else to do it for the spring term."

"You and I both screwed up," Conrad said. "We'll both feel better we've made amends."

"Huh. Maybe *you* will," Jamie muttered.

"Jamie!" Conrad's tone of voice startled his son

into looking up and then ducking his head. "Grow up. Be grateful you didn't kill someone. Your punishment for what you did could have been far, far worse. I want your promise that you'll do a good job for these folks."

There was a long silence which neither parent broke. At last, Jamie looked up at them. "Okay. I promise."

"Ms. Levin will testify to everything that you just told me?" Captain Dubrow asked Villegas. Dubrow tossed into her mouth some of the few remaining M&Ms in her holiday snowman double bowl.

"Yes, and the AG has the recording that Molly, uh, Ms. Levin made. It's a clear confession. Even if there's some lawyer trick to get the recording thrown out in court, Molly's testimony was firsthand and should be evidence enough. But the recording could be used to corroborate that testimony. She also took a photo of one of the stolen silver sculptures in Ms. Goossens's apartment. We have that sculpture—or what's left of it —in our possession with a clear chain of custody."

"'Molly,' huh?" Dubrow said and raised an eyebrow. "If I didn't know you were married, I might wonder if you were getting too close to your *civilian* informants. By the way, how was your dinner with the Rasmussens?"

How does she know these things? Villegas wondered. "Who told you about that?"

"Little birds, little birds," Dubrow said, linking her thumbs and wiggling her hands. She then ate the last M&M.

"It was fine," Villegas said. When she continued to look curiously at him, he relented and provided some details. "We went to Feast downtown. Ever been there?"

Dubrow nodded. "Very nice wine list."

Villegas smiled. "Yep. And Mary Rasmussen is a gem. Don't know why..." He stopped himself. "Terry's fortunate."

Dubrow nodded approvingly.

Then she examined her hand, frowned, and pulled a tissue out of the box to scrub at her palm. She disposed of the tissue and returned to the conversation. "Terry told me that Konsinski got a very generous deal from the Army. No court-martial. Just community service?"

"Yes. Ms. Levin found that out. She and Mrs. Konsinski are friends. And Mrs. O'Day returned the blackmail money—all of it— to the Konsinskis. A bit surprising, given our experience with her."

"Did she win her case with Edison?"

"Not really. Looks as if Edison may settle. All the parties involved have gone silent while the negotiations are going on. But if they do pay her, it'll be to shut her up and avoid all the negative publicity. They still insist she screwed up somehow."

"What do you think?"

"I think she's very fortunate if she gets any settlement at all," Villegas said. "Remember I found that she went off the road at the only possible place in miles that she could have without getting seriously hurt? Very propitious choice of spots for an accident." He smiled a bit complacently. "I'm with Edison. I never thought that car was hacked."

"Last one," Mike said, wrapping a delicate glass bell in tissue paper before putting it in the box marked "Christmas Ornaments." "Now to tackle the tree." Mike and Molly were dismantling the holiday decorations they had put up two weeks earlier.

Molly looked dubiously at the large rectangular carton Mike had carried in from the garage. "Did the tree really fit in that?"

"I forgot you weren't here when I put it up. Yep, it splits into three pieces and the branches fold up like an umbrella. Usually takes a little persuasion." He illustrated by laying the three sections in the box and leaning on each to make them fit.

"Looks like a coffin. I feel kind of bad scrunching it up and closing it in there."

"No anthropomorphizing, please. This tree is a bunch of plastic pieces. It's not Shelley."

"You know," Molly said, surprised, "I guess that *is* why I'm feeling sorry for the tree. I didn't even realize I was thinking about her. Thanks, Dr. Phil!" She put a knee on the top of the box so that Mike could secure it with packing tape.

"I don't look forward to testifying against her. If I hadn't gone over that morning and gotten her to confess, she'd be back in Chicago." She stood staring at the boxed tree. "Audrey might have found those clippings, but I really don't think Shelley would have confessed to anyone but me." Molly's voice wobbled as she added, "She trusted me."

Mike stopped taping and put his arms around her. "You've got to separate the Shelley you liked a lot from the Shelley who cold-bloodedly set out to kill Tom. She's a terrific con artist! Have you forgotten that I could have had Tom's death pinned on me? I could easily have been the one to hear the jail cell door close behind me. Believe me, I had nightmares about that sound."

"You're right, of course. And her lawyer can argue that she didn't intend the datura to be lethal."

"Except that she seemed supremely indifferent as to whether he died or not," Mike observed. "I think she saw a rough justice in what she did. She knew no jury would consider Tom responsible for her brother's death, and she didn't feel directly responsible for Tom's."

"But in her case, a jury is likely to see it differently."

"And they should. Tom didn't know Brian would kill himself when he sentenced the kid. Shelley may not have known exactly what would happen when she poisoned Tom, but she hoped for the worst. We can't have individuals deciding what they think is justice."

"Granted. Don't worry, I'll tell the truth and let the system decide on what's the right punishment. I just wish...." Molly's voice trailed off.

"...that Tom had given Brian a fairer sentence?"

"No. Well maybe. More that I wish I'd somehow figured out what Shelley was up to and could have talked her out of it."

"I doubt you could have. She'd set that plan in motion a long time ago, when she tracked Tom down, moved here, figured out how to get close to him, and then decided to poison him."

"I'd just rather we prevent murders than solve them," Molly said morosely.

"Oh, no worries," Mike said cheerfully. "Human nature being what it is, we'll have plenty of opportunities for both. Hey, by the way, I've got a bit of news that will amuse you. The Sunrise library asked if I would be willing to lend them one of Andrea's paintings to hang in the foyer. I invited Josie—you know, the woman who volunteers there almost every day—to come look at my collection and select one. You know which one she chose?"

"The one over your mantel," Molly guessed. "Your own favorite."

"Yep. The datura flowers."

ACKNOWLEDGMENTS

Retired professors Dorothy Leonard and Walter Swap (AKA "Andre Charles") live in an "active adult community," and therefore have general knowledge about the pursuits of our fellow denizens, including community politics, supper clubs, hiking venues and, of course, pickleball. However, our academic pursuits never intersected with police procedures or hallucinogenic desert plants. In *Overkill,* we have relied on a number of individuals who have generously shared their considerable expertise to fill in these and other critical gaps.

Dr. Leslie Boyer, University of Arizona emerita professor of pathology, shared her expertise on poisonous desert plants and how their chemical compositions may be revealed through thin layer chromatography. Oro Valley Police Department Public Information Officer, Michael Duran, and Lieutenant James Steinmetz, retired, Middlebury Heights Ohio Police Department, helped correct our misconceptions of murder investigations gleaned from television crime shows. Any remaining errors are ours alone. Don Teiser helped us identify possible charitable organizations where Jamie Konsinski, our young wayward computer hacker, could use his considerable skills.

Several beta readers provided valuable suggestions and caught some glaring continuity errors. Thanks to Alison Wilkinson, Norma Hudson, Bonnie Bethea, Michelle Barton and Jef McAllister.

Once again, we thank Cornelia Feye, for her careful editing and tending to all the publishing details that would have driven us nuts.

ABOUT THE AUTHOR

Andre Charles is the pseudonym for Dorothy Leonard and Walter Swap, retired professors. In addition to the first book in the Molly & Mike mystery series, *The Bell Tower*, they have co-authored books on group creativity, innovation and knowledge. The Arizona retirement community they live in, bears a remarkable similarity to the fictitious Sunrise Acres. Visit the authors at: www.andrecharles.com.

Made in the USA
Middletown, DE
17 October 2023

40748355R00201